The Chimera's Curse

Julia Golding
AR B.L.: 5.9 Alt.: 908
Points: 11.0   MG

The CHIMERA'S CURSE

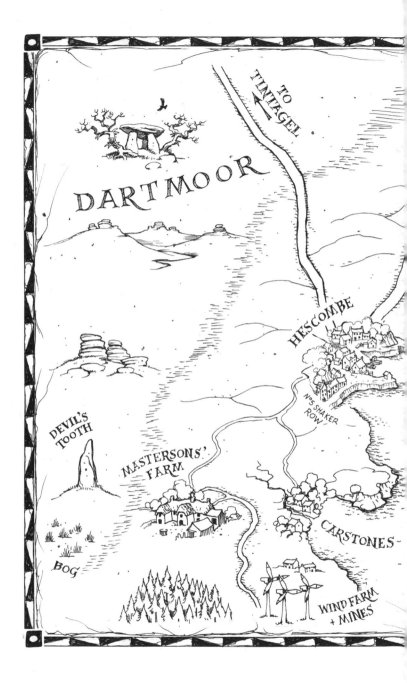

EDGE OF DARTMOOR NATIONAL PARK

REFINERY

CHARTMOUTH

MILSOM ST.

MALLINS WOOD

COASTAL PATH

THE STACKS

HESCOMBE CHANNEL

BOOK FOUR
THE COMPANIONS QUARTET

The CHIMERA'S CURSE

JULIA GOLDING

Marshall Cavendish

Text copyright © 2007 by Julia Golding
Illustrations copyright © 2007 by David Wyatt

Marshall Cavendish Corporation
99 White Plains Road
Tarrytown, NY 10591
www.marshallcavendish.us/kids

Library of Congress Cataloging-in-Publication Data
Golding, Julia.
The chimera's curse / by Julia Golding ; [illustrations by David Wyatt].—
1st Marshall Cavendish ed.
p. cm.—(Companions quartet ; bk. 4)
Summary: Connie and Col band together to save the world for all creatures,
including the mythical ones of which few humans are aware, from the shape-shifter Kullervo's army
and, along the way, Connie finds herself transformed in an amazing way.
ISBN 978-0-7614-5440-3
[1. Animals, Mythical—Fiction. 2. Human-animal communication—Fiction.
3. Secret societies—Fiction. 4. Supernatural—Fiction.
5.Friendship—Fiction.] I. Wyatt, David, ill. II. Title.
PZ7.G56758Chi 2008
[Fic]—dc22
2007029776

Book design by Vera Soki

Printed in China
First Marshall Cavendish edition, 2008
Originally published in the UK by Oxford University Press, 2007

10 9 8 7 6 5 4 3 2
ⅲℸⅽ Marshall Cavendish

C𝒽imera: (from classical mythology) A fabled fire-breathing monster, with a lion's head, a goat's body, and a serpent's tail (or according to others, with the heads of a lion, a goat, and a serpent), killed by Bellerophon.

Modern use: an unreal creature of the imagination, a mere wild fancy.

(from *The Oxford English Dictionary*, by permission of Oxford University Press)

Contents

Hunt

Come to me, Universal. You know you are mine. Connie Lionheart stirred restlessly in her sleep. A hot wind whispered in the curtains, carrying the scent of the parched land. The breeze bore the sound of waves folding onto the beach. It was a sultry night, and the sheet clung uncomfortably to her body.

Come to the mark. Come to me. You know you must.

Connie surfaced from sleep, struggling like a swimmer caught in weeds, thrashing to reach air. When she woke, she found the bedclothes twisted around her. She threw them off and sat up to gulp some water from the glass on her bedside table, her hand shaking slightly. The voice had crept into her dreams again: the voice of Kullervo, the shape-shifter, her enemy—and her companion creature. He said the same thing each time, repeating the message again and again so that she could hear its echo during the daylight hours as well as in the stillness of the night. She knew where he wanted her to go: he wanted her to meet him at the mark he had made deep in her mind, the breach in the wall between her and his dark presence. But she would not give in to him.

Sentinel! Connie called out in thought. *Help me! He's here again.*

Sentinel the minotaur, the creature appointed by the Society for the Protection of Mythical Creatures to guard the universal, sent his shadow-presence instantly to her side. He was hidden in a cave in the cliffs not far away, keeping watch, but he did not need to be with her in body when he could come to her through the bond between them. His presence burst into her mind, stamping out any residue of the dark creature that had visited her dreams. With bull head dipping from side to side, he gored and pierced the shadows, reducing the shape-shifter's presence to tatters and finally to nothing but a faint whisper of mocking laughter. And then even that echo was snuffed out by the minotaur's bellow of anger. Satisfied all was now clear, shadow-Sentinel bowed to the universal, his hand clasped to his heart and his curved bull's horns lowered.

He has gone, he growled. *You may sleep in peace.*

Too shaken to lie down immediately, Connie remained sitting and hugged her knees, her fear creeping back now that she was alone again. It had been much easier to repel Kullervo before Argand, her golden dragon companion, grew too big to fit through her bedroom window. Each night they had curled up together and she had shared the dragonet's dreams, leaving no room for Kullervo to creep into her mind. But now Argand slept on the moors with the rest of her family and Connie was on her own.

She lifted her shaggy mane of black hair off her neck in a vain attempt to cool herself. Connie knew she was living on borrowed time: Kullervo would seek her out again. These nighttime visitations were just his way of teasing her; his real attack would come in some way she did not expect, and he would try to trick her as he had already done three times in as many years. It was difficult to remain constantly alert. After all, she had a life to lead in Hescombe: she had to go to school, see her friends, have fun like any other ordinary teenager.

Connie shuddered. But, of course, she wasn't ordinary. As the only universal companion in existence, the only person who could bond with all mythical creatures, her life was never going to be conventional or safe. Kullervo would always hunt her because he needed her powers to achieve the destruction of humanity. The prospect paralyzed her with fear. Connie rubbed her forearms, trying to drive away the tremors that set in when she thought of the threat hanging over her. Sometimes, she wished she could forget what she knew. She clung on to the times when she could pretend to be normal, when she could relax and forget the burden and blessing of her gift. Like tomorrow, for example: tomorrow she was going for a picnic with her great-uncle; her brother, Simon; and her friends Jane and Anneena—none of them knew anything about mythical creatures so there was not a whiff of an encounter planned. She would seem to the world like an ordinary girl on her summer vacation, her extraordinary secret well hidden.

Holding on to this comforting image, Connie turned over and eventually drifted off to sleep.

⊲⊱

At the Mastersons' farm, Shirley's party was in full swing. Col was sitting on the front doorstep, can of Coke in hand, watching the dancers. The birthday girl's silky blonde hair swirled as she danced, and she was laughing loudly among the crowds of young people. Col felt a twinge of envy at Shirley's ability to fit in so effortlessly with the non-Society friends she'd invited; he had to acknowledge that, recently, being a member of the Society had gotten in the way of how he would like normal people to see him. He feared that these days at his school no one would say he was the least bit cool, not when his best friends, Connie and Rat, stood out for being so strange.

Col crushed his empty can. He wished it didn't matter to him but it did. Worse, he had no idea what to do about it. Only a few years ago he had been so confident in class, easy in his skin; now he spent all his time worrying about how others saw him. He wouldn't dream of dropping his friends, but neither Rat nor Connie showed any sign of change, so the problem wasn't going to be solved that way. It just didn't feel right to spend most of his time embarrassed by their behavior.

Col put his head in his hands and groaned. He was an idiot. He didn't deserve them. They were both extremely gifted and Connie was truly unique. Perhaps *he* was the problem?

The song ended, and some of the dancers drifted off the floor. With a jolt of surprise, Col noticed that Shirley was headed in his direction with a group of her school friends in tow. Long limbed, tanned, pretty, they were an intimidating sight. He suddenly felt very nervous: a pack of girls bearing down on him tended to have that effect. Assuming nonchalance he didn't feel, he grabbed a fresh can from an ice-filled bucket and pulled the tab, letting it fizz onto the step.

"And this is Col," Shirley said, sweeping her arm toward him. She quickly ran through the names of her friends. Pinned by their gaze, he felt as if they were silently grading him on a scale of ten.

"Hi." He managed a general greeting, giving himself zero for originality.

But it seemed to do the trick. On that signal, the girls clustered around him, giving him their full and very flattering attention. Slowly, he began to relax, thinking he was doing okay as they quizzed him about his school and his taste in music. That was until they started on his friendships.

"Shirley said you were friends with that girl Connie Lionheart," one dark-haired girl said sweetly.

Col swung around to her. "Yeah. Do you know her then?"

"I've heard a lot about her." The girl took a sip of her drink and exchanged a smile with Shirley. "Didn't you both get stuck up a tree?"

"Er, yeah." Col took a nervous gulp from his own can.

"Is she really your girlfriend?" The girl gave him an amused look, eyebrow arched in disbelief.

Col felt the blood rush to his cheeks. "Of course not. Who gave you that idea?" It had to be Shirley. He liked Connie; they were closer than he could explain, thanks to all they had been through together, but girlfriend . . . !

"We didn't think so," a second girl butted in. Clearly his love life had been much discussed even before they approached him. "Everyone says she's so . . . so odd."

Col knew he should speak up in defense of Connie. She was much more than the label of "odd" they had given her, but what could he say? He was acutely aware that Shirley's crowd would think badly of him if he said anything. He shouldn't care about their opinion, but he did.

"We're good friends," he said lamely, letting the comment go, "just good friends."

Satisfied, Shirley indicated to her group that it was time to move on. "Aren't you going to dance, Col?" she asked as they began to wander away.

"No," he said bluntly, hating her for showing up his lack of loyalty to Connie, and cursing himself for succumbing to the pressure.

She gave him a triumphant smile. "Fine. See you."

The companion to weather giants returned to the dance floor and soon had her hands draped around the neck of a dark-eyed boy that Col recognized as Jessica Moss's selkie companion, a changeling creature that could transform into a seal. Jessica must have brought him, knowing that he could mingle inconspicuously with the other young people. Thinking about Jessica—freckle-faced, with a mass of reddish-brown curls—Col spotted her sitting on her own in the yard on the hood of one of the cars. Jessica looked about as miserable as Col felt as she watched Shirley and her companion dancing. Getting up from his post by the front door, Col walked over, a fresh can of Coke in hand.

"Want something to drink, Jess?" he asked.

Jessica looked up at him with a grimace. "Thanks, Col." Taking the can, her eyes snapped back to the dance floor. "Look at her. She's been longing to get her claws into Arran for ages and now she's succeeded."

Col followed Jessica's gaze and saw that Shirley now had her head bent against the selkie's neck.

"Forget it." Col slid onto the hood beside her. "He'll soon figure out she's not worth it."

"I'm not jealous," Jessica said quickly, though from the flash in her eyes Col doubted this was the case. "But he's so green, so soft-hearted."

Col kept his smile to himself. "Don't worry. He won't abandon his companion. It just doesn't work like that."

Jessica sighed. "I s'pose not. It's not very likely that he'll find a future with a weather giant companion, is it?"

"No chance. Too much rough water."

Jessica relaxed, sitting back so that she leaned against Col. "Thanks. So, how are you?"

"Oh, I'm fine. Trying to put in the flying hours for my Grade Four exam."

"I know what you mean." Jessica yawned. "I was up at the crackle of dawn for my swimming training." She gazed at the rest of the crowd, her brow furrowed. "How come only you and I get invited to this party out of all of us in the Society?"

Col scanned the groups of dancers under the flashing party lights, the knots of people by the drinks' table; he didn't know many of them well, but he recognized the local in-crowd when he saw it. "We're not the only ones. I was with the dragon twins earlier, but I think they left to go flying."

"Still, what about Connie and Rat?"

Col gave a hollow laugh. "Don't you know Shirley well

enough, Jess, to know that she wouldn't invite them? Not Rat's kind of thing anyway."

"S'pose not. But what about Connie?"

"Shirley didn't ask her. I don't know if it's because she's insanely jealous of our universal or because Connie's not cool enough for her friends from Chartmouth." Col fell guiltily silent, remembering how he had just inadequately defended her only a few moments before.

"Oh." Jessica wrinkled her nose in disgust. "Well, I like Connie. Does that make me uncool?"

"I s'pect so—in Shirley's eyes at any rate." Col noticed that Shirley now appeared to be kissing Arran's neck.

"Huh! Excuse me if I don't make her opinion the guide to what I like and don't like!" Jessica's eyes sparkled dangerously as she saw what was going on.

The song ended, and at last the dancers broke apart. Arran looked in their direction and noticed Col with his arm around Jessica. Immediately, the selkie abandoned Shirley and headed for them with a determined look on his face.

"Hello, Arran," Col said levelly as the selkie came to stand in front of them. "Enjoying the party?"

"Hello, Col," said the selkie, his voice a snarl. Arran turned to his companion. "I've had enough, Jess. Can we go now?"

Jessica sat up abruptly from leaning against Col and accepted Arran's hand to slide from the car.

"Tired of your dance partner already?" she asked, swatting his arm. The selkie shuffled his feet awkwardly, looking down. If he had been in his seal shape, his whiskers would have drooped in shame. "See you, Col," Jessica said brightly, blowing him a kiss.

"Bye," Col said. "See? Nothing to worry about," he muttered as Jessica and Arran walked off hand in hand.

⚜

Getting up late the following morning, Col decided he'd hack across the moors to see Rat. He still felt annoyed with himself for how he'd behaved at Shirley's party. Being a member of the Society meant he spent much of his time hanging out with people who were frankly all a bit eccentric. This had never bothered him much before, but last night had brought home to him that he wanted to be . . . well . . . cool again.

Am I being a jerk? he wondered, looking at himself in the mirror.

Probably, he admitted with a shamefaced grin. That's what Rat would say.

Rat's reaction he could handle, but why did he get tied up in knots any time someone mentioned Connie? He felt he should defend her, yet didn't; he wanted to be with her, but then felt embarrassed when she started doing things like talking to seagulls in public. He was in awe of her gift. She couldn't help it, but she always made him feel as if he was standing in her shadow. These days everyone saw the universal first and had no time for an insignificant pegasus companion. And why *would* they notice him? He'd done nothing worth mentioning.

Fetching his chestnut horse, Mags, from the stable, Col turned him toward the beach, planning a shortcut along the shore, hoping the ride would restore his good humor. On this route, the only hazard they met were encampments of tourists marking out their territories with striped screens, sun-tents, deckchairs, buckets and spades.

"How much for a pony ride?" called a cheeky-faced boy of about seven or eight, popping out from behind a rock and running beside Col's stirrup for a few paces.

"Get lost!" Col grinned. But softening, he added, "If you're still here when I come back, I'll give you a ride for nothing."

"Done!" shouted the boy and zoomed off down the beach, arms outspread like an airplane, to splash into the scintillating water.

Col spurred Mags on. He was doing what he did best: riding. Surely nothing could go wrong with such glorious sunshine and not a cloud on the horizon?

Connie lay on the picnic rug, feeling full and deliciously lazy after an ample lunch. The picnickers had not gone far from her great-uncle's cottage, just up to the edge of the moor, to a field where the Mastersons' flocks grazed the sun-bleached grass. Uncle Hugh snored gently in his folding chair, newspaper dangling precariously off his knees, sun hat slanting over his eyes. Jane and Anneena were talking in quiet voices not far away. Simon, her younger brother, was picking apart a strand of dry grass, and now started throwing bits onto his sister.

"Stop it, Si!" she said wearily, waving the nuisance away like a fly. "Why don't you annoy someone else for a change?"

Simon continued to dribble bits of grass onto her, his short black hair bobbing around at the periphery of her vision as he stretched over.

"Do you have to do that to Connie, Simon?" came Anneena's voice from the other side of the picnic rug. Anneena was sitting up, fanning herself with her straw hat.

"Brothers can be such a pain," said Jane grumpily. She had an older brother and was used to such tormenting.

"Look, why don't we go for a walk?" suggested Anneena. "We could find some shade in the trees over there."

"A walk?" Connie groaned. "In this heat?"

"Yes. You shouldn't lie out in the sun: you'll burn."

"Okay. Let's go," Connie said, sitting up, feeling momentarily dizzy as the world righted itself.

"I'm not coming. It'll be boring," said Simon sullenly.

"Fine," cut in Anneena. "You stay here and clean up then."

Simon got to his feet. "I'm coming," he said quickly.

The four of them headed toward the pine plantation, eager to reach the shade once they started walking in the glaring heat. As they entered under the boughs, the contrast with the bright day could not have been greater; brown shadows clung to the tree trunks, obscuring the depths of the wood from view. A thick layer of pine needles muffled their footfalls, releasing the heady scent of resin as they were stirred. The air was stuffy, like a room that had been shut up for many years. Connie felt a prickle down her spine and shivered.

"I'm not sure it's any cooler in here," said Jane doubtfully. "Shall we go back?"

Anneena and Connie were ready to agree but Simon was standing very still, staring fascinated into the trees.

"No, I want to go further in," he said firmly. His thick black eyebrows, which almost met in the middle, were set in a determined frown.

"Come on, Simon, let's get out into the fresh air again." Connie pulled on his sleeve, but he shook her off. Her skin was prickling, her body tense, on the verge of making a run for it. Anything to get out of this creepy wood.

"No," he said angrily. "You dragged me in here. It's not fair to make me go just because you've changed your mind."

"He has a point," said Jane. She brushed her fair hair off her face where it was sticking to her skin.

Connie now noticed that her brother was gazing into the shadows, a rapt expression on his face. She paused for a moment, focusing her thoughts on the creatures around her. Then she caught it, too. There was something slinking through those trees—a creature whose presence she had never felt before—something dangerous.

"I think we'd better go back," she said quietly, laying a hand on Simon's arm to convey to him that she understood.

He shook her off roughly. "I'm going further in."

"But it's not safe," Connie said in a low voice, hoping Anneena and Jane wouldn't hear. She didn't want them to question her.

"Not safe! It's not the Amazon jungle, you know. What do you think will get me in Hescombe—a particularly hacked-off squirrel? What'll it do: throw pine cones at me or something?" Simon said in frustration.

Connie could have pointed out that dragons, stone sprites, minotaurs, and frost wolves were not unknown on the moors—to the Society members, at least. But Simon was not a member of the Society and showed no interest in undergoing an assessment, though Connie had reason before today to suspect that he had a gift.

"I know," she said, struggling to be reasonable as her instinct grew that they must retreat and quickly. "But please trust me for once. It really isn't safe for anyone to go in there, not until we know *what it is*." She held his gaze, trying to convey that she, too, sensed the creature in the shadows ahead.

"Know what *what* is?" asked Anneena, intrigued by this exchange, looking eagerly from one to the other. "Did you see something?"

Connie shook her head. "No, I think Simon and I might've heard something moving about."

She was saved further explanation by an ear-splitting whinny and a shout, followed by a thump, not far away to their right. Now they could all hear something large crashing through the trees, and Connie caught the glimpse of a long black tail disappearing into the undergrowth. Without hesitation, they all ran in the direction of the cry.

Simon was first to reach the scene. He found Col sitting on the ground, holding his head and groaning.

"Are you all right?" Connie pushed past her brother. "What happened?"

"Mags threw me," Col gasped, an astounding statement from him as his riding skills were famous.

Connie gave a whistle, and the chestnut horse galloped back into the clearing, eyes wide with fear. Mags nestled against her for comfort, skin quivering.

"How come you fell?" Simon asked. "You never fall."

"I dunno." Col shook his head to clear it of the ringing in his ears. "We were riding along, minding our own business when we—" He stopped, suddenly remembering what he had seen. "Connie, there's something loose on the moor. A big cat maybe. I saw its eyes in the bushes over there." He gestured toward a thick tangle of fallen trees and new saplings. "It leapt out, Mags reared, and I fell."

"A big cat?" Anneena offered her hand to pull Col up from the ground. "Are you sure?"

Col gave Connie an awkward look. Society members were sworn to keep mythical creatures secret, and if this was one of them then he'd just made a monumental blunder. Anneena would never give up on such a tempting mystery. "I'm not sure. Maybe it was just a deer or something."

"It wasn't a deer," Simon stated. "I know it wasn't. Let's go look for it."

Connie frowned at her brother. This was getting out of hand and she still felt they were in desperate danger. "You can't go. You're forgetting that Col's hurt. Aren't you, Col?" she said, giving him a heavy hint.

On cue, Col clutched his ankle. "Yeah. I think I've sprained it."

"Let's go back to the cottage and get you some ice. Simon, you'd better take one side, I'll take the other." Forcing her brother to assume his part as one of Col's human crutches, Connie led the retreat, leaving two amber eyes watching her from the shadows.

2

Fire Imps

Ice pack in place, Col sat on a sun chair in the back garden of Rat's house, surrounded by the defunct engines sacrificed to Mr. Ratcliff's hobby of car mechanics. Mr. Ratcliff himself was asleep in the hammock slung where the drying line normally hung. Mrs. Ratcliff was clattering in the kitchen, singing tunelessly, making what she called "hedgerow jam" and what her son and husband called "Mam's Poisoned Spread."

"It'd be okay if she just stuck to blackberries and things." Rat groaned. "But she will branch out—chuck in a bit of anything that catches her eye."

"Like what?" asked Connie, plucking the petals off a daisy. "He loves me, he loves me not," she counted absent-mindedly.

"I dunno—like nettles and cow parsley—anything really."

Connie threw the daisy aside and made a mental note to dispose quietly of the jar Mrs. Ratcliff had given her great-uncle for Christmas.

For Rat's benefit, Anneena had just finished running through what had happened in the plantation and was now speculating about the strange creature.

"It's not the first time, of course," said Anneena, fanning herself with her sun hat. "There've been reports of a beast on the moors for ages."

"Oh?" said Connie guardedly. She had certainly never sensed the presence of this particular creature before and was still wondering what it was. It seemed so strange, so contradictory—dark and prowling like a big cat, snake-like in the way it slithered through the undergrowth, but also nimble, certainly fast enough to make a rapid escape.

"Yes. I saw a story last month from over Okehampton way about a flock of sheep being raided. Paw-prints everywhere, according to the farmer."

"I don't think that was the same beast," said Rat with a grin. He stretched out his thin, wiry body on the scrubby lawn dotted with bright yellow dandelions. His sharp profile twitched with suppressed laughter.

"Oh?" asked Anneena. "Why not?"

Rat opened his mouth but was lost for words.

Col knew why: it must have been the frost wolf, Icefen, in one of his wilder moods. Col wouldn't have been surprised if Rat had encouraged him. Come to think of it, Rat might even have been riding him at the time.

"It's a long way from here, isn't it?" Col supplied for his friend who was notoriously bad at lying. Rat twisted over onto his belly and gave Col a grateful grin.

"But how many wild animals do you think there can be, Col?" asked Anneena dismissively.

Far more than you know, Col thought, but he shrugged for Anneena's sake.

"Isn't it more likely that it's the same creature?" Anneena persisted. "You can get all the way from here to Okehampton on open moor. It's unlikely to be spotted. Not unless someone's looking for it."

Connie turned quickly to Anneena, hearing a familiar determined note in her friend's voice. Jane had picked up the same signal.

"Looking for it?" Jane asked slowly.

"Yes. Aren't you even the least bit interested to find out what's going on out there?" Anneena waved her slim hand vaguely in the direction of the moor. "If a big cat's escaped from a zoo, it's got to be caught before it does any more harm."

"Yes, but—" Connie began.

"And we know this area better than anybody. We could track it down." Anneena had a glint in her eyes. They all knew that she liked nothing better than to have a project.

"I don't think it's a good idea," said Connie firmly. "It's

too risky. You can't go tracking unknown wild animals, Anneena. You wouldn't stand a chance if you met it."

"I don't want to meet it. I just want to gather as much information as I can about it. Once we've got a good idea of where it hunts, we can pass on the information to the proper authorities."

"We?" asked Jane in a wary tone of voice.

Anneena looked around the unenthusiastic faces of her friends. "Well, I hoped it would be 'we.' That creature is probably suffering out there—terrified and hungry. Can't be much fun surviving in this drought, can it?" She turned her large brown eyes to appeal to Connie. "And if you met it, it'd probably just roll over and let you tickle its tummy."

"Ha!" Connie gave a skeptical laugh. She knew too much about hostile creatures to expect such a warm welcome.

"You didn't see it, Anneena," Col warned. "It's no kitten."

"Oh, come on, you guys! What else have you got to do with your summer?"

"I'll help you, Anneena," said Rat, to Col and Connie's surprise.

"Are you sure?" asked Connie.

"Yeah. I've got a good idea about the beast's habits already." He winked at Connie. "I know enough to keep Anneena occupied."

"Rat!" Connie protested.

But Anneena cut in quickly, thinking that Connie was

trying to undermine her idea. "Thanks, Rat. I really appreciate your support." She glared around at the others, saving her hardest stare for Connie.

"Okay, okay," said Jane, surrendering to the inevitable. "I'll help."

Anneena looked pointedly at Connie and Col.

Connie sighed. "I will, too. But you must trust me if I say it's too dangerous; you must promise to leave the moor immediately."

"Don't take any notice of her," chipped in Simon, who had been sitting forgotten, listening in on the conversation. "She's just being a nag as usual. I'll help."

Connie frowned at Simon, but he was studiously avoiding her eye. Sibling relations were definitely at an all-time low.

"Thanks, Simon," said Anneena, somewhat surprised by this offer. Simon was normally found inside destroying aliens on his computer, not volunteering for a challenge outdoors.

Col spoke last. "I'm with Connie on this. I'll only help if we follow her lead. We all know she's the one who understands animals."

Simon snorted. Col glared at him, making Simon swallow his comment.

"Okay," said Anneena, happy to have gotten her way. "We'll start by looking up recent news reports of attacks and see if we can establish a pattern." She looked around the circle. "Any volunteers to come with me to the library in Chartmouth?"

"Libraries: not my thing, Anneena," said Rat quickly.

Anneena must have agreed with him for she was now looking expectantly at Jane and Connie.

"Okay. I can come on Monday morning," admitted Connie.

"I'll come, too," volunteered Jane.

Connie and Jane shared a private, exasperated look. They both loved Anneena dearly, but sometimes being her friend could be exhausting.

⬦⬦⬦

Astride Mags once more, Col trotted behind Connie as she pedaled her bike down the lanes bright with nodding summer flowers and grasses. Since Col's father had married Connie's aunt last year, Col had been spending more time 'round at Shaker Row and it was becoming a second home to him. He had decided to go back with Connie to ask his father about the creature on the moors: as a member of the Society, Mack might have some ideas.

Col would also have liked to ask Connie for her opinion, but she did not seem disposed to talk at the moment. Instead, he watched in silence as butterflies fluttered in a circle over the universal's head, drifting in and out of formation like tiny ballroom dancers. Jane and Anneena were just in front, riding their bikes side by side, talking animatedly about the moorland beast.

Col turned his thoughts back to the scene in the plantation and shuddered. He hadn't caught a proper look at the animal, but he remembered the wave of malevolence that accompanied its pounce. It had felt so powerful; he would put money on it being some kind of mythical creature. But which one? The Society had good relations with most of the beasts and beings on Dartmoor, except mischievous creatures like the kelpies, horse-shaped sprites who liked to confuse walkers and lead them into bogs. But that kind of harm was mostly a wicked trick, rarely fatal; the creature in the plantation had been different. It had wanted blood.

Connie's thoughts were preoccupied not by the creature but by her brother's behavior in its presence. She was relieved to leave Simon behind at her great-uncle's cottage on the headland, where he was staying for the summer. They were definitely not getting on as well as they used to. But she was going to have to confront him about his gift, talk to him about the Society at the very least, before he did something rash.

"So, what do you think?" Col asked her as soon as they waved farewell to Anneena and Jane on the outskirts of Hescombe.

"He's not himself," she said.

"What?" Col had no idea what she was talking about.

"Simon: he definitely sensed the creature before I did, up in the plantation just now."

"Oh," said Col. This put a new spin on the whole adventure. "D'you think?"

"What else can it be?"

"Do you think he's another universal?"

Connie frowned, digging back in her memory to recall the other times she'd been with her brother in the presence of animals. He had a special bond with her aunt's cat; he'd shown that long ago.

"I don't know. None of the mythical creatures have ever mentioned it to me and, in my own case, I know they sensed it without my having to ask them."

"So what about entering him for an assessment?"

Connie shook her head. "He's not interested. Both Evelyn and I have asked him before, but he's taken it into his head that the Society is my thing, so he hates it. And Mr. Coddrington is still in place as the assessor for our region; I really couldn't face explaining the difficulty to the Society." Though losing his post as Trustee and being almost universally disliked for his attempt to oust Connie from the Society, Mr. Coddrington had clung on to his official role as an assessor at its London headquarters. Nothing had ever been proven against him, so they couldn't fire him.

"Dr. Brock then?" suggested Col.

"Yes, that's an idea. Or Horace Little. He's a friend of Uncle Hugh's, so Simon might listen to him."

They stopped outside the gate to Number Five.

"Do you want to come in?" Connie asked hesitantly, looking at Col with her mismatched eyes—so like his—one green, one brown. She was aware that there was a certain tension between them ever since she'd kissed him on the cheek a few months ago. Col no longer seemed easy in her presence. She now regretted doing it.

"Dunno," said Col, glancing at his watch, even though he would like to have stayed. "I'm not sure I have time. I did want a word—with Dad, that is . . ."

The decision was taken out of their hands by Mack Clamworthy. He had been on the watch for their return and spotted them hovering by the gate. He came striding down the path: a handsome man in good shape, with spiky black hair, square jaw, and twinkling brown eyes. It was his Harley-Davidson by the gate that Connie had just propped her bike against. She picked up the bicycle quickly, knowing how protective he was of his beloved motorcycle, though for once he seemed completely oblivious of his prized possession, not giving it a second glance.

"Col, Connie, just the people I want!" He threw open the gate and gave his son a bear hug, from which Col struggled to extricate himself. "Come in, come in." He made no attempt to hide that he was in an extremely good mood.

Col and Connie exchanged puzzled looks, but there seemed nothing to do but follow him inside. They trailed behind him down the garden path and around to the back door. The kitchen windows were wide open, the mobile of scavenged feathers and glass tinkling melodiously over the sink. The dishes in the sink were piled high. Clearly no one had done any housework since breakfast, which was not unusual in this household.

Mack strode into the hall and bellowed up the stairs. "Evie, Connie and Col are back. Are you coming down?" He turned to grin at them. "She's just having a rest. The heat got to her." Rubbing his hands gleefully together, Mack paced across the stone floor, but said nothing more, waiting for his wife to arrive.

Col sat down at the table and tapped his fingers impatiently. He wished now he had slipped away and gone straight home. Connie, equally perplexed, helped herself to a glass of water at the sink, leaned against the edge, and waited.

When Evelyn came in, with her long brown hair bundled up in a crimson scarf, Connie saw instantly that her aunt looked distinctly unwell. She poured a second glass of water and held it out to her.

"Here, have this. You don't look good."

"Thanks, Connie," said Evelyn, taking the water and gazing at it as if she would rather not drink it. "I'm fine. Really, I'm fine."

Connie took a step forward and put her hand to her aunt's forehead to see if she had a fever. Connie gave a small gasp.

"You're not . . . ?" Connie asked.

"I am," said Evelyn with a weak smile. "Feeling ghastly, but I am. How did you know?"

Col looked from one to the other. Connie, at least, now seemed to understand what was going on here, but he was still in the dark. Was Evelyn seriously ill? Surely not?

"Will someone please tell me what's going on?" he demanded, feeling a sharp pang of concern.

Mack strode over to his son and clapped him on the shoulder. "How would you like to hear that you are going to have a brother—"

"Or sister," added Evelyn.

"—or sister? In March, we think."

Col's jaw dropped. "You're not . . . ?" he asked Mack.

"Yep. Going to have a baby. Well, Evie's going to have the baby. I'm just the proud father." Mack went over to his wife and gave her a gentle squeeze.

"Poor kid," said Col with a broad grin.

"So you're pleased?" Mack looked a little worried. Mack and Col both knew that he had not been the perfect father to Col, absent for much of the time.

"'Course I'm pleased." But for all his delight, Col couldn't help feeling jealous of the new baby. He or she would have Mack as a proper father, something Col had never been allowed.

Evelyn turned to Connie. "And what do you think?" she asked her niece.

Connie had just been wondering if this new turn of events would mean that she was still welcome at Number Five. There wasn't much space and she had the attic bedroom, leaving just one for guests.

"It's great news. I'm really pleased." How could she not be when it was so clearly what Evelyn and Mack wanted?

"So tell me, Connie, how did you know?" Evelyn was looking at her shrewdly with her bright green eyes.

Connie rubbed her throat. How could she explain? "I felt him—or her," she added quickly. "I could feel another life." She did not want to go on to say what else she knew. Why spoil the surprise with something that was for the moment only a suspicion?

❧

When Col left the impromptu celebration in the kitchen, he found that Mags was not alone by the front gate. The boy he'd met hours earlier on the beach was waiting for him on the steps that led down to the shore, absentmindedly brushing the sand from his feet, his nose red after a day of playing in the sun. He sprang up when he heard the gate clang shut and flashed a gappy-toothed grin at Col.

"See, I'm still here!" he said in an eager voice.

Col groaned inwardly. He would have very much preferred to head straight home so he could be alone with his thoughts about his father's news—but a promise was a promise.

"Where's your mum and dad?" Col asked, looking up

and down the beach. It was deserted, the tide in, and the long, yawning shadows cast by the cliff made it far less inviting than it had appeared earlier in the day. The sea had lost its sparkle and now lapped with a dull gray sheen against the seaweed-strewn stones. A red light flushed the sky as the sun slipped beyond the horizon.

"They've gone back to the hotel," said the boy, gesturing over his shoulder toward the harbor. "They know I'm with you."

That was a bit odd. The boy didn't even know Col's name but had just assumed that he would keep his word and let him ride. And the boy's parents had let him stay out this late on his own? Col's grandmother wouldn't have done the same when he was the boy's age.

"I can't give you a long ride because Mags here has been out all day and needs to get back to his stable." Col patted his horse on the neck and gave him an apologetic look. Mags shook his mane, forgiving Col his foolish generosity. "But I can take you for a quick trot on the beach. Have you ever ridden before?"

"Nope," said the boy happily, already attempting to scramble onto Mags's back as if the horse was a jungle gym. Col grabbed him by the back of his T-shirt and pulled him down.

"Not like that," he said, half-amused, half-irritated. "Here, put this helmet on. Then put one foot in the stirrup, and I'll help you up."

Once the boy was safely in the saddle, Col shortened the stirrups and took Mags's halter. With a click of his tongue, he led the way down to the beach. Mags snorted in disgust as the boy bounced up and down, crowing with delight.

"Look, mate, he's got feelings, you know: he's not a pogo stick," Col called up.

"Sorry!" said the boy, still laughing. "This is great. I've always dreamed of riding a real horse."

Col whispered something in Mags's ear, and in unison they began to trot along the strand. The boy was now bouncing for real on the horse's back, clearly in seventh heaven. They reached the limit of the beach, forward progress cut off by the tide, and Col turned for home.

"What's that?" called the boy, pointing over Mags's head up in the air.

Plumes of dark gray cloud were rising from the cliff top. Col caught the scent of smoke. He led the horse and rider into the shallows so he could get a better look. There was an orange glow above them, like a fringe of flaming hair on the brow of the hill.

"Some idiot's started a fire," Col answered. "Shift up. We've got to call the fire brigade." He swung up behind the boy and urged Mags forward, cursing himself for leaving his phone at home.

The boy was still staring with wonder at the fire.

"I can see people in the flames, dancing!" he said excitedly. "Let's go up there!"

"No," said Col sharply. "There can't be—not in the fire." However, he could see that there *were* shapes very like people leaping into the sky. But they were not human. The fire imps were rejoicing in the blaze. He wondered that the boy had seen them so quickly. Most people just dismissed them as odd silhouettes in the flames.

"But I must go up!" the boy cried. His eyes shone with a fanatical gleam as he twisted around in the saddle to stare up at the fire. "They're calling to me!" He began to slip from Mags's back as if he intended to scale the sheer cliff face in his desperation to reach the imps. Col gripped his arms firmly and yanked him back on.

"You're not going up there." He kicked Mags into a trot that swiftly turned into a gallop, and the boy was forced to concentrate on staying seated. Mags surged up the slope from the beach back to Number Five. Col dismounted, pulling the boy after him. "You're coming with me." He did not trust the boy on his own, sure that he would run back to the fire the moment he was left alone.

"But—!" protested the boy, reluctantly allowing Col to propel him up the path to the back door, his eyes still fixed on the blaze.

Col banged the door open and pushed him into the kitchen, much to the astonishment of Connie and Mack, who were just sitting down to supper. Evelyn had returned to bed, not feeling up to eating. Mack rose abruptly to his feet, chair clattering to the floor behind him.

"I've got to use your phone," Col said. "The headland's on fire."

Mack tossed him the handset. "And who's this?" Mack asked, looking the boy up and down. Col shrugged, having just got through to the emergency switchboard.

"I'm Liam," said the boy defiantly, his chin tilted up to face the imposing figure of Mack Clamworthy.

"Sure you are," said Mack with a grin, taking an instant liking to the lad. "Sit down. Col won't be long."

"Would you like something to drink, Liam?" Connie asked. She got to her feet and took a glass from the draining board. If she had been him, she knew she would not have liked being stared at by two strangers.

Liam, however, had other things on his mind besides standing in an unfamiliar kitchen. "There're people up there—dancing around in the flames!" he said. "I saw them with my own eyes. I've got to get back to them." He half-turned as if to make a dash for the door.

"Hey there!" Mack blocked the exit. "Calm down!"

Connie paused, her hand gripping the cool glass at the tap. She closed her eyes and felt out to the cliff top, sensing the presence of the fire imps, darting in and out of the tongues of fire curling up from the bone-dry grass. When she opened her eyes, she saw Col looking at her, and he gave her a slight nod of confirmation.

"Didn't you hear them calling us to come and join them?" Liam asked Col. His gray-green eyes, the color of smoke, were wide with a mixture of exhilaration and anger that no one seemed to understand or believe him.

Col shook his head. "No. I didn't hear a thing."

"But you must've!" Liam said desperately, his fists clenched. "Their voices were like . . ." He paused, struggling to find the right words. "They sounded really clear to me like—"

"Like crackling twigs, hissing logs, and popping sparks," said Connie softly. Liam turned to stare at her in amazement.

"You heard them then?" he asked.

"Yes, I've heard them," said Connie. "Now, Liam, what would you like to drink? You want a drink, don't you?"

"Yeah," said Liam, licking his sunburnt lips and giving her a wary look. "Have you got Coke?"

"Sorry, only water or orange juice."

"Juice then."

In the distance, the wail of a siren announced the arrival of the first firefighters on the cliff top. Connie handed Liam his drink and led him to a chair. The others were silent, content to let the universal deal with the situation. "I know what you heard, Liam, but it's not safe to follow those voices until you know more about the creatures," she said.

"Creatures?" Liam was gazing at Connie like he couldn't take his eyes off her. Col knew that there was something special about the effect Connie had on some people, those who were most sensitive to her gift, but seeing her with

Liam made him realize anew that there was a mesmerizing power within her. She contained a spring of energy that bubbled up and out to other living beings. He couldn't look away from her, either.

"Yes, creatures." Connie knelt beside Liam and put a hand on his arm. "You've seen the fire imps tonight. Your companion species, I think. But you must keep it a secret from everyone until we've had a chance to talk to your parents. You see, we want to introduce you to other people—people like you."

Mack gave a discreet cough. "He's a bit young for an assessment, Connie," he said. "You-know-who'll never agree to do it." He was right: Ivor Coddrington would not consider examining anyone under ten.

"It's a bit late for that, isn't it?" said Connie. She was no longer afraid of the assessor, her declared enemy within the Society. His opposition to the existence of a universal was now just a fact of life. "Liam's seen them—he's heard them."

"Yeah, you're right as usual," Mack conceded.

"I'll take it to the Trustees if I have to. Anyway, perhaps it's not Mr. Coddrington we need to ask. Liam, where do you live?"

"London," said Liam, looking puzzled by this exchange. "Vauxhall."

"That's near Brixton, isn't it?"

"Yeah."

Connie smiled. Here was the answer: Horace and Antonia Little, her friends in Brixton, would help. Antonia was a member of the Company of the Elementals, creatures made of the four elements of water, earth, wind, and fire. And London had a different assessor. That meant she needn't approach Ivor Coddrington for help.

Col glanced up at the clock. It was half-past eight. "We'd better get you back to your hotel," he said to Liam. "Your mum and dad will be worried about you."

"No, they won't," said Liam matter-of-factly, getting up to go. "They'll be down at the pub by now. As long as I'm in bed when they get back, they won't care."

Col again swallowed his surprise that no one seemed to be looking out for Liam. "Well, I've got to get back. My gran will be wondering where I am. Come on."

Liam took a reluctant step to follow him. "Can I come back tomorrow?" He looked to Connie as if he half-expected a rejection.

"I'm not here tomorrow," Connie said. Liam's face fell.

"Okay," he said in a small but bitter voice. "Fine."

"But if you're still here on Tuesday, come by," she added swiftly. Liam smiled.

Col grabbed a slice of garlic bread from the table. "But I'm here tomorrow. I'll look out for you on the beach. Maybe Dad and I should try to meet your parents?"

His father got up and slung his jacket over his shoulder, keys jangling in its pockets.

"I was thinking of calling in at the Anchor to see if I can spot them tonight," said Mack. "I'll break the ice over a couple of beers. Let me walk you two back."

Liam, who had been looking delighted by these invitations, now seemed worried. "I'm not sure," he said, biting his lip. "They can be a bit weird, my parents."

Mack laughed. "Don't worry, Liam. I do weird—ask anyone in Hescombe. I'm sure we'll get on like an imp on fire."

Mack led the boys out of the house, leaving Connie to the now-cold supper. In the silence as she ate, Connie let her thoughts stray to the hilltop. Had the fire really been an accident? She caught a whisper of a slinking presence and tasted sulfur at the back of her throat. It felt uncannily like the creature from the moor.

She got up to scrape the plates, trying to shake off the instinct that she was under threat. Whatever had started the fire, water was putting an end to the imps' party; their cries were rising up in indignant hisses as they were doused by hoses. Their fragile bodies of flames were snuffed out, leaving their spirits to wander on the wind until the next blaze ignited.

What did it mean, all this about Liam and the revelation of his gift? She had known the moment he had spoken, just as she had sensed Simon's bond with the mysterious creature of the moor. And then there was the baby in her aunt's womb. Her ability for divining the gifts of others was becoming more acute with each passing day. Not only could she now sense the presence of mythical creatures, Connie was coming to know their human companions, like an antenna buzzing with the transmissions of many radio stations. But the gift came at a price. As she spent so much of her time resonating to the presence of others, it threatened to squeeze out her own sense of self.

Connie thought back over her nights of disturbed sleep. If only she had the ability to tune out Kullervo's wavelength, perhaps then this gift would be more bearable, but there seemed no prospect of being able to do this. His presence was a current that flowed under all the others, wearing her down, ingrained in her so deeply that she could not hope to block it out any more than she could turn the tide.

3
Devil's Tooth

Connie spooned the chocolate-coated froth off the top of her cappuccino, savoring the milky sweetness on her tongue. Anneena was bent over a pad, comparing notes with Jane after their session in the Chartmouth library. Outside the air-conditioned coffee shop, the weather was cloudy but still hot and dry. A woman walked past with an elegant poodle mincing along at her high heels. Catching sight of Connie in the window, the poodle barked a greeting. Connie raised her little finger in a tiny wave.

"Now, this is really interesting." Anneena's voice broke into Connie's daydream. "There's an article on local wildlife in this drought. It says that many animals are being forced out of their normal habitats to find food and water. I bet that's what's happening to our creature."

"Maybe," said Jane. "It's been a funny year—hardly

any rain since the beginning of July."

Taking another sip off her spoon, Connie wondered what the weather giants made of it all. They were particularly angry at the changes brought to the climate by humans. Many of them had already gone over to Kullervo's side, and he was urging them to take violent action. She wouldn't put it past them to be withholding the rain on purpose.

"The writer says the drought's due to global warming," continued Anneena, reading off her handwritten notes.

"Maybe," said Jane again. "But no one knows anything for sure. You should hear Dad on the subject."

"I don't really think there's any doubt that we're doing the damage," Connie said quietly, remembering what the mythical creatures had told her over the years.

"But no one's sure how much and how fast," Jane explained. "It really worries me."

Anneena flipped her notebook closed. "Me, too. What about companies like Axoil pumping out all those greenhouse gases? They won't change unless someone makes them."

"True," said Jane, watching the cars growl by. "But the rest of us don't live completely green lives, either. I feel like a fraud most of the time."

Connie grimaced. She knew what Jane meant. It was easy to go on about the environment but much harder to do anything about it.

"So what else have we learned about the beast of the moor?" Anneena asked, changing the subject. "I've got a list here of recent sightings and attacks."

Jane pulled out a map, opened it up on the table, and pointed to each location. "The pattern before July seemed fairly random and wide-ranging. But just before our sighting, there was a report from a mile further on the moor of a dark brown, cat-like creature on the road—only seen in headlights and gone before the witness could get a second look."

Anneena craned her head over the map. "The plantation is the only place to hide in that area. It might well be living there for the moment. Why don't we keep watch for a few evenings to see if we can spot it moving around?"

Connie put her cup down abruptly. "But I thought you didn't want to get too near it?"

Anneena shrugged. "No good going on this old news. We've got to find out more about it ourselves. Perhaps even get a photo." She shot a hopeful look at Jane. "I don't want to pet it or anything—just to see it."

Connie was alarmed. This was all getting out of control. She couldn't understand why her friend had got so wrapped up in this mystery. "Why, Anneena? There've been stories about a beast on the moor for years, and you've never worried about it before."

"But we almost saw it, Connie!" said Anneena as if she was astounded that her friend didn't share her enthusiasm.

This was awful. Anneena had no idea what she was getting herself into.

"You know I don't like it, but if you're set on keeping watch for the creature, promise you'll take me with you," said Connie firmly.

Anneena gave an offended laugh. The bracelets on her arms jangled as she stretched them above her head. "That's a strange offer. First you say you don't want to go, then you say you've got to come along. But don't put yourself out. I'm sure I could get others to help. Your brother wanted to."

That settled it. Connie knew she definitely had to be at hand if Simon was going near that creature again. "I've got to be there. You don't understand, Anneena."

"And you do?" her friend asked, irritated now.

"Yes."

"In that case, why don't you share your *special* knowledge with the rest of us?" Anneena gathered up her things and thrust them in her bag. She flicked her long black hair off her shoulder in an angry gesture.

"Anneena." Jane tugged at her friend's jacket, determined to prevent the fight from escalating. "You know Connie's good with animals. You shouldn't turn down her help just because you're feeling a bit miffed."

Anneena's annoyance dispersed as quickly as it had arisen. She put her bag down. "Oh, you're right as usual. Sorry, Connie. Of course, you have to be there. It's just that this beast thing is really getting to me. I have this weird feeling that we are fated to meet."

Connie said nothing, hoping Anneena's instinct was for once way off target.

⚛

"Anneena's crazy! We should keep as far as we can from that creature!" exclaimed Col.

Connie had just filled him in on her morning with Anneena and Jane in Chartmouth. They were walking through the Mastersons' yard on their way to their training sessions: Col to fly with Skylark and Connie to meet her mentor, Gard the rock dwarf. The yard was buzzing with activity. Over by the barn, Dr. Brock was talking intently to the two dragon companion twins. All were dressed in their leather flying jackets, planning an evening expedition.

"Argand wants to see you, Connie," Dr. Brock called. His white hair, still ginger at the temples, shone in the late-afternoon sunlight.

"Tell her I'll try to come out after my class," called back Connie. "I'll meet her in the usual place."

"Don't keep her out late!" warned Dr. Brock. "Castanea was furious last time you two were out alone. She said that it was well past midnight before Argand came home."

"You know Argand," said Connie, pausing beside him for a moment. "I wanted to go home much earlier, but she insisted we stay out for the moonrise. She said she'd come

42

and watch it on the beach in front of my house if I refused to remain on the moor with her."

"Ah."

"I thought that the family next door were probably not ready to see a dragon outside their front garden so I stayed."

Dr. Brock gave her a smile of understanding. Tom and Greg, the dragon twins, laughed sympathetically.

Tom, who was the companion to one of Argand's siblings, commiserated. "Castanea can be a bit fierce. I still bear the scars."

"Always keep out of range of her tail, that's my motto," added Greg.

"I'll try to remember that." Connie gave them a rueful grin.

A crowd of young people from Sea Snakes were just getting into a mini-bus for the trip down to a quiet cove they used for their training. Jessica and Arran greeted Col warmly, any bad feelings from Saturday night clearly forgotten. Then they both hugged Connie. The others Connie knew less well—a mermaid companion, a companion to the Nereids, as well as a stern-looking boy who was companion to Charybdis, the whirlpool sea monster. Though the Sea Snakes knew Connie only slightly, they all called out greetings to her, eager to catch the attention of the famous universal if only for a moment.

"We'd better get a move on or we'll be late," said Col,

picking up the pace, annoyed that he was being ignored again, though he knew he should be used to it by now. "So what do you think's out there?"

Connie shrugged. "I'm not sure. I can feel it's very wild—really dangerous."

"Yeah, I could've told you that."

"And it's not used to humans, like one of our companion species would be. The problem is, I can't get a fix on its nature: one moment, it seems very cat-like, then it slithers out of focus like a snake sliding under cover." She paused, forehead wrinkled in a frown as she tried to sort out her confusion. It was no good: what she sensed would not settle into anything definite.

"If you don't know what it is, I'm not sure anyone would," Col said loyally.

She shook her head. "I hardly know anything, Col. There's so much to learn about being a universal. But Anneena's right about one thing: it's in that plantation, deep inside. I was thinking that maybe I could persuade Anneena to set out watch as far from it as possible. That way we probably won't see anything and, knowing her, she'll soon get bored. The only problem is Simon."

"Simon? Why's he a problem?" asked Col, vaulting over a fence. Connie followed more slowly, jumping down on the other side.

"Well, if he can sense it, too, he'll probably lead Anneena right to it."

Col thought for a moment. "Leave Simon to me. I'll see if I can't do something."

"Thanks," Connie said gratefully. "That'd be a great help. If I say anything, he'll just do the opposite to annoy me."

A strange warmth uncurled in the pit of Col's stomach. It felt good to have Connie's gratitude, to have her smiling at him as if he was the most wonderful friend she had. He only wished he deserved her admiration.

"Don't worry, Connie. You can count on me," he said, swearing to himself that he'd prove it.

⁂

Connie's usual place for meeting Argand was up on the Devil's Tooth, an isolated crop of granite sticking out of the moor and the first tor reached after leaving the Mastersons' land. She could still see the roofs of the farm buildings below her as she made her way up the valley, though the farmhouse itself was swallowed up in the long shadows cast by the setting sun. Down in the darkness, she knew that the stocky black figure of Gard was watching her go, following her progress through her footfalls as she climbed up out of the mild valley onto the dry expanse of the moor. She waved to him.

I'll be fine from here, she told him, sending her thoughts diving down into the earth and along the granite rock bed under their feet. *I can see the Devil's Tooth ahead of me now. You don't need to wait for me. Argand will be along any moment.*

Be careful, cautioned Gard. *Call if you have need.*

I will.

Reaching the brow of the first rise, she paused to take a breath. A cattle-grid marked the beginning of the moor. A narrow ribbon of gray tarmac wound over the next hill, curling around the base of the Devil's Tooth. The tor jutted out of the top of a hillock like a fang gnawing at the sky. It was an eerie but beautiful sight, colors softened this evening by the wash of pinks and blues on the horizon. Clouds were fringed with intense shafts of flame as the sun set, dazzling Connie for a moment as she looked into the heart of the inferno. She stood back to let a Land Rover pass, its wheels juddering over the grid. The sheepdog in the back barked excitedly at her, scratching at the rear window in greeting. She laughed and waved, but the car was soon out of view, heading back down into the valley for the evening. Overhead, three suspiciously dragon-shaped silhouettes flew high, heading out to sea. Dr. Brock and the twins were airborne, at last.

Balancing her way across the grid, Connie left the road to take a more direct route up to the tor.

It wasn't far; she usually managed the climb in ten minutes or so, though she was slowed down tonight by the lingering heat of the day. Her brow was soon beaded with sweat, and she wished she had thought to bring a bottle of water. Trying to distract herself from her thirst, she opened her mind to her surroundings. Having just come

from a long session with Gard, she was alert to the nature
of the earth she was treading on, probing down into the
layers, passing through the thin covering of soil and grass
to the bones of the moor below. A hot wind ruffled the
parched grass at her feet. The normally emerald green
moor was bleached in the sun, balding where the dry grass
had been worn away by the passage of hooves and feet.
She could feel the vegetation crying out for relief, for the
gift of a shower of refreshing rain, but the skies remained
empty. She would have been grateful for a spot or two of
rain herself at that moment, she thought, running her
tongue over her lips.

It was then that she felt it. There was a creature near
her. *The* creature. Its presence flickered into her mind then
darted out of perception, eluding her attempts to pin it
down. Connie looked around, but could see nothing. The
wind continued to rustle the grass. The brown bracken
swayed slightly. Had that been the breeze or was something lurking in the cover of the waist-high stems?

Connie hesitated. Should she call Gard? To say what?
That she was being stalked, for that was what it was
doing, wasn't it? But surely she didn't need to be afraid?
If it thought it could trap a universal like this, then it
had another think coming. She had an appointment
with a dragon; no beast would dare come near her once
Argand arrived.

Picking up her pace, Connie clambered up the last few

feet to the base of the Devil's Tooth. She quickly examined the stones, seeking out hand- and footholds to take her to the top. If she got up there, no one could reach her without giving plenty of warning of their approach. Perhaps this was her chance to see the creature and find out what it was? Suffering a few scrapes along the way, she hauled herself up. Once on the crest, she was rewarded by a cooler gust of wind fanning her face.

From up here, she had the sensation she was on a gray ship looking down on the twilit sea. She did not like heights, and felt as if she was swaying on real waves, her head beginning to spin. She sat down to anchor herself against the stone. The granite still throbbed with the heat of the day, its cracks and crevices groaning as they contracted after hours of baking in the sun. Feeling more secure now that she was seated, Connie gazed around for any sign of the creature. Nothing. Had she imagined it? After all, she had spent much of the day thinking about it; she had probably let her imagination run away with her.

Just then a flicker of flame between her and the road below caught her eye. Straining to make out what was happening in the gloom, she saw fire consuming a patch of bracken. Like a swarm of locusts, the sparks spread with voracious rapidity, cutting off her retreat back to the farm.

A dark shadow slunk away from the blaze, slipping swiftly out of sight.

Connie grew suddenly conscious of her own exposure

up on the Devil's Tooth. A moorland fire was an unpredictable thing; there was no doubt she was in danger if she stayed where she was for long. Fortunately, the wind was blowing from behind her, driving the flames away from the tor. She had time.

"Argand!" Connie called, cupping her hands around her mouth. "Help!" Surely the golden dragon was nearby? The sun had almost set. She should be here at any moment.

There was a shower of sparks to her left some distance from the original blaze. At first, Connie thought that it was Argand sailing out of the sky to her aid, but then she realized a new fire had started. The grass surrendered to the flames without a struggle, expiring in a crackle of orange. Once again, Connie thought she glimpsed the prowling form of a creature, long tail whipping behind it as it leapt out of the way. Was it trying to flee the fire? Or was it starting the blaze? The acrid scent of smoke now came to her on the wind. Spinning around she saw that behind her a patch of flame had sprung into life, this one creeping toward her, driven by the wind. Desperate now, Connie looked out to her right into the only expanse of darkness and, sure enough, the rash of fire was ignited there, too. The creature was trying to trap her in a ring of flame.

Argand! called out Connie. Trust her to be late when she was most needed! *Gard!*

Yes, Universal? The presence of the rock dwarf was with her in an instant.

I'm trapped. Fire on the moors! Get help!

We're coming. Stay where you are. I can sense another creature near you. But Gard was over a mile away. He could do little on his own and would need time to find help from the other creatures. All the dragons and pegasi were off flying. Who could reach her in time?

The fire was gaining a grip on the earth, a jewel-bright tide crawling over the surface like lava. Billows of choking smoke dotted with orange sparks whirled up into the air. Then came a subtle change in the wind, a shimmer on the horizon, and Connie sensed the approach of the fire imps. From all directions, their wispy bodies plummeted out of the sky like shadows of seabirds diving on a school of fiery herring. Once in contact with the heat, the imps ignited, their bodies bursting into joyous flame. Connie saw them writhing with delight, long hair flaring up to the heavens. They shook their pointed fingers defiantly at the sky, daring it to douse their celebration, but the sky was empty, having nothing to shed to quell this festival of fire. The hill on which the Devil's Tooth stood was now crowned with thorns of flame.

Hurry up! Please! Connie called out to Gard, her fear mounting. She could feel the heat on her cheeks, and her eyes watered as the smoke stung them. A new presence, a dark tide, seemed to be rising in her mind. She began to feel dizzy and sick, fighting unconsciousness. Resting her head on her knees, she gasped and coughed.

A touch on the back of her neck made her sit up abruptly. Opening her eyes, she found herself looking into the fiery irises of the golden dragon. Argand crooned anxiously, her forked tongue flickering over her companion's cheek.

"Get me out of here," croaked Connie. She threw her arms around the dragon's neck.

But never carry before, said Argand doubtfully. *What if drop you?*

No choice. Try. Please. Connie could feel her lungs bursting for clean, fume-free air.

With a leap into space, the dragonet took off from the rock—and immediately plunged down into the flames, unable to support the weight of her companion.

Hauberk! the dragon screamed to Connie.

Just in time, Connie wrapped herself in her companion's unique protection against fire, donning it like a suit of golden mail against the shafts of flame. They thumped to the ground but Connie managed to cling on, gripping the fringe of scales that ran down Argand's neck. Blazing tongues now licked harmlessly around Connie's ankles. The fire imps shrieked in delight, whizzing around the universal and her dragon, releasing showers of sparks.

Let's get out of here, said Connie. *Hop if you have to.*

With an ungainly shuffle, Argand began to jump forward, using her wings to help her. The wings acted like bellows, sending gusts of fire heavenward with each downdraft. Connie was thankful that she had learned last year to use the hauberk; without it, she would have been a blackened crisp by now. With a final bound, Argand clattered down, her wings sagging like a collapsing golden tent. She landed on the tarmac road, a firebreak stopping the flames at its very edge. Connie looked back up the hill and saw that the conflagration had reached the base of the Devil's Tooth. She had escaped just in time.

What is that, Companion? Argand asked, pointing with one claw to the fiercest part of the blaze. Connie turned to look and saw with horror that there was a small figure— but not a fire imp—dancing hand in hand with those creatures.

Oh no, it's Liam! You've got to save him! She slid off Argand's back and pushed the dragon back toward the fire. *He doesn't know about the imps, yet.* He did not know how they could turn on you in an instant like a blaze fanned by a sudden change of wind, withdrawing their protection, the most fickle companion species.

But how save him? asked Argand, puzzled.

He's small. You might not be able to fly with me, but I'm sure you'd be able to carry him for a short flight back. Please! Connie's gaze was fixed desperately on the cavorting boy, willing the imps to keep their good humor a few more moments.

I try, agreed Argand.

The dragon took off and climbed into the sky to gain height for her rescue attempt. Every second that passed was agony for Connie, sure that the imps would suddenly turn on their young companion. Judging her opportunity, the dragon swooped down, her claws held out in front, and scooped the unsuspecting Liam out of the fire. The imps screamed in fury, hissing and spitting at the dragon. Liam yelped: one of the sparks had scorched his bare legs.

Argand wheeled over Connie, spiraling down to Earth, and dropped Liam at her feet. She landed a few paces away and began to preen her wings; the arch of her neck and the sly pleasure of the smile on her long narrow snout radiated pride at her achievement. Liam stared in astonishment at the dragon and then looked up at Connie.

"Why did it do that?" he asked in a voice on the verge of tears. "I was having fun!" He seemed more surprised by the abrupt end to his party than the fact that he had just been grabbed by a dragon.

"It wouldn't have lasted," said Connie, putting her arm around him. "How's your leg? Can you walk?" Liam nodded. "Good. We've got to get out of here. Let's go."

The smoke was billowing across the road. The fire imps were shooting sparks in their direction. The creatures would punish them if only they could reach them.

"But can't I go back?" Liam protested.

"No," said Connie firmly, steering the boy farther from the blaze. "Thanks, Argand. You were brilliant." The dragon bobbed her head, accepting the praise as her due. "I'll see you soon. You'd better get home, too."

Towing Liam down the hill, Connie had not gone far before she ran into a group of Society members, led by Gard, hurrying up from the farm. Bounding along behind them was Rat, perched on the back of Icefen the frost wolf. Rat broke into a relieved grin when he saw Connie.

"So, you don't need us then?" he said, his eyes shifting curiously to the boy at her side.

"No, thanks to Argand. I'd have been toast by now if she hadn't pitched in just in time." Connie felt numb. Though quite capable of talking, even able to speak lightly of what had happened, she could not take in the fate she had so narrowly escaped.

Gard, usually so calm, was visibly shaken by the near miss. "Are you unscathed, Universal?" he asked in a cracked voice.

"I'm fine."

"I tried to find a winged beast, but there were none on the farm." The polished facets of his coal-black face gleamed as if catching light from the glow of the flames behind Connie. "All we could do was call the fire brigade and hope it was not too late."

"Let's not talk about this now," said Connie, with a shiver. "Liam's injured. Let's get back."

"Liam?" asked Rat.

Connie nodded to the boy who was holding tightly onto her hand and gazing fearfully at the strange collection of beasts and beings around him.

"Here, Liam, I'll give you a ride back to the farm," said Rat cheerfully, holding out a hand to the boy.

Liam took one look at the slobbering jaws of the wolf and gave a whimper.

"It's fine. You can trust Rat," Connie coaxed. She pushed him forward. Mr. Masterson stepped out of the crowd and helped lift Liam up in front of Rat. "I'll see you in a few minutes—I promise," she said.

With a whisk of his brush-like tail, Icefen bounded down the road. He took the shortest path back to the house, eager to put distance between himself and the punishing heat of the fire.

Gard turned to Connie. "So, Universal? What happened?"

❧❧

Mr. Masterson gave Connie and Liam a lift back into Hescombe. They had to pull over several times to let the fire engines pass—the second major incident in as many days. Connie sat on the backseat with her arm around the sleepy boy. She was feeling tired, too, having just relived the events up on the moor for Gard and the other Society members. Her numbness was fading, and her body began to tremble. She had almost died and had only herself to blame—for she had dropped her guard, arrogantly assuming she could cope with anything, and had walked straight into danger. But what creature was it that wished her dead?

"Liam?" Connie said gently. "What were you doing up on the moor?"

"Followed you." Liam yawned, snuggling down against her. "Followed Col out to that farm, then followed you."

Connie was shocked. Liam was not a member of the Society yet, but this meant he had seen many of their secrets.

"What did you see?"

"Oh, loads of brilliant creatures. I liked the dragons best—after the fire imps, of course." He stretched like a cat settling itself to sleep on a welcoming lap.

"Did you see anything on the moor—when you followed me, I mean?"

"Nope."

"Promise you won't tell anyone about what you saw today?"

"'Course not. It's our secret, isn't it?"

"Yes, that's right. Our secret."

Silence fell in the back of the car, broken only by the purr of the engine. Connie bent over Liam and could tell from his even breathing that he had fallen asleep. What were they going to do about him?

4

Bite, Burn, or Venom?

The next evening, Connie spent a long time sitting on her great-uncle's doorstep contemplating the plantation, trying to pick the safest spot away from the beast for Anneena's wildlife watch. Its presence was very faint tonight; if it was in the trees at all, it was far away on the side fringing the open moor and nowhere near the cottages. If they camped near the wind farm, they should have an uneventful night. But how was she to persuade Anneena and, more importantly, Simon to adopt this plan?

Anneena and Jane biked up at eight o'clock. Anneena's front basket was weighed down with blood-stained white plastic bags. She brandished them triumphantly at Connie.

"Look, I got this from our restaurant kitchen! My uncle said the meat might lure a few foxes our way. It might attract something bigger, but I didn't tell him that."

Jane was checking her camera, changing the lens for poor light conditions. "Ready, Connie?" she asked with a commiserating smile.

Simon came out of the house with a pack on his back and a flashlight strapped to his belt. His eyes were shining with excitement.

"Uncle Hugh's packed some supplies for us—a thermos and some chocolate," he said. "He thinks we're just camping out. I'm so looking forward to this!"

"Where's Rat?" asked Anneena. "Shall I go and get him?"

"No," said Connie quickly. "He's tied up tonight. He's sorry he can't make it." Rat was on patrol with Icefen. The wolf and rider were currently hidden in the northern part of the plantation, watching the edge of the wood that was nearest to the sheep, thinking that this was the creature's most likely evening hunting ground. Col was doing an aerial sweep of the area on Skylark before coming along to join them later.

Anneena clucked her tongue in disappointment. "I thought he was eager to help out. So no Rat and no Col."

"Col's coming, just held up," Connie added.

"Oh? He didn't tell me. He never said he had something else to do tonight."

This gave Connie an idea. Here was her excuse. "He has. But he'll be finished by eleven, and he'll meet us up by the wind farm. I said we'd start our watch there."

"Is that a good idea?" said Jane. "I mean, a wild creature

will probably be spooked by those masts. We're not likely to see anything there."

Be quiet, Jane, thought Connie. Did her friend always have to be so clever? "Oh, I don't know. Let's give it a few hours. Anyway, we've got Anneena's bait, haven't we? It might come out for that."

Simon began to grumble his disagreement.

"Fine," said Connie sharply. "If you want to leave Col wandering around looking for us all night, then go ahead, choose another spot. I'm going to stay where I said we'd be."

Faced with this ultimatum, the others had to agree. With no further arguments, they set out, past the humming transmission station, across the field under the wind turbines, arriving at the southern edge of the plantation. It was already night under the closely grouped boughs of the pine trees.

"Where shall we set up camp?" asked Anneena.

Before Connie could speak, Simon jumped in. "I think we should skewer the meat on sticks along the edge here, not far from these bushes. The creature'll want to feel he's got cover nearby if he's to come out." He looked up into the sky, feeling for the wind. "And the breeze is coming in off the sea. We should place ourselves downwind. What about by that fallen trunk there?" He pointed to one of the many trees that Connie had felled earlier in the year when she and Kullervo raised a whirlwind.

It was a good plan, thought Connie. Too good, for it

had a chance of working. But, unfortunately, Anneena had also noticed that Simon knew what he was talking about.

"Great. Let's do that. Would you put out the bait for us, Simon?"

With a grin, glad to have his plan approved under the nose of his supposedly more experienced sister, Simon took the bag and proceeded to peg out the meat. The three girls took the rest of their stuff over to the trunk.

"I didn't know Simon was so clever," Anneena said to Connie, "you know, switched on to animals like you are."

Connie did not share Anneena's obvious approval. In her eyes, her brother was being a complete pain, making her life even more difficult, but she bit her tongue, knowing that she would only make it worse by saying anything now.

Simon jogged back to where they were hiding, wiping his hands on his jeans.

"There, that's done. Not the best spot, but give it time, we might draw him out," he said.

The four sat in silence, watching the night grow darker and darker. Connie handed around cups of coffee when an hour had passed. So far so good: no sign of anything. There was a rustle of wrappers as each broke into their chocolate and then silence again. Connie sat with her senses fully tuned. Col and Skylark were patrolling the moor between here and the Devil's Tooth, just in case the creature decided to roam that way again. Gard was not far away, his presence felt through the soles of her feet.

Sentinel the minotaur waited alert just inside the entrance to the old tin mines over the hill. Icefen and Rat had become distracted; Connie could sense they had left their post and were now running through the flocks of sheep, Icefen unable to resist his instinct to give them a fright. And the creature? She was almost sure that the creature was waiting in its lair in the heart of the plantation. Connie allowed herself a small smile. Soon Col would be here to help.

Another hour crept past, and the coffee was all drunk. Simon began to get restless.

"It's not working," he said abruptly. "He's never going to come so near to houses. Let's go in a bit further and see if we can lure him out."

"No!" said Connie. "What about Col?"

"Oh, stuff Col," said Simon. "Why waste our evening's watch if he can't be on time? You stay here for him if you want. I'm going in."

"You're right," said Anneena, the boredom of watching nothing having got to her, too. "I'll come, Simon. Jane and Connie can wait for Col."

"I think we should all wait here," repeated Connie, but she knew she was losing the argument: Anneena and Simon were already on their feet. Jane looked torn, not wanting to be left behind if there was a chance of really seeing something. She fiddled with her camera strap.

"Look, if we don't go far, Connie can wait on her own

for Col and then give us a shout when he gets here," she suggested.

"Yeah. Give us a shout, Connie," said Simon, hurrying off to pick up one of the meat lures to carry with him.

"But it's not fair!" protested Connie to her friends. "You said you'd listen to me. It's not safe."

"Don't be silly," said Anneena in exasperation. "The creature won't be interested in us if there's a ready supply of meat waiting for it." She set off on the heels of Simon who, to Connie's horror, was already striding purposefully into the plantation as if he knew exactly which way to go. She'd lose him if she waited any longer.

And somewhere in the thicket of trees, the creature was on the move.

"You're not leaving me behind!" she called, stumbling along after the three of them.

Simon laughed, already lost in the shadows ahead. "I thought you'd change your mind if you saw there was any chance of missing out on the fun!"

"Fun!" Connie shouted back with disgust. "This isn't a joke, Simon!" She caught up with Anneena and Jane.

"Sssh!" hissed Anneena. "You'll scare it off with all that racket."

"Good," Connie replied bitterly. But in her bones she knew that the creature was not frightened away: it was slinking closer and closer. "We've got to get out of here. Where's Simon?"

But Simon had gone. The tall, slim trunks of the pines stretched away on all sides like gray pillars in a dark hall. The darkness was almost tangible under the trees; Connie felt she was taking it in with every breath so that it filled her lungs, drowning her.

Anneena was no longer so confident now that they had lost the youngest member of their team. "Simon!" she called out. "Simon!" Her voice was swallowed up in one gulp by the night.

A tangle of bushes on their left rustled, but there was no breeze under the trees. Connie felt an ominous presence drawing closer. What was it? Cat, but not just cat.

"I don't like this," said Jane in a small voice. "It's creepy."

Connie closed her eyes. If Simon had a gift, surely she should be able to sense where he was just as she could with other companions? As soon as she turned inward, she heard Gard's voice in her head.

It's near you, Universal. Get out of there!

Gard, quiet! I've got to find Simon. A pause. Both of them sensed him, Gard through Simon's footprints, Connie through his gift.

Twenty paces ahead, Gard confirmed. *But the creature's moving swiftly; you haven't got time.*

But it's heading for him, isn't it? Not for me. Connie began to run toward her brother.

"Simon!" she shrieked into the darkness. The stifling blanket of night seemed to muffle her call. Jane and Anneena were searching for Simon behind her. Not understanding that Connie knew exactly where he was, they had turned the other way. At least they were heading away from danger. "Simon!"

She almost ran into her brother. He was standing stock-still with the pathetic meat lure held out in front of him.

"He's coming, isn't he?" he said triumphantly. "You know it, too, don't you?"

"Yes, I know," she said, grabbing his arm. "And we've got to get out of here."

But it was too late.

Out of the trees bounded a huge leonine creature, the size of a shire horse, with a mangy black mane. Its muzzle was open in a roar, displaying a row of yellow-white teeth. Connie glimpsed the malevolent gleam of amber eyes and caught a whiff of its hot breath.

A chimera.

"Run!" she shrieked, dragging at Simon's arm, but he was still holding out the pitiful bait, no more than a cocktail snack for this giant. The creature swept it aside disdainfully, catapulting the stick into the air and knocking Simon to the ground. It hesitated for a second, standing between the two of them; Connie on its right, Simon on its left. It seemed momentarily in doubt as to whom it should strike first, swinging its head to and fro, its whiskers twitching, its long black tail curling over its back like a scorpion's sting. Connie stumbled backward, still screaming at Simon to move, but her brother was in a daze. He was staring at the creature as if it was a vision of beauty rather than terror. She realized that he was held in the spell of seeing his companion creature for the first time.

"Simon, move! It's not trying to encounter you: it wants to kill us!"

Her shout seemed to make the creature's decision. It took a pace toward her, its jaws gaping in a hideous grin of anticipation. She turned and fled, but almost immediately tripped over a tree root in the dark and fell spectacularly onto her face, stunned as her head made sharp contact with the ground. The creature gave a yelp of pleasure. There was no need to hurry: this little prey could not escape the chimera's teeth, the nimble cloven goat's hooves of its hind legs, nor its serpent tail. Pulling herself up onto her knees, Connie could sense dimly that her friends in the Society were mobilized to come to her aid. Icefen was even now leaping back into the plantation; Sentinel was charging up from the mines; dragons had been sent; but none were close enough to step between her and those jaws which must be mere inches from the back of her neck.

"Yah!" There was a yell behind her. Connie spun around to see Simon had jumped between her and the creature, brandishing a branch he had grabbed from the ground. "Get back! Leave her alone!" he shouted at the beast. He whacked it over the nose, shattering his defense into scores of splinters. His intervention gave Connie the seconds she needed to get to her feet. She turned to face the creature and saw immediately that Simon's blow had riled it into madness. But it was not leaping on his throat: it was gathering itself for another kind of attack.

"Get behind me!" Connie cried, tugging at Simon. He resisted. "Don't be an idiot! Get behind me." As they scrambled away, she succeeded in pushing her brother so that she stood between him and the chimera.

Even as Connie did this, she was diving deep into her mind, swiftly conjuring up the universal's shield. She raised it in front of her, the powerful mental tool taking shape in the air as a frail circle of silver mist. She had no idea if it would work against a physical attack, but it was either that or they would die. The chimera let out a roar of fury, releasing a lash of flame from deep in its throat. The fire licked at the shield, evaporating the mist in a hissing steam, but still Connie held it up. Her fingers could now feel the heat of the fiery breath battering against her protection, blistering the back of her hand.

Its fire resisted, the chimera drew breath, ending the outpouring of flame. It leapt forward and struck with its front paw, claws cutting into Connie's side and sending her spinning into the undergrowth. It jumped after her, pouncing before she had even hit the ground. Grabbing her by the back of her jacket, it bounded into the trees and away from the annoyance of the other human.

Dangling in its mouth, Connie could hear Simon's cries behind her and knew that he was following. She would have shouted at him to run for help, but she was nearly strangled by her own jacket. Her right side was in excruciating pain, bleeding freely from the deep scratches in her flesh. She knew she was going to die. Frozen with terror, she could not have cried out even if she had the breath.

Then, as rapidly as the creature had carried her off, it dropped her onto the ground and rolled her over with its paw. She was staring up into the chimera's callous eyes, her senses almost overwhelmed by the reek of its breath. A heavy paw was placed in the center of her chest, pinning her down. A second head darted into view: the hooded cobra that formed the tuft at the end of the chimera's whip-like black tail had come to gaze on its victim. A drop of venom dripped from its fangs and hissed like acid as it hit the ground by her ear. The paw pressed harder; Connie could now sense the presence of the creature trying to force its way into her mind. It wanted to encounter its prey. She let it in, thinking that this was her only hope of escape: maybe if she bonded with it, she could turn it from its determination to kill?

As soon as the door in her mind opened, she regretted her decision. The attack in the physical world was terrifying enough, but now she was swept up into a vortex of stormy emotions. The three different natures of the chimera—

lion, goat, and serpent—were in a constant battle with one another. But this was not like another conjoined creature she had encountered, not like the minotaur's formalized dance of man and bull: this was a chaotic frenzy of teeth, fang, and hoof. The ascendancy shifted second by second, giving the creature no stable identity. Connie cried out with pain as first she was filled with the fire of the lion, her appetite for blood voracious, tantalized by the delectable flesh of the goat that was forever out of reach. Next, she was squeezed into the writhing form of the snake, hungering to sink its fangs into the haunches of its own lion and goatskin, yet knowing that if it did so it would end its own life. Finally, she stretched into the agile form of the mountain goat, bounding in breathless haste from rock to rock, always desiring to flee the enemies that surrounded it front and rear, but unable ever to leave them behind. The creature was damaged, crazily divided against itself. Its only moments of calm came when all parts were joined in the hunt of another, a common focus for their hatred.

Connie heard its thoughts in her head. Each transition coming with a pain so exquisite she felt she was being torn apart.

How shall we kill the universal? asked the serpent, its tongue flickering between its teeth. *Bite, burn, or venom?*

The lion head yawned, fire glowing at the back of its cavernous throat.

Let's stamp on her, then fly! cried the goat hysterically.

The other two ignored this voice. *Each will have his turn,* said the lion magisterially.

Me first! hissed the snake. *It's my turn.*

The lion growled.

You had your chance but you failed to burn her alive! the serpent argued. *You'll still have your turn. But it's no sport for me biting after you've had your way.*

Please! begged Connie, screaming to get her voice heard in this debate, but the three-natured creature kept slipping away from her, not interested in hearing any last-minute pleas from their quarry.

Snake, then lion, conceded the lion.

Then me! Hooves after! bleated the goat.

Agreed, said the lion, though with no more concern for the goat's wishes than it would have for the vultures that cleaned up after its kills.

The last thing Connie saw was the snake's head lashing down like a whip-stroke. Its bite felt as if hot needles had been driven into her neck. She grew rigid, her eyes misting over. With vague, dreamy relief, she knew that she was unlikely to be conscious when the next stage of the attack began. All went dark.

⚜

Col knew there was something seriously wrong as soon as he arrived at the deserted camp. He could hear screams and cries from in the trees. He plunged forward, pushing his way through the branches in the direction of the loudest cries. After running for a few agonizing minutes, he could see a flashlight beaming wildly ahead as someone sprinted at full speed toward the uproar.

"Connie!" he shouted. "Wait for me!"

But the flashlight-carrier did not pause. With a sickening jolt, Col realized the screams had stopped. Finding this more unnerving than anything he had heard so far, he put on an extra burst of speed, arriving at Simon's shoulder as they both sprang out of the trees into a clearing.

The chimera was standing over Connie, saliva dripping from its jaws as it licked its lips, preparing to bite. She lay stretched out on the bed of pine needles—still, white-faced, and death-like—the only sign of a wound coming from the blood seeping from her side. Their entrance distracted the creature: it looked up, momentarily dazzled by the light that Simon had the sense to shine full into its face. Then, on the other side of the clearing, a huge, white, rough-pelted wolf leapt from the trees. A small figure slid from its back as the frost wolf collided with the chimera, knocking it away from Connie. Simon and Col had to dive to one side as the two beasts rolled over in a furious knot of teeth and claws, kicking up twigs and cones in their frenzied struggle, snapping saplings off at the roots. The three boys dashed to Connie to drag her clear of the fight before the creatures rolled back and squashed her. Col tried to lift her from the ground, but she hung limp in his arms.

"She's not dead, is she?" Simon sobbed, paying no heed

to the roars and growls as Icefen and the chimera crashed, clawed, and bit each other.

Col did not know what to answer. "Let's get her out of here," he said, half dragging her away.

There came the pounding of hooves behind them, and Sentinel galloped onto the battlefield. Without a word, he scooped Connie from Col's arms and bounded away from the fighters.

"Follow me!" he called to the boys.

They had a hard job keeping up with the minotaur, even though he was the one carrying the burden. Col helped Simon along, realizing that the boy was close to collapse. After a nightmarish time of stumbling behind the fleet-footed creature, they reached the edge of the trees. The minotaur paused, snuffing the air. Connie dangled in his arms like a broken puppet. Sentinel laid her gently on the floor.

"Other humans approach. I leave the universal in your care. Fetch healers!" He plunged into the trees, heading back to where Icefen was still battling the chimera. He had no sooner disappeared than Jane and Anneena came running up, their flashlights darting over the leaf litter until they lit on Connie. Anneena let out a piercing scream.

"Shut up and do something!" shouted Col. He was dialing for an ambulance on his cell phone.

Jane bent over Connie, feeling for any sign of life.

"She's bleeding from her side. She's quite cold, but I can

definitely feel a pulse," Jane said in a steady voice as she slipped off her sweater to cover her friend.

The competent touch of Jane's hand on her forehead roused Connie from her dark dreams. Her eyes flickered open, but her vision was blurred. Two Cols and two Janes swam in and out of focus.

"Col?" she murmured.

Col quickly knelt at her side. "Yes?" he said urgently.

"Fetch Windfoal. Poison." Her eyes closed again, and she sank back into unconsciousness.

Col swallowed, feeling as though he had an apple-sized lump in his throat. Connie wanted the healing powers of the unicorn: but that was impossible. Windfoal must be far away at the moment. They would have to make do with non-mythical sources of help for the present.

"We've got to carry her down to the road," Col said, getting a grip on himself now that he had worked out what he must do first. "Rat, help me with her head. Jane, Anneena: you take her legs."

The awkward human stretcher bumped its way as quickly as it could down the field, passing under the slowly revolving blades of the wind turbines. Behind them, a loud roar from the plantation signaled that the battle of beasts had reached its climax. Col glanced nervously over at Rat.

"Icefen won," Rat muttered back, his face taut with tension.

Jane and Anneena had also heard the commotion. "It's the beast that got her, isn't it?" said Anneena, close to hysterical tears. "It's all my fault. She told us not to go in!"

Col felt too angry with her to try to comfort her. Yes, it was her fault, he thought savagely.

"No, it's my fault." Simon sobbed. "I didn't understand. I thought I could speak to it. I never want to see it again. It's evil—wicked."

Col hoped that the girls would put these disjointed sentences down to the ramblings of distress, but clearly there was a problem for the Society here in the shape of Simon Lionheart.

They reached the road. At Jane's prompting, Simon ran on ahead to rouse his great-uncle. He had not been gone long when the blue lights of an ambulance appeared at the head of the little valley. Jane waved her flashlight to show the driver where they were waiting, and the white van came to a stop, headlights flooding the patch of road where Connie was lying. Uncle Hugh came panting up in his tartan dressing-gown and slippers, at the same moment as the paramedic jumped out of the vehicle. The Ratcliffs emerged from their house, anxious to find out what all the fuss was about.

"What happened?" Hugh gasped, seizing his niece's cold hand.

"Stand back, sir," said the paramedic as he checked the pulse on her neck. Connie winced and moaned with pain, her eyes still shut. She raised her hand, trying to push the medic away from her throat, but he caught her wrist gently and laid her arm back by her side. Spotting the blood seeping through her clothing, he straightened up and turned to Hugh. "We're taking her to the hospital. I want someone who can tell me what happened to ride along with me."

"I'll come," said Col quickly.

The paramedic's colleague appeared with a stretcher from the back of the ambulance. Together they lifted Connie on and wheeled her into the clinical white light of the treatment area. Col got in after them. The last image he saw as the doors closed was Hugh comforting a sobbing Simon.

"I'm coming in the car!" Hugh called after him. "Tell Connie I'm coming!"

Tell Connie? Just at the moment, Col could tell her nothing: she was beyond his reach. He tried to stifle the terrifying thought that she might never return. He sat silently to one side watching the paramedic make his friend comfortable. The medic took out a pair of scissors and began to cut away the torn clothing so he could tend to the wound in her side. Col flinched as he saw the four scratches scored into her skin.

The paramedic whistled through his teeth. "What on Earth did this?"

"Something big—a wild cat," Col answered hoarsely.

"It must be a hell of a monster to do this much damage," the man said. He bent closer. "She's lucky: it doesn't look as if it went very deep. The jacket saved her, I'd say."

Lucky? thought Col desolately. He wouldn't have called her that.

5

Unicorn

It was now three days since Connie had been admitted to Chartmouth Hospital and the doctors were worried. At first, her injuries had not seemed life-threatening. Whatever it was that had attacked her in the wood—the theories in the local press ran from rabid fox, to stray dog, to escaped wild cat—had left deep scoring in her side, but this had been successfully treated with stitches and was healing well. The burns on the back of her hands had been dressed, though quite where she got them remained a mystery. The problem was that she was still delirious, suffering from weakness of the limbs and neck, a strange lack of taste in her mouth, and she was having trouble breathing. She surfaced from her drowsy state only for brief spells. The doctors decided she must have picked up a blood infection from the scratches, but so far they had failed to isolate it in the samples they had taken. One keen-eyed intern from Nepal suggested that she showed the same characteristics as someone suffering from a venomous cobra bite, but when the consultant heard this theory he told the trainee bluntly to stop dreaming and keep his mind on his job. Cobras in England? Utter nonsense!

Conventional medicine having failed, the Society decided it was time to take matters into their own hands and send for Windfoal as Connie had requested. The unicorn was now waiting outside the hospital, which was why Mack, Col, and Rat were walking down the long shining corridor armed only with a bunch of flowers and innocent smiles. Ignoring the nursing staff, Mack strode into the youth ward and scooped Connie off her bed before her roommates could protest. Connie groaned as he swung her up, just managing to hang on to consciousness.

"Just a quick trip to the parking lot, and we'll bring her back unharmed, I promise," Col assured the girls as he backed out of the ward on his father's heels.

"It's her horse, you see," added Rat for good measure. "She'll never get better until she's satisfied it's okay, so we've brought it here."

"Right, quick as we can!" said Mack once they were out in the main corridor. They made a dash for the elevator. "Come on, come on!" He thumped the controls as it seemed to take ages to arrive. Mercifully it was empty when the doors opened. They entered, feeling relieved to have gotten this far without being stopped.

"Did you have to tell them about the horse?" Col asked Rat with exasperation, thinking that his friend was getting carried away.

"'Course. We're parked right outside. I'll bet you any money they'll all be looking out of the window to see what we're doing."

It was a good point. As a cover story, it had its merits. Maybe Rat wasn't as crazy as he looked, conceded Col.

They reached the ground floor. Connie cradled in his arms, Mack marched determinedly through the crowds, out through the sliding doors, and into the parking lot. Stationed in the "20 minutes only" slot by the entrance was the horsebox with Kira Okona, Windfoal's companion, leaning against it, checking her watch anxiously. Seeing them emerge from the hospital entrance, she opened the rear doors so Mack could carry Connie directly inside. Laying the universal gently on the hay, Mack stepped outside to leave her in Windfoal's care.

Five minutes later, Connie leaned against the unicorn, resting after Windfoal had purged her blood of the elusive venom of the chimera. Her head was now clear, the unicorn's healing touch having burnt away the poison that had been gnawing at the bond between her and this world.

"You came just in time," Connie whispered. "I couldn't have held out much longer."

Windfoal whickered her agreement, nuzzling her young friend affectionately. Her horn gleamed with a soft golden light in the darkness of the van, casting everything in a warm glow. Even Windfoal's normally silver-white coat seemed tinged with honeyed gold.

"I'd better go. I think everyone's in trouble because of me," Connie said regretfully.

Windfoal pushed her toward the door with her velvety nose. *Come and see me soon, Universal,* she said through their bond, *so we will heal those scars as well.*

Connie nodded and slid the door open, reluctant to leave the peaceful haven of the horsebox. Col, Mack, and Rat were standing in a worried huddle, watching a posse of people headed in their direction. Kira started the engine. Three nurses, backed up by two uniformed security guards and a doctor, approached at a run. Col cheered up when he saw that Connie was on her feet.

"Let me handle this, okay?" she said to them. "You'd better go."

She walked over to meet her reception committee, reassured to hear the doors of the van slam behind her. The priority was to get Windfoal away before too many questions were asked.

"Connie!" exclaimed the staff nurse from her ward, "what on Earth are you doing? You're not well enough to be outside in nothing but a nightgown! And no slippers!"

The van engine rumbled to life. The grit of the parking

lot surface crackled as Kira pulled out of the spot.

"I'm fine. All I needed was a breath of fresh air," said Connie.

The doctor, a young woman with short bleached hair and owlish glasses, came forward and took Connie's arm. "I must say you do look much better," she said, leading her back toward the hospital. "I thought you were getting nowhere fast this morning when I checked you over, but now . . . Well, let's take you inside and see what's what."

After a thorough examination, the doctor pronounced Connie remarkably improved.

"I don't know what miracle you found, Connie, but I wouldn't mind some of it," the doctor said with a smile as she noted the healthy, almost golden, glow of Connie's skin. "Just the stitches to take out tomorrow and then you can go home."

Connie was relieved to hear that she was to be discharged so quickly. Now that she was returned to full consciousness, her memories of the terrifying night in the plantation had come flooding back. Uppermost in her mind was Simon: How was he? What was the Society to do about the disastrous revelation of his gift? And what about the chimera? Had Icefen mortally injured it or was it still out there, waiting for her?

That afternoon, she had two sets of visitors. First, a stricken Anneena and more composed Jane arrived bearing a bunch of roses. Anneena gave a muffled squeal of delight when she saw Connie sitting up, leafing through a magazine the girl in the bed opposite had lent her.

"Connie! I'm so, so sorry! But you're better! You look better than better: you look great."

"Yes," said Jane with a thoughtful expression, head cocked to one side, "you do look well. What've they done to you?"

Connie smiled.

Anneena leaned forward and took her friend's bandaged hand. "I'm really, really sorry, you know that, don't you?" Putting her other hand on her heart, she added, "And I promise I won't go looking for that beast again."

"I know," said Connie, returning her friend's pressure on her fingers with difficulty through the bandages. "Let's just hope it's the last we've seen of the . . . of it."

Anneena sat back, satisfied and appearing more her old self. "Oh, it's still out there, unfortunately. There was no sign of it when they combed the plantation; lots of blood," Anneena looked down as all of them were thinking that some of the blood must have been Connie's, "but nothing else. We don't know what drove it off, and the ground was too dry for it to leave any tracks, but my dad says it'll have gone onto the moor to hide so it can lick its wounds." She paused, her eyes sliding up to Connie's face. "He's banned me from going up there again. I'm to stay in Hescombe until the creature's been caught and destroyed."

"Me, too," said Jane. "My parents are worried it may've

got a taste for humans. What do you think your aunt will tell you?"

Connie shrugged. Her case was a bit more complicated. She had not yet considered what the fallout would be for her freedom to roam.

At that moment, her aunt and Dr. Brock appeared in the doorway: Evelyn willowy and energetic, any hint of her previous queasiness now gone; Dr. Brock at her shoulder, his lined face radiating pleasure at seeing Connie sitting up.

"Second shift," said Jane, getting up to make room. "See you when you get home, Connie."

"Thanks for coming," she called after them.

Evelyn waited until the girls had gone and then folded Connie into a tight hug. Connie again had the unnerving sensation of perceiving the little life inside her aunt.

"Connie, you look so much better. Windfoal's cured you then?" Evelyn said happily, not bothering to keep her voice down. The girl opposite, who had no visitors this afternoon, looked up curiously.

Dr. Brock raised one brow in warning and bent over to kiss Connie on the cheek. "Best not say too much about that just yet. Our companions, both big and little, send greetings, Connie."

"Thank father and daughter for me," said Connie smiling back at him, not without a pang of envy that he would be seeing Argand so soon and she was stuck inside for another day, at least. "So where is it now?" She could tell from their faces they both knew she was talking about the chimera. "And how's Simon?"

Dr. Brock sighed, taking a seat in the plastic chair Jane had vacated. "Well, the two questions are linked, as you well know, because with you in here, only your brother can answer the first. The rock dwarves say they can't sense it— something to do with stone sprite interference. But Simon's not been seen by anyone except Hugh since the attack. He's been hiding away in his room."

"You've got to talk to him, Connie," said Evelyn. She angrily stuffed the roses into an empty vase on Connie's bedside table, snapping one from its stem. "I'm afraid he's been damaged by what happened. He doesn't want to accept what he is—won't talk to any of us."

"Of course, I'll talk to him—as soon as I can."

Dr. Brock leaned forward and said in a confidential voice, "The Trustees have convened an emergency assessment for him, and for that little boy, Liam, you identified. If you are well enough and can persuade Simon to come, it's to be held next week at the Society headquarters. And"—he dropped his voice even lower—"they also want to take counsel with you on the chimera. It's quite unheard of—a chimera in these parts. I have to admit that we're suspicious of the coincidence. Your brother a companion to it—you, its quarry."

Yes, thought Connie, put like that it did seem strange. If someone had known about Simon before she did and had wanted to create a trap for her, what would be better than using her brother to lure her into the mad creature's path? If they knew this much, they would have known that only she had the gift to sense the danger and would not abandon Simon to face it alone. But the creature itself gave no hint that it was doing anything but following its own crazed impulses.

"I see," she said without committing herself to a comment on what Dr. Brock had said, not wanting to speak her fears aloud. "Of course, I'll try to persuade him. Simon owes me one."

⚜

It was without much grace that Simon agreed to accompany his sister on the trip to London. He said he would go for her sake, but warned that he was doing so under protest. He wanted nothing more to do with his "gift" as she insisted on calling it, nor did he want to see any more monsters, bull-headed or otherwise. Connie felt desperately sad for him: he was clinging on to the illusion that he could just pretend none of it had happened. He had even grown angry with her when she had forced him to admit what he had seen and felt on that fateful night.

The visit coincided with Col's Grade Four theory examination, also to be held at the Society headquarters, and Connie was relieved to have his help in getting a reluctant Simon onto the train and for keeping up a light three-way conversation with her brother and Mack all the way to Paddington. She sat leaning against the window, feeling washed out; her right side still ached and was painfully sore when anything touched it. At night, Kullervo's voice still taunted and tempted her to join him at the mark. She had to wake repeatedly to drive him off with Sentinel's help, leaving her exhausted when dawn finally arrived. In a perfect world, she would have preferred to spend the day quietly at home. But it wasn't a perfect world, and a meeting with the Trustees was not something she could miss.

"They've got absolutely no chance of winning." Col was still arguing sports good-humoredly with Simon as they got out of the taxi onto Liam's street, south of the River Thames. Connie wrinkled her nose, smelling decay and neglect in the doorway of the low-rise block of flats. Col stopped teasing Simon about his team and gazed around him, also dispirited by what he saw. Black bags of garbage were piled in a heap by the overflowing dumpsters. Graffiti, pointlessly repeated initials, defaced the drab brick walls. A derelict car up on wooden blocks obstructed the entrance.

"Come on," said Mack, the only one who seemed unperturbed by their surroundings. He squeezed his way around the car. "Let's go on up."

They climbed two evil-smelling flights of concrete stairs and arrived at a landing. It ran down the front of the apartments like a walkway in the sky. It was less gloomy up here; bright window boxes decorated some of the homes;

a little boy rode past on a multi-colored tricycle, ringing his bell happily. They stepped out of his path, and then moved aside quickly again as his dad jogged by in hot pursuit of the speeding toddler.

"It's Number Eighteen," said Mack, checking a piece of paper. "Last in the row." He knocked. After a few moments, the door opened and a skinny woman, hair straggling on her shoulders, peered outside.

"What d'you want?" she asked. She took a drag on a thin white cigarette she held shakily in her right hand.

"Suzanne? It's me, Mack Clamworthy. We've come to take Liam out for the afternoon. Do you remember me calling you over the weekend about it?"

Suzanne lifted her tired, pale eyes to him and a glimmer of recognition passed over her face. "You'd better come in then." She turned in to the hallway, steadying herself by resting her hand on the shiny wallpaper decorated with overblown roses. "Liam, baby, your friends are here!"

The little boy erupted out of a door at the far end of the hall, hopping with delight.

"Great!" He sprinted toward them as if intending to leave there and then.

As neither Mack nor Suzanne said anything, Connie caught Liam gently by the shoulder. "Shoes, Liam?" she asked, pointing to his bare feet.

He grinned up at her. "Oops," he said and ran back into the room he had come from.

Feet stuffed in tatty sneakers, Liam breezed back into the hallway.

"See you later, Mum," he called, nearly pushing Mack out of the door in his haste to be gone.

"Bye, baby," she said, taking another drag on her cigarette.

"I'll bring him back around six," Mack told her when she forgot to ask. "And you can reach me on my cell phone." He thrust a piece of paper into her hand, which she put absentmindedly into her pocket.

"Fine. Have fun."

6

Playing with Fire

Col glanced at his watch for the hundredth time as the taxi crawled slowly down the Strand, one of the busiest streets in London.

"I'm going to be late!" he muttered. "The test starts in five minutes."

"You'll be there on time." Mack yawned, turning the page of the newspaper he had brought with him. "Anyway, I thought you said Grade Four would be a breeze for you and Skylark." He winked at Connie. Simon and Liam looked up, their interest caught by a discussion they did not quite understand.

Col swallowed. His palms were sweaty and his throat dry. A flutter of nerves in his stomach made him feel sick. He was angry that his father, as usual, was failing to provide a sympathetic ear to his problems. Mack had never understood what it was like to be in his shoes.

"I said the practical exam will be a breeze, but the theory paper, that's different."

"You'll be fine," said Mack with annoying calm. "When I was your age, I passed all my tests with top marks. Don't forget: you're a Clamworthy."

"Shut up, Dad," said Col.

Connie intervened before father and son could rub each other further the wrong way. "Give it another minute, Col, then you can always get out and go the rest of the way on foot if we're still stuck at these lights. We're almost there now."

Col's hand hovered by the door, but at that moment the lights changed and the taxi grumbled on for the final hundred yards, dropping the passengers at the entrance to the alleyway leading to the Society headquarters. Col abandoned his father and the others, calling over his shoulder: "See you later. I'll meet you in the foyer when I'm done."

He disappeared into the dark tunnel of the alleyway, leaving them to follow more slowly.

"Connie, what's going to happen to me?" asked Liam—not as if he was afraid, but as if he wanted to relish each exciting detail. Connie saw that Simon, though pretending to be fascinated by the railings of the old houses they passed, was listening intently.

"Nothing bad. They'll do a test on you to make sure that I've got your gift right."

"A test? What will I have to do? I can't read much, yet."

Connie gave him a reassuring smile. "You won't need to do anything but follow a few simple orders and then answer some questions. You won't need to read anything."

"And then?"

"Usually, after the test, you'll be given a mentor to help with the rest of your training—your mentor will teach you how to talk to your creature safely."

Simon gave a skeptical snort. Connie knew what he was thinking: it was doubtful any training could teach you to encounter a crazed chimera without losing a limb. She had to admit she agreed with him.

Mack strode purposefully under the arch into the courtyard of the palatial headquarters of the Society for the Protection of Mythical Creatures. Its warm, caramel-colored facade—decorated with ornate carvings depicting creatures from the four companies—glittered with three rows of high windows; the slate roof was topped with a lantern dome that sparkled like a lighthouse. The sun blazed on the cobbled forecourt, making the walls gleam like gold cliffs rising from a sparkling gray-blue sea. None of this splendor gave Mack a moment's pause, but both Liam and Simon stopped in their tracks.

"Are we allowed in?" asked Simon.

"Of course, or we wouldn't have brought you here," said Connie, leading the way over the cobbles. She remembered very well how daunted she had felt on her first visit.

"What's this?" asked Simon, pointing up at the compass motif in the circular window over the doorway.

"It's the symbol of the universals," said Connie briefly as she passed under it.

Simon gave her a sideways look. "That's what you are, aren't you?" When she looked surprised, he added, "I heard that minotaur call you—that name."

This was the first time Simon had willingly referred to the events of the previous week. Connie nodded. "That's right. That's my sign."

Simon said nothing more, but Connie took heart from the fact that he was no longer trying to block out what he had seen and heard. The indisputable presence of the Society headquarters appeared to be changing his mind. She only hoped this more cooperative mood would last.

Mack was waiting for them in the marble foyer, leaning against the porter's window, laughing with him about something.

"I've signed you all in," he said loudly, his voice booming around the cavernous space. He tossed them each a badge, which Connie promptly dropped. Mack groaned.

"I should put her down for the England cricket team, shouldn't I?" he joked with the porter. "She'd fit in with the current bunch."

Connie was forcibly reminded of his son: both Clamworthys had the ability to ignore atmospheres that would daunt others. She scooped her tag from the floor and saw that it had a silver compass next to her name.

"What are these for?" she asked. On her previous visits, she'd only had to sign in.

"For the Chamber of Counsel," said the porter. "You're not allowed in there without one of those. Do you like yours? I got my wife to run that off the computer specially. Needless to say, we didn't have any in stock for you."

Connie smiled shyly. "Yes. Thank you—and thank your wife, too."

"Off you go then," said the porter, waving them to the double doors opposite, which were nestled between the two curving flights of stairs leading up to the library above. "The meeting's already started. You're the last to arrive."

Mack led the way over to the entrance and pushed open the doors with a boom. Connie, who had never entered this chamber before, was astounded by what she saw. A huge room stretched before them, the same dimensions as the library on the floor above, but unlike that book-filled space, the walls here were lined with mirrors, reflecting themselves infinitely on all sides. It was like stepping inside a crystal ball—she felt momentarily giddy. Liam gasped. Simon moved closer to his sister.

The floor was polished white marble, veined with blue-gray. In its center was an inlaid four-pointed star made out of silver. As Connie approached, she recognized it as her sign. Looking straight ahead along the eastern point, she saw Storm-Bird perched on a golden rod suspended from the high ceiling. Its head was tucked under its wing, but as Connie's feet touched the center of the compass, it awoke, croaking a greeting. A rumble of distant thunder rolled toward her as the giant crow-like bird fluttered to the floor. Seated cross-legged at Storm-Bird's feet was its companion, Eagle-Child, dressed in a tan suede jacket and trousers, his long black hair streaked with white. The front panels of his jacket were decorated with wings made from tiny blue and red stones. He raised his hand, palm outward, in greeting to the universal. Glancing behind her, she heard the steady clip-clop of hooves on the marble. Windfoal, the unicorn, had stepped forward to take her stand at the western end of the Chamber of Counsel, her white coat making the marble dull by comparison. Kira Okona followed and took a seat on a wooden armchair by the unicorn's side. Kira was dressed in bright African cottons, her braided hair concealed today under a flamboyant blue and white headdress.

From the expression on Simon's face as he stared to his right, Connie guessed he had spotted the ancient green dragon, Morjik. His gnarled green hide seemed even rougher than Connie remembered in contrast to the smooth stone floor. He looked like a volcanic island rising out of a sea of milk. His ruby eyes gleamed hotly, lit by the fire within. A tendril of smoke wound up from his snout, curling to the ceiling where it hung in an umbrella-shaped cloud over his head. His companion, Kinga Potowska, an elderly woman but still a formidable dragon-rider, looked up and smiled at Connie; her determined eyes glinted speculatively as she next turned her gaze on the two boys who trailed in the universal's wake.

Finally, Connie raised her sight to the northern-most point of the chamber to where the newest Trustee pair was seated. The representatives of the Elementals—Chan Lee, an older Chinese man neatly dressed in a collarless black suit, and the rock dwarf Jade—sat side by side, both still as stone. The rock dwarf, her body swathed in a green cloak, pushed back her hood to gaze on the universal. Connie was struck by her beauty; used to Gard's craggy features, she had not expected this. Jade reminded Connie of an exquisitely carved chess queen she'd once seen in a shop selling Far Eastern curios: wide almond eyes, long graceful neck, elegant fingers that lightly grasped a small silver mallet. But the most alluring thing about Jade was the beautiful polished sheen to her skin, a rich blue-green hue flecked with crystal.

Greetings, Universal, came Jade's voice, sliding through the veins of marble floor to the soles of Connie's feet. *We meet at last.*

Connie bowed her head respectfully.

Kinga stood up and came a few paces forward, holding out her hand to the newcomers.

"On behalf of the Trustees for the Society for the Protection of Mythical Creatures, may I welcome you all into our circle," she said, gesturing around at her colleagues. Connie, feeling exposed standing in the middle of the vast room with only the two boys beside her, looked for Mack and saw that he had gravitated instinctively to the southern end of the chamber and had seated himself on the far side of Morjik. She wished he hadn't abandoned her so quickly. His belief in her abilities often outstripped her own confidence. She looked down shyly, noticing for the first time how her feet were in the very center of the compass as if drawn to that spot like a magnet.

"Please, take a seat," continued Kinga.

To Connie's surprise, Liam immediately headed off toward the rock dwarf and sat himself down at the hem of her robe. Connie saw Kinga look inquiringly over at the Trustee pair for the Elementals. Mr. Chan nodded slightly, and the rock dwarf gracefully rested her hand on Liam's hair and gave him an affectionate pat.

"That is settled then," said Kinga in a pleased voice. "Liam is confirmed as a fire imp companion."

Connie's face must have registered her astonishment for Eagle-Child laughed. "There are more ways than one of carrying out an assessment, Universal, as you should remember from your own experience," he said. "When the candidate stands in the center of all the Trustees, we do not need to resort to the substitutes used by the Society's assessors in our absence."

Connie glanced at Simon. He was still hovering in the

middle of the room beside her, looking angry and confused. Why had it not worked for him then?

"Simon," Connie asked softly, "do you know which way you should go?"

Simon shook his head miserably; he bit his lip. Gazing around the circle, Connie noticed that the Trustees, too, now looked uncertain.

"Stand out of the circle, Connie," said Kinga after a brief pause. "Perhaps your presence is confusing us."

Quickly, Connie moved toward Mack to a point as far away from the Trustees as she could go. The last thing she wanted was to mess up Simon's introduction to the Society, knowing how hostile he had been to the whole idea in the first place. Simon now stood alone in the center. Her heart ached for him. She wished he would listen to the prompting of his gift and make up his mind.

"He is ours," said Kira finally after a brief consultation with Windfoal.

"Surely not?" challenged Kinga.

"Ours," growled Morjik.

Tension rippled in the air between the dragon and unicorn like a heat haze. Simon swayed. Connie feared he was going to make a run for it.

"He cannot be in two places at once!" interrupted Mr. Chan in a clipped, high-pitched voice. "Honorable colleagues, one of you must be wrong."

Mack stood up from where he had been lounging

against the wall and scratched his head. "Troublemakers, these Lionhearts," he said to Connie, evidently amused to see the dispute among so august a company.

On another occasion, Connie might have made a smart response about the Clamworthys, but she was too concerned for her brother. Then she had an idea.

"Let me stand with him," she said coming forward. "Let me see if I can confirm his gift."

"What do you mean, Connie?" asked Kira.

"It's just a skill I seem to have gained. I can now sense where human companions are by their gift," Connie said in a quiet voice, aware how strange this would sound to her listeners.

"But that is astounding, Connie," said Kinga, looking up at Morjik then back at Connie, as if the dragon had confirmed her thoughts. "Why were we not told? How long have you been able to do this?"

"Since the beginning of the year. Since the shared bond."

"You may, of course, try," said Kinga. "But we must talk further about this."

Connie came to stand at her brother's side. "I'm just going to put my hands on your shoulders, okay?" she said.

Simon shrugged. But she could tell he was relieved not to be alone any longer in the center of that room. "If you must," he said in a falsely casual tone.

Connie ignored this. She closed her eyes, dipping into her mind to see the room through the bonds that filled it, rather than the physical presence of those gathered. She could see the strong silver links of her own bond stretching out along all four points of the compass to the creatures: dragon, bird, unicorn, and dwarf. Then, less distinctly, she could make out the connections between creature and companion. Curiously, she turned her mind to Liam and saw that he was wrapped in a misty chain that, though it stretched to no creature in the room, was the same color as the earthen links that connected Mr. Chan to Jade. Confident now that she knew what she was looking for, Connie rested her hands on Simon and turned her thoughts to his gift. Immediately, she saw it— or really, "them." Snaking out from his feet toward the Company of Sea Creatures and Reptiles was an orange, swirling ribbon, but a second grass-green rope stretched straight toward the unicorn and the Company of Two- and Four-legged Beasts and Beings.

"He's both," she said simply on opening her eyes again. "Like the chimera, he's both."

"But that's impossible," said Kira.

"No, it isn't," Connie replied. "I'm all four. What's impossible about my brother being bonded to two companies?"

"But you bond with all creatures, Connie," said Kira. "He's only a chimera companion."

"Is he?" Connie asked, her eyes now turning to Morjik and Windfoal.

"The great snakes," growled Morjik.

Windfoal whinnied. Kira said: "The Amalthean goats and the Nemean lions."

Simon's confusion had not lifted. "What're they talking about, Connie?" he asked his sister anxiously.

"Simon, I don't think you *are* a chimera companion," Connie said, her heart feeling lighter than it had since Simon first sensed the creature, "at least, not *just* a chimera companion. You also bond with the creatures that produced the chimera—the Amalthean goats, the Nemean lions, and the great snakes."

"My friend, you are unique, like your sister here," said Eagle-Child, staring at Simon as if to read the secret of his strange powers. "I have never heard of a companion bonding with more than one creature—other than the universal."

"So what are we to do with him?" asked Kira, looking to Kinga and Morjik.

"What does the universal advise?" asked Kinga.

Connie found the answer came easily to her now that the mystery was solved. "Well, if Simon is happy, I think you should place him in the Company of the Two-Fours for now as two of his companions are in that group. You should mentor him on all three species. I don't think he wants to go any further with the chimera; do you, Simon?"

Simon shook his head, for once not arguing with something suggested by his sister.

"Then come," said Kira, beckoning to the boy. "Sit by Windfoal and me."

With the first smile Connie had seen on his face for days, Simon nodded to his sister and went to sit at the western point of the chamber. As if the last piece of a puzzle had just been slotted into place, Connie sensed the energy in the room was once more in balance.

Mr. Coddrington is just going to love this, she thought, watching Simon pat Windfoal's neck cautiously. She remembered how the assessor had resented her presence outside the normal four companies; now he had someone who was in two: it would mess up his filing system nicely.

"All that leaves," said Connie, looking around the room, "is the question of where I should sit?"

⚞⚟

Col doodled absentmindedly on the test paper, reading through the answers he had written so far. All around him in the wood-paneled room, other candidates were scratching away at their responses. He could just see Jessica's curly head several rows away bent over her Grade Five sea-craft paper; Shirley was two rows to his right absorbed in her Grade Four storm-raising test, a lock of pale blonde hair dropping over her face, hiding her eyes. He wondered briefly what Grade Four consisted of for weather giant companions: Light wind and rain? Short, sharp showers? Minus points for brewing hurricanes? He hoped somebody had told the examiners about her taste for casting nasty lightning bolts and hail stones, and would deduct points from her as a result. But seeing as the only weather giant companion in Britain apart from Shirley was her mentor, Mr. Coddrington, he supposed it was a done deal that she would get top marks.

His thoughts turned to Connie. She had looked really tired on the train, lacking her normal sparkle. He hoped the trustees weren't giving her a hard time about the chimera, as none of it had been her fault. Ever since the attack, he'd been feeling guilty that he had failed to protect her. No one had protected her. Despite its best efforts, the Society had proved unable to keep its universal safe. Col's pen punctured the paper as he stabbed it in frustration. He couldn't bear it if anything happened to Connie.

But this train of thought wasn't going to get him through the exam.

With a deliberate effort to calm himself, Col turned back to his answer paper. Only thirty minutes to go but he was making good progress, having covered care and first aid, encounters, and intermediate maneuvers. He'd now reached the final section, which examined flying protocols, the rules of the airways.

Question Twenty: Name the circumstances in which you can use the Thessalonian Roll, and what safety precautions must always be observed.

Col had a sudden vivid recollection of Skylark plunging down toward the treetops of Mallins Wood with the Kullervo-pegasus on his tail, but he knew that this was not the answer the examiners were looking for. He put his pen to the blank sheet of paper before him.

The Thessalonian Roll should only be used after the pegasus and rider have passed their Grade Eight flying exam. It should only be done over water to reduce risk of serious injury if the rider falls off.

He looked down at the answer. What he had written was a load of garbage. It was the technically correct answer as he had revised it, but it wasn't the truth. Behavior like that wouldn't protect the universal when under attack. A spark of rebellion ignited in him as he remembered his confrontation in Mallins Wood, and he picked up his pen again.

P.S. The roll also comes in useful when avoiding a more agile enemy, such as Kullervo, even if you've not got Grade Eight. In these circumstances, soft landings are unlikely to be available so you have to go ahead and do it anyway.

There, that should wake them up a bit.

"How was yours, Col?" Jessica asked him as the candidates poured out of the examination hall onto the landing near the library.

"Okay," said Col, not committing himself to a more definite answer. He didn't want to tempt fate by saying that he thought it'd gone well. His only fear was that the examiner might deduct marks for his postscript about Kullervo. Maybe he shouldn't have done that, he thought, now that the rebellious mood had passed. "Yours?"

Jessica made a face. "Much harder than Grade Four. Some of the questions were really tricky."

"I'm sure you did fine," he said, glancing up at the clock again. "I'll see you later."

"Okay," said Jessica, a little surprised. "But I was going to the café. Don't you have time to come?"

Shirley Masterson arrived at Jessica's shoulder. "Did someone say 'café'?" she asked. "I'm dying of thirst. Shall we go?"

Jessica looked reluctant to be stuck with Shirley on her own. "I was just asking Col if he had time," she said, looking pleadingly at him and succeeding in making Col feel sorry for her.

"I'm supposed to be meeting the others."

"Others?" inquired Shirley, looking around her to see who else was there from Hescombe.

"Dad, Connie, and a couple of new members you don't know."

"Should've guessed you'd be meeting her," muttered Shirley.

Col shrugged. "I've gotta go. I might see you in the café later if Connie's still with the Trustees." He was rather pleased to see Shirley's expression sour with envy as she heard that the universal was once again receiving VIP treatment. "See you." He bounded off down the stairs, taking them two at a time.

When he came into the foyer, he found Mack, Liam, and Simon waiting for him.

"There you are!" said Mack. "How was the exam?"

"Fine. So, what happened? Where's Connie?" Col asked, looking at Simon. He was surprised to see that, though a bit dazed, Simon had cheered up since this morning.

"Connie's still talking to those Trustee people—and creatures," Simon said, grappling with the new language of the Society.

"And?" prompted Col.

"I'm a fire imp companion!" said Liam, sparking with excitement.

"Well, we knew that, didn't we?" said Col, ruffling the boy's hair. "That was stating the blindingly obvious, wasn't it?"

"And I'm a companion to the great snakes—" began Simon.

"Not the chimera?" interrupted Col too quickly.

"Let him finish," growled Mack. "You're going to like this."

"—and the Nemean lions and Amalthean goats," concluded Simon proudly, though he was still not quite sure what this all meant.

"No!" said Col, staring at Simon.

"Yeah," said Mack. "Connie found it out. Just as well, or

Simon here would've been the rope in a tug of war between the unicorn and the dragon. Both wanted him."

"And Connie's still in there?"

"Yep. I said we'd meet her in the café. Horace and his granddaughter are waiting for us. They want to meet Liam, so does Liam's mentor. We'd better get along there before they give up on us."

As Mack led the way to the south wing of the building and the café on the ground floor, Col followed behind with the two newest members of the Society. He couldn't quite believe what he had just heard: Simon, companion to more than one creature! It had been shocking enough when Col had first heard of Connie's gift, but at least universals were a known part of the Society's history. Simon seemed to be a wild departure from all established rules and practices.

The café was bright and airy, doors opening along the far wall onto the gardens that ran down to the banks of the Thames. The white-painted wrought-iron tables, laden with homemade cakes and tall cool drinks, the lush potted plants and striped awning over the patio gave the room a summery, celebratory feel. The place was buzzing as Col's fellow candidates toasted the end of their written papers for that year. Giving Shirley and Jessica a brief wave, Col accompanied his party to a table where Horace and Antonia Little were already seated. Horace, an elderly black man with grizzled white hair, stood up to greet them. His granddaughter, her hair braided in a geometric style, had clearly also just finished her exam as she was gulping down her lemonade while looking back over her question paper. She gave Col a nod of recognition and then looked curiously at the other two boys. With the Littles was a small, bird-like lady with a headscarf. She had the olive-toned skin of someone from the Middle East and did not appear to understand much English when Horace tried to introduce her to the newcomers. Col began to wonder if this lady, Mrs. Khalid, was really the best mentor for Liam that the Society could've found.

"So, Liam," said Horace genially, "I hear you live near us. I hope you'll let us come and see you."

Liam nodded eagerly, but his eyes kept straying to Mrs. Khalid. Col had the impression that there was some communication going on between the two of them that did not need words.

"I'll introduce you to the other Elementals in our area," said Antonia. "There's no one exactly your age, but there's a couple of ten-year-olds."

Suddenly, Mrs. Khalid thrust her hand into the pocket of her baggy robe and pulled out a white candle in a stubby earthenware holder. The table fell silent.

"Lee-am," she said softly. "Watch."

She struck a match and lit the flame expertly, cupping her hands around to protect it from the breeze blowing in through the open doors. Abruptly, a little body of flame ignited, no bigger than a maple leaf, and began to dance in the heart of the candle flame. Mrs. Khalid slid her finger into the fire, and the creature jumped onto her knuckle and curled around it like a burning ring. She removed her finger from the wick and pointed it to the ceiling. The fire imp wound up to the tip of her finger and then danced on the very end, its little arms and legs flickering, sending out golden sparks with each stamp of foot and clap of hands.

"Wow!" breathed Liam. "Can I have a go?" He leaned forward as if to touch the creature, but Mrs. Khalid gently caught his hand in her free palm.

"Wait," she cautioned. "Watch what he do."

After exhausting his delight at dancing on the fingertip, the fire imp turned a deeper shade of golden red. His tiny head turned from side to side as if looking for a new vent for his energies. Seeing nowhere to go from his position high in the air—away from any other objects—his tiny ember-bright eyes glittered with annoyance, and he stamped his foot down on the finger that held him aloft.

"Ouch!" said Mrs. Khalid with a wry smile. Col could tell that she had been expecting this and was not that hurt. She wagged her other index finger at the creature and made a noise that to Col's ears sounded like the spitting of damp wood on a campfire. "Chtsh! Bad imp."

Liam had been transfixed by these small events. "He hurt you?" he asked Mrs. Khalid with surprise.

She nodded.

"Why?"

"He is not my pet. He do not like to be kept in one place. Look, I send him back into air." With a snap of her fingers, she quenched the flame on her fingertip.

Liam looked up as if he expected to see the creature hovering over their heads. "Where's he gone?" he asked.

"To join brothers and sisters. He do not come back unless I call," said Mrs. Khalid, leaning forward and blowing out the candle. Looking at her hands resting on the table in front of her, Col noticed that there was a network of shiny red scars. Being a fire imp companion clearly took its toll.

"So, can I call him?" Liam reached for the candle.

"Not yet. You learn about danger first. Start small with imps like my friend before dance with big ones again." Her eyes were serious as she held Liam's gaze. "You must read signs when mood about to change. Red glow is one, but there are others. I heard you needed golden dragon and universal to save you on your first encounter—"

"But I wasn't in danger!" protested Liam. "We'd only just started dancing. It was great!"

"You in more danger than you know, Lee-am. The universal and her dragon will not always be there for you. You must learn to play safely with fire imps."

Liam nodded, his face reflective as he absorbed this new perspective on his adventure. He did not look entirely convinced.

Col sincerely hoped the lesson had sunk in. He hated to think that this might be the start of Liam's career as an arsonist as he sought bigger thrills and more danger than he could handle. Mrs. Khalid appeared to have been thinking along the same lines.

"I have sons," she said proudly, "but not fire imp companions. Companions to the sylphs and the kelpies, yes, but not to fire imps. You be my fire imp son?"

"You'll teach me all this?" Liam asked Mrs. Khalid, his face glowing as if she had conjured a fire inside him.

"I teach. You meet my sons. They are good boys. Bigger than you. Twelve and fourteen. They look after you on streets when you come to my house. I send them for you. I live not far from you. Come have meal with us after school on Wednesdays. You learn then."

"Brilliant!" said Liam.

Col smiled, an image popping into his mind of Mrs. Khalid cooking surrounded by fire imps. He had been wrong. The Trustees had clearly known exactly what they were doing when they chose Mrs. Khalid as Liam's mentor. The boy now had a whole new surrogate family. With the Littles also close by, Liam had become attached to an extended network of friends. All of them would look out for him; Col didn't need to worry about Liam anymore.

7

Guy de Chauliac

Connie sat cross-legged in the center of the compass in the Chamber of Counsel.

"If you are ready, Universal," said Kinga, "we will continue our discussions through the shared bond. All will then be able to take equal part."

Connie nodded.

"You are still weak, Connie," added the unicorn companion. "The chimera's attack has taken more out of you than you realize. Windfoal says we must be careful. Signal when you are too tired to continue."

"I will," Connie said.

Kira looked to the other Trustees. "First, let my companion heal the scars in the universal's side. She will be more comfortable after that."

There was a brief pause while Windfoal and Connie

bonded together. The stream of silver balm unwound from the tip of the unicorn's horn and twisted itself around Connie's waist like a bandage, easing the tightness and pain of the scars left by the stitches. Connie immediately felt better.

"I am ready for the shared bond," she said at last, and sat with head bowed as she waited for the three other mythical creatures to approach. With Morjik and Storm-Bird, she welcomed back old friends, but the encounter with Jade came with the thrill she always experienced on meeting a creature for the first time. The rock dwarf's presence stole up through the floor like a stream of liquefied emeralds, the slow creep of the rock-forming powers of the earth speeded up so Connie could sense the crystallization of Jade's thoughts in her head without waiting millennia. With his companion came the shy, neat presence of Chan Lee. The shadow-Mr. Chan bowed low, asking permission to enter the bond, which Connie immediately granted, and he took his place in the shadow-Chamber of Counsel created in her mind. Finally, she raised a silver image of herself to sit in the middle of the shadow-chamber, a focus for her thoughts and speech.

Now that the Trustees and universal could all hear one another through the mediation of Connie, the discussion began in earnest.

What shall we do about the chimera? asked Eagle-Child. *Was it hunting alone?*

I don't know, said Connie. *I don't think I understood it properly. I've never met anything like it before. I think the creature's unstable, somehow driven into madness by fighting against itself.*

It is the chimera's curse to be thus, said Windfoal sadly, *to be always divided in its own nature.*

Like our world. Morjik grunted. *We are like the chimera, tearing each other apart.*

Maybe, said Windfoal, *but the chimera has always been like this. We have not. We were once whole and healthy, living in balance. We can be so again. I do not know if any healing can be brought to this creature.*

Connie shook her head. *I don't think it can ever be peaceful.*

So, said Kira, *if the chimera is that disturbed, we cannot hope to turn it from its path by persuasion. We must find it and remove it to a safe place. We also need to find out if it was the agent of another. I, for one, do not believe its presence on Dartmoor was a coincidence. Chimeras are rarely found outside the Mediterranean.*

*I didn't sense anything other than the chimera when it attacked me—*Connie stopped. She suddenly remembered how during the fire up on the tor, at the point of losing consciousness, the dark tide she associated with the presence of Kullervo had swept upon her. As these thoughts could be sensed by those sharing the bond, she had no need to put them into words.

He was there? said Kinga.

Maybe. I don't know for sure.

It is probable, honorable colleagues. With the brother to universal a companion, said Mr. Chan with a deferential bow to Connie, *the shape-shifter does not need to do more than place chimera in locality and wait. Companion will seek out creature: we all know this.*

I agree, said Connie. *But I don't understand why Kullervo would do this? To kill me or capture me?*

I'd say he was trying to assassinate you, said Kinga with a disgusted curl to her lip. *That venom almost did the task.*

But that would mean he's finally given up on turning me to his side, said Connie. *Which would mean—*

Which would mean he found another universal. He does not need you, concluded Mr. Chan.

Revenge now on his mind, said Jade in a silky voice.

The prospect of Kullervo finding another universal filled all of them with dread. The shadow-chamber became obscured by a cold, damp fog as Connie could not contain her bewilderment at the new thought that Kullervo would now stop at nothing to eliminate her. The worst was not the fear for her life—but his rejection of her—though she should not want him, he was still her companion. And if they did not find the other universal first, who knew what Kullervo would persuade him or her to do? She was also ashamed to feel a twinge of jealousy; she hated to think someone else shared that bond.

Stupid thought, she told herself, hoping the others had not sensed this traitorous feeling.

Be comforted, Universal. Morjik growled, dispelling the fog with his warm breath. *Too many assumptions made. We do not know if there is another universal. We do not know that he wants to kill you. Scare, yes. Drive you to him, yes. But kill?*

Morjik's right, said Eagle-Child. *The chimera may only have been following its nature. If our side had not intervened to save you, maybe Kullervo's plan was to come and get you at your weakest.*

Connie wasn't sure if this prospect was very comforting, but at least it wasn't a sentence of death.

We need the chimera, concluded Kira decisively. *We have to take it away from the universal, but we also must ask it if it is working for Kullervo and what its orders were. That will answer many of our questions. But how can we catch it? Do you know where it is, Universal?*

On the moor. But I don't know for certain. It eludes me, you see. I've never been able to pinpoint it until it's very close. I don't think I want to get that close again, Connie added with a shudder that made the floor of the shadow-chamber quake. *Sorry.*

Brothers and sisters, what would we do with it even if we did catch it? asked Eagle-Child, looking around at his colleagues. *It is not an easy beast to constrain even for a dragon or a giant.*

Kullervo did so, grunted Morjik.

Yes, said Kinga. *If the creature is Kullervo's tool, we must assume that it is obedient to him part of the time. Kullervo must have found some inducement to make it bend to his will. If we knew what that was, perhaps we, too, could bring it under control long enough to make it safe and find out what we need to know.*

Storm-Bird croaked. Eagle-Child shifted uneasily. *It is not the Society's way to capture and control,* the Native American said in a firm tone. *That is the way of exploitative humans— and of Kullervo.*

What do you suggest we do then? asked Kinga. *Allow it to run amok on the moor, trapping Connie in Hescombe because we cannot allow her out? You'll be caging her if you refuse to let us capture this creature.*

You are right, Companion to Dragons, said Eagle-Child fairly, his humility defusing any frustration that was building in the southern quarter of the room. *I ask only that we make sure our means are not those of our enemies, even if our end is better.*

We should find out more about the creature, said Jade in a soft voice. *Let us see what knowledge you have here in your British headquarters. If that fails us, we should send abroad to other great collections of the Society.*

I'll summon the librarian, said Kira, jumping to her feet.

Er . . . said Connie, restraining the overeager Trustee with a misty cord across the exit from her mind, *hadn't I better end the encounter first before you leave?*

Sorry, Connie. Kira laughed. *Yes, I remember what it was like to end the shared encounter too abruptly. I'd not like to experience that again.*

Slowly and calmly, Connie reeled in the links that

extended from her to the creatures, ending the shared bond for now. All opened their eyes, blinking to find themselves back in the glittering surroundings of the real Chamber of Counsel.

"As I was saying," said Kira with a warm smile at Connie, "I'll fetch the librarian."

Barely five minutes had passed before Kira returned with Mr. Dove, the white-haired librarian Connie had met on her first visit to the headquarters. He followed the Trustee, staggering under the weight of a large leather-bound volume. He almost toppled over with the combined hindrance of the book and his attempts to bow.

"Mr. Dove has kindly agreed to help us in our search for knowledge," said Kira to her colleagues. "Here, why don't you put that book on this table?" She pulled forward a gilt-decorated, three-legged table that had been standing against the wall.

"Thank you," said Mr. Dove breathlessly, mopping his brow with a red silk handkerchief. "Much obliged." He glanced apprehensively over at Morjik, then darted a look at Storm-Bird, and took a swift sidelong survey of Jade. Connie dipped into her mind, glimpsing a hint of pale light dancing over his sparse crop of white hair. Yes, he was a companion to the will-o'-the-wisp; no wonder the large creatures disturbed him.

Lastly, Mr. Dove's eyes fell on Connie, sitting hunched

up on the center of the compass. He gave her a respect-
ful bow.

"Universal, a pleasure to meet you again." His eyes crin-
kled in a smile. "I should have guessed you would be here."

"Mr. Dove," said Kinga, stepping forward, "we would be
grateful if you could tell us what stores of knowledge the
library possesses on the subject of the chimera."

Mr. Dove reached in his top pocket and pulled out a
pair of half-moon glasses which he perched on the end of
his bony nose. With a slight cough, he addressed the company: "This book is the index to all records we keep on the
different mythical creatures. They are all listed alphabeti-
cally by name. If we have anything, it will be here."

He opened the book, sending clouds of dust into the air
as the covers thumped onto the tabletop. He ran a long,
tapering finger down the list: "Chaonian Bird, Charybdis,
Chichevache . . . ah! Here it is—Chimera, or Chimaera,
pronounced Kai-meer-a. The entry is very brief, I'm
afraid, as you don't see many of those in England. In fact,
this is the first one I've come across. Now, let me see." He
fell silent as he peered at the details once written down by
quill. "Should have all this on computer, I suppose," he
mused. "I have a terrible time reading some of the hand-
writing, but then, it somehow makes me feel more
connected to my predecessors than a print-out." Kinga
coughed at his elbow to remind him of the urgency of
their business. "Yes, yes, here it is: we have one book on the

subject. It is called *A Treatise on Conjoined Creatures and Multiple Monsters*, by Guy de Chauliac, translated by Edward Alleyne." He sniffed. "A rather offensive title if you ask my opinion. We would never call any creature a 'monster' these days, but I suppose we have to make allowances as they were unenlightened days back then."

"And where is it?" Kinga asked abruptly.

"Well," said Mr. Dove with a smile at Connie, "normally, I would have to tell the reader that it was out of bounds, but you are in luck."

"Why?" asked Kinga, beginning to pace as she restrained her urge to be rude to the long-winded old man.

"The book is in the universal's reading room. The young lady before us is the only one who can reach it."

Kinga spun on her heel to face Connie. "You remember the title, Connie?" Connie nodded. "Then we would be grateful if you would make haste to read all you can in the time we have left. Morjik and Windfoal must leave under cover of darkness; their barge will be here at midnight so that gives you a few hours."

"But the library closes at six!" protested Mr. Dove, looking at his pocket watch whose golden hands showed that it was five o'clock already. Kinga looked hard at him and raised one of her dark eyebrows. Morjik released a puff of red smoke. "But of course, we'll arrange a special extended opening tonight," Mr. Dove added quickly, licking his dry lips.

"Good." Kinga gave him a curt nod.

"But the universal is tired!" intervened Kira. "We must not work her so hard."

"I'm fine," said Connie, suppressing a yawn. She was more eager than any of them to find out about the chimera if it could help them capture the creature. "Could you please send a message to my brother and the Clamworthys that I might be some time? They'll probably want to take Liam home."

"Of course," said Kinga. "I'll take care of that."

"And we'll arrange for some refreshments for you," added Kira.

Mr. Dove was about to protest at the idea of food and drink in the library, but one look at the pointed horn and ebony hooves of Windfoal made him think better of this.

⚓

Up in the universal's reading room, Connie took more time than usual to recover from the encounter with the great snake that guarded the entrance. The bite-like bond it demanded on each entry reminded her too vividly of the chimera's fangs, and she felt sickened, her hand rising involuntarily to protect the place on her neck where the serpent had bitten her. Her skin still seemed to smart, and there were two lumps under her fingers where the teeth had sunk in, which throbbed slightly with remembered pain. To calm herself down, she poured a cup of coffee, took a mouthful of cheese sandwich, and enjoyed chewing it under the disapproving nose of the door-ward, which now lay curled up at the head of the winding stair, blue ribbon trailing from its mouth as it sucked on the golden key she had given it.

Time for her task.

Brushing the crumbs off the table, she got up to locate the book she wanted. She guessed it would not be filed under one of the four companies on the outer wall as the subject matter crossed the bounds of these categories. So instead, she knelt down in front of the low circle of bookshelves devoted to subjects to do with the gift of the universal. She ran her finger down the spines of the books on which she had so far barely made any impression. So much knowledge for her to gain! Here her life's work was laid out before her. Hidden among the fat volumes filed under "C" was the book she sought: a slim, handwritten manuscript bound in black leather. The pages crackled as she opened it, releasing the smell of dust and decay. At first, she thought it was written in a foreign language as she could make out little on the page she had randomly selected. Laying it open on the table, she saw that she was wrong. The language was English, but English as people seven hundred years ago would have spoken it.

Connie was about to give up in despair, as she understood only two words in five, when she turned a page and found a bundle of yellowing notepaper slipped between the sheets. It was dated December 1940 and bore the name "Reginald Cony." Connie realized she had stumbled upon the notes made by the last British universal, the uncle that the Trustee Frederick Cony had told her about before his own death last year. She leafed through the pages. Reginald appeared to have been taking notes on behalf of a Society member and had addressed a letter to someone called George Brewer. But Reginald must have forgotten to take the notes with him, and the letter ended abruptly mid-sentence.

Dear George, she read, *I hope my last set of notes reached you safely through all the snow and ice. The griffin messenger said that the passage over the Arctic Circle was particularly hairy at the moment. I hope I can complete these today, but what with the frequent interruptions of the air-raids, I'm not confident. I got my call-up papers, as expected, so this will be my last opportunity to come here for some time. The lantern dome offers spectacular views of the bombers coming in from Germany but it isn't the safest place to be. We're moving as much as we can down to the basements, but I'm afraid the universal's collection will just have to run the risk as I'm not going to try getting past the door-ward with a bundle of books. I don't think it understands about human war.*

No, it wouldn't, agreed Connie, smiling to find that her predecessor had shared her mixed feelings about the guard.

Now, as I wrote in my last letter, I fear de Chauliac spends most time on the chimera. I won't bore you with the details. . . .

Oh do, urged Connie, but it was hopeless: she was decades too late to influence this correspondence.

But he does mention the shape-shifter a couple of times. It seems that Kullervo is able to calm the chimera's madness by turning into a chimera himself. This way the different parts of the chimera can communicate with their Kullervo-counterpart, and he is able to persuade the creature to do his bidding. So if you run across a chimera up there, it's probably under Kullervo's sway and I'd advise you to steer clear.

And here's something else that might interest you. I've just read the note made by the translator, one Edward Alleyne. He notes that Guy de Chauliac had made a special study of the conjoined creatures as a way to combat Kullervo, so you were on the right track there. He notes that both he and de Chauliac were fellow-universals. There were apparently ten identified ones in Europe alone in the 1340s! Can you imagine that! At the moment there's only poor old me and Miguel in Argentina, and you know that I can't speak a word of Spanish, nor he a word of English, so we're not much company for each other even when we do meet.

De Chauliac, Alleyne, and their fellow universals had worked out that Kullervo was spreading the Black Death through rats. Over a third of the population in the known world had died by the time they figured this out, and they knew that they had to act quickly. De Chauliac did do something—Alleyne said he "passyd oute of thys world by the mark." So you were right: Kullervo does have to be challenged at the mark, but I think it is something only a universal can do, so I advise you to

Here the letter ended. So it had never been delivered to George Brewer, whoever he was. Connie supposed another bombing raid had sent Reginald scurrying to the basement, and he had not returned to collect his letter. What had he been about to advise his friend to do? She leafed through the book to the note he referred to, wondering whether with his guidance she could make anything of it.

𝕲𝖚𝖞 𝖕𝖆𝖘𝖘𝖞𝖉 𝖔𝖚𝖙𝖊 𝖔𝖋 𝖙𝖍𝖞𝖘 𝖜𝖔𝖗𝖑𝖉 𝖇𝖞 𝖙𝖍𝖊 𝖒𝖆𝖗𝖐 𝖆𝖓𝖉 𝖙𝖍𝖊𝖗𝖊 𝖜𝖆𝖘 𝖜𝖊𝖕𝖞𝖓𝖌 𝖆𝖓𝖉 𝖉𝖔𝖑𝖔𝖚𝖗 𝖔𝖚𝖙 𝖔𝖋 𝖒𝖊𝖘𝖚𝖗𝖊. 𝕺𝖚𝖗 𝖈𝖔𝖚𝖓𝖘𝖊𝖑𝖘 𝖆𝖗𝖊 𝖌𝖗𝖎𝖊𝖛𝖔𝖚𝖘𝖑𝖞 𝖑𝖊𝖘𝖘𝖊𝖓𝖊𝖉. 𝕭𝖚𝖙 𝖍𝖊 𝖉𝖊𝖋𝖊𝖆𝖙𝖊𝖉 𝕶𝖚𝖑𝖑𝖊𝖗𝖛𝖔 𝖋𝖔𝖗 𝖙𝖍𝖞𝖘 𝖙𝖎𝖒𝖊.

Well, that was clear enough. Whatever Guy de Chauliac

had done—"challenged at the mark"—it had worked. She had the vivid image of a medieval Guy on horseback like some knight-errant of old, riding to face his opponent on the jousting field. But the challenge had cost him his life.

She closed the book and slipped the unfinished letter into her pocket, hoping the snake had not seen. She felt she might get away with taking the letter and the notes, but not the book. If ever there was a volume that she would like to smuggle out of the reading room, this was it, but she knew from past experience that was out of the question as far as the door-ward was concerned. Picking up the remains of her picnic supper, she followed the snake down the winding stair, her mind still up in the lantern dome with Reginald and Guy.

⊰⧓⊱

"So, now we know how Kullervo is controlling the chimera," said Kinga, handing the notes back to Connie. "Not a method we can use, I fear. None of us can change into a chimera."

"Not so," growled Morjik, his sulfury breath blooming around his nostrils in vibrant yellow flowers of smoke. "There is a way."

Connie had thought of it, too, but had hoped no one else would.

"What do you mean?" asked Kira, her dark eyes bright with interest.

"He means," said Connie wearily, "that if we gather

together a Nemean lion, a great snake, and an Amalthean goat, then through the shared bond they can communicate with the chimera. I can mediate."

"Not only you," said Jade softly.

This was the bit Connie had really hoped they would not think of, but she should have realized that the ageless rock dwarf and ancient dragon would have had many years in which to learn such secrets.

"Simon, too," she admitted reluctantly. "But he's not even begun his training. You can't seriously expect him to help?" Her weariness was becoming almost unbearable; she was finding it increasingly difficult to control her emotions. The Trustees exchanged looks over Connie's head as she sat once more hugging her knees in their midst. "Please, tell me you're not serious. He's only just turned twelve!"

"But you were only eleven the first time you faced Kullervo, Connie," said Eagle-Child. "Do not treat your brother as an infant. He is fast approaching manhood. In my tribe, he would soon be initiated as an adult."

The unicorn companion was looking at her with a worried frown, sensing that the universal was exhausted.

"And as far as we know, the chimera is not instructed to kill him on sight. It would surely be safer to use his skills and train him for this task than risk putting you in the creature's path again?" said Kira calmly, moving toward her.

"No!" Connie leapt to her feet, swaying with tiredness. "I can't let you do this. You don't understand what it's like!"

"No, we don't," said Eagle-Child, "but Simon will. It is his gift. You should not deny him this."

"I'm not denying him anything. I'm just trying to stop you from killing him in some stupid attempt to save me. I'm not exchanging my life for his!"

The room fell into stunned silence as Connie's last words echoed around the chamber. She had not meant to be so outspoken, but she stood by every word she had said.

Windfoal neighed and rippled her mane.

"Connie, you're tired and upset," said Kira coming forward to lay a hand on her elbow. "We've overtaxed you today. It is our fault. You should rest now."

Connie was shaking slightly with a mixture of anger and fatigue. It would be unwise to say any more in her current condition, she knew that, but she had to make them understand! When would she have another chance to speak to the Trustees?

"You don't see it, do you? That letter isn't really about the chimera—that's just a sideshow. It's about Kullervo— this whole situation is about Kullervo. That's what Guy de Chauliac and Reginald Cony both realized. We should be talking about challenging him at the mark—about me challenging him at the mark—not about the chimera!"

The silence that followed turned icy. Connie could sense the Trustees thought she had gone too far. Kinga and Morjik were angry with her; Windfoal and Kira were afraid.

"What are you all looking at?" Connie asked with a defiant tilt to her head when no one spoke. "Are you afraid to hear the truth?" Anger was making her feel like quite a different person—not a shy teenager, but a universal, proud of her inheritance and ready to defend it.

Windfoal stamped her foot. "We're not afraid of the truth, Universal," said Kira sternly. "We are afraid for you—and of you. It is you who does not know what she is talking about if you think the way to defeat Kullervo is to challenge him."

"Connie, listen," said Eagle-Child. "You do not even sound like yourself. You are talking about traveling a lonely path, repeating the same mistakes of the universals of the past."

"But it wasn't a mistake," said Connie beseechingly, turning to Eagle-Child. She could usually count on him to be on her side. It was very serious if even he did not agree. "Look at what Guy de Chauliac did: it ended the Black Death, for God's sake!"

Eagle-Child shook his head. "You have read only one account—a biased one by a friend of his. By another universal. The histories of the Society around the world tell how Guy de Chauliac failed in his challenge. He was taken by Kullervo before he could complete the ordeal. It is a horrible death you are talking about—a torture beyond your imagining."

Connie was taken aback. They had already known

about Guy? What else did they know that she didn't?

"But Edward Alleyne said he succeeded," she said miserably.

"He did. In part," said Eagle-Child. "He satisfied Kullervo's lust for destruction for that time. But Guy did not achieve his aim, which was to vanquish Kullervo once and for all. Do you want to pay that price? Your suffering as the sacrifice that will make Kullervo cease his attack for a brief time? And when he has exhausted you, thrown you aside, he'll come back for more—new victims, new forms of devastation."

Connie sat down again, no longer wanting to be in the middle of the room, at the center of everyone's attention, yet she didn't know where else to sit.

"But he knew there was a way to defeat him, didn't he?" she said, still stubbornly defending the memory of her predecessor like the sole fighter left after a hopeless siege. "He was on to something."

"He failed," concluded Eagle-Child. He rose gracefully to his feet and came to sit cross-legged in front of her, his open, bronzed face smooth and calm. Only the flicker of fire in the depths of his eyes betrayed his anxiety. Connie's head was bowed so that he could not see her expression. He gently slid his hand under her chin to raise her face. Tears trickled down Connie's cheeks as she met his gaze. "We forbid you to go any further down this path, Universal. Do you understand?"

Connie could feel the minds of all the mythical creatures snaking toward her, seeking to strengthen the prohibition of the Trustee for the Winged Beasts. She did not want them in her head; too much else was going on there at the moment. In one swift move, she raised her shield against them, blocking entry, and jumped to her feet, knocking away Eagle-Child's hand.

"I understand," she said bitterly. "But I don't agree." And, turning on her heels, she fled from the chamber.

8

Alone

Connie kept silent on the train journey home the following day. Col watched her out of the corner of his eye as she leafed through a book she had borrowed from the main section of the library—*The Early History of the Society, 1000–1500*. It looked like a boring read to him: cramped, close-printed text with no illustrations. If she wanted to wade through tedious textbooks she only had to wait until school next week. She was probably just covering up her bad mood by pretending to be interested in it, he decided. It was what he would've done. He knew that she had fallen out with the Trustees, which he had to admit was pretty serious, but he didn't know the details. Maybe he should try to cheer her up and see if she wanted to talk about it?

"Hey, Connie, do you want a mint?" he asked, holding

out a packet he kept in his pocket for Mags.

She shook her head mutely.

"Yeah, I'll have one!" said Simon, making a grab for the sweets. In complete contrast to his sister, Simon could not have been in better spirits.

"Hands off." Col laughed, chucking him a single mint, which Simon caught.

"You show more promise as a fielder than your sister," teased Mack, ruffling Connie's hair. She flinched away and Mack quickly withdrew his hand, which as usual had been stung by static upon touching the universal. "Why do I always forget about her defenses?" Mack said ruefully, waving his fingers in the air to shake away the pain. He turned back to Simon, to whom he'd been talking before Col offered around the mints. "And what did they tell you then?"

"They said I'm to be put on a fast-track training program," said Simon proudly. "They've a special task for me."

The Early History of the Society slid to the floor with a clunk. "Yeah? What?"

"They want me to help capture the chimera so Connie can get out and about again."

"That's cool," said Col, glancing over at Connie, who was bent forward, hair in a curtain around her face, as she picked up the book. Was this the problem? he wondered. Did she not like being ordered to stay in Hescombe? Another thought struck him. Or was she jealous of Simon being given this special treatment? But you couldn't get more special than being a universal. Simon's gift, though unique, was not in the same league as hers.

"That's what I said when they told me." Simon bubbled with enthusiasm. "They're to make special arrangements with my school so I can carry on the training on the weekends. Apparently, one of the teachers is a member of the Society—Mr. Hawthorn, the science teacher—I'd never've guessed. He seems so normal. They're going to bring in a Nemean lion especially for me."

"That's good, isn't it, Connie?" said Col, turning to her.

She paused, then said: "I'm glad they're going to train Simon properly."

Col sensed there was an unspoken reservation. "But?"

She shut her book with a snap. "But they shouldn't be using Simon to catch the chimera: it's too dangerous."

"Oh, come on!" protested Simon. "You're always trying to spoil my fun."

Connie looked as though she felt like strangling her brother. "Don't be so stupid."

"Stupid!" Simon was riled now. "You don't understand. You never understand."

"Ha!" said Connie, getting up to push past Col, who was blocking her path to the aisle. "I think you'll find I'm the only one who understands. I'm going to get a coffee." Grabbing her book from her seat, she disappeared in the direction of the dining car.

Mack, Simon, and Col exchanged looks.

"Girls!" said Mack with a shrug. "Hormones, mood-swings; Evie's the same."

Simon nodded and returned to his update of what the Trustees had told him that morning. Col did not join in the conversation. Neither did he agree with Mack's diagnosis that Connie was merely being moody. She was normally one of the calmest people he knew. Something was up, and he very much wanted to know what was going on. So, slipping out of his seat, he quietly followed her.

He found Connie standing with an untouched cup of coffee, leaning against the grubby ledge that served inadequately as a table in the dining car. Outside, the rows of houses and industrial buildings had given way to rolling green hills. They had escaped the coils of London and were heading home.

"Want anything else?" he asked, gesturing to her drink.

"No, thanks. I don't recommend the coffee."

Col bought himself an orange juice and came to lean beside her. They stood together in companionable silence watching the world pass by. He had the sudden strange sensation that the train was standing still and it was the trees and the cows that were being whisked away at great speed.

"So, what's the matter, Connie?"

She did not speak for a moment, biting her lip as she looked down at the plastic spoon she was fingering. It snapped in two.

"And don't say 'nothing.' You and I both know each other better than that."

She could not resist his sympathy. Yes, she could tell him. He would stand by her. She threw the splinters of the spoon into the trash and took the plunge.

"You know I had a . . . a disagreement with the Trustees yesterday?"

Col nodded, keeping his eyes fixed on the distant hills in the hopes that it would be easier for her to speak if she did not feel under interrogation.

"Well, I think I've discovered a way, or an idea about a way, of finally defeating Kullervo."

Forgetting his resolution, Col turned to stare at her. "That's great! Amazing! What is it?" He thought for a second longer. "So, what's the problem with the Trustees?"

Connie tapped the spine of the book she had tucked under her arm. "I'm not the first to find out about it. There've been other universals who've tried, but they've failed, or at least, only partially succeeded. That's what we argued about. The Trustees think it's too dangerous and won't work."

Col's enthusiasm was dampened. "So what is it?"

"I'm not sure exactly, but it involves challenging Kullervo at the mark—the place where he enters our world. I think in the past this was a real place, but in my case, it's . . . well, you know where it is."

He did indeed. He vividly remembered visiting

Connie's mental wall of encounters and seeing the breach made by Kullervo: the dark void that whispered like waves on a distant sea.

"And what do you have to do in this challenge?"

"I don't know, yet. But I think the Trustees do since they told me those who failed were . . ." She stopped and took a sip of her coffee, wrinkling her nose at the bitter taste.

"Were what?"

"Were tortured to death."

Col choked on his mouthful of orange juice. "Connie! No wonder they don't want you to have anything to do with this! And you were just telling off Simon for getting into danger! You must be crazy even to think of it."

"Of course, I don't want to get hurt!" she replied angrily, crumpling up an empty sugar packet. "I'm not stupid. But think what it would mean if I succeeded."

"Yeah, right. And if you don't, as all the others have found out, you die a gruesome death. Good thinking, Connie."

"I thought you'd understand," she said in a small voice, turning her shoulder from him slightly.

"What? Understand your mad death-wish? Sure, I understand," he said, his voice laced with sarcasm. He couldn't believe she was really suggesting putting herself at such grave risk.

"It's not mad," Connie said defiantly. "Or if it is, it's only because I'm being driven mad by his voice in my head every night. I can't stand it. And if I can get rid of him forever: think how many lives that would save!"

Col sighed. "I'm sorry, Connie. I didn't know he was still bothering you." He placed a hand on her arm. "Look, it's just that none of us want to see you get hurt. We couldn't bear that—I couldn't bear that. Listen to the people you trust. You know they're only trying to do what's best for you. Don't go it alone on this one."

"I don't want to 'go it alone'—I want everyone's support for what I've got to do. I want to do this properly—avoid the mistakes made in the past."

"Stop right there. You know I'm on your side, Connie, but I can't support you in such a suicidal plan. Don't even think about it. Anyway, the Trustees won't let you do it." He could sense she was raw with pain, so he put his arm around her and gave her a hug. "You know it's not because we don't believe in you, don't you? You're an amazing person, Connie." He had to get through to her. "Promise me you won't do anything stupid?"

Her voice, coming from the muffling center of the hug, was close to a sob. "I can't . . . promise." She pushed him away and stood back to look into his eyes, her voice now firm. She would not allow even Col to stop her from doing what she knew was right, even when it was so tempting to take the easy path of falling in line with his wishes. "But thanks, Col. I know you're my friend—my *best* friend. And I promise I'll think over what you've said. Okay?"

It would have to do. "Okay," said Col, still looking at her

warily. "Hadn't you'd better drink up? We're almost there."

"Can't swallow the stuff," she said, throwing her cup into the trash. "Let's get back to the others."

※

Connie's disagreement with the Trustees, which normally would have greatly concerned Evelyn, was overshadowed by two other arguments. The first, Connie realized later, she should have foreseen. It arrived in the form of a telephone call that evening from her parents in Manila. If the phone could have given Connie warning of what was to come, it should have glowed throbbing red as she picked it up.

"WHAT IS ALL THIS!" bellowed her father. She held the receiver away from her ear. Her father was clearly attempting to get his voice heard from the other side of the world without the use of modern technology. "Simon has just called full of nonsense about joining that Society of yours!"

"Ah."

"I can't stop him, of course," he continued, "not with you being a member."

That was a shame, thought Connie. It would at least take away one problem if Simon wasn't allowed to train.

"But I blame you for this!"

"Me?" Connie was stung at the injustice of the accusation. "What've I got to do with it?"

"What've you got to do with it! You only took him up there and enrolled him without our permission. I thought your aunt was bad enough, but I didn't think my own daughter would go against what you must have known would've been my express wishes. Why on Earth have you involved your younger brother in that crazy society of yours? I expect your aunt's to blame, too, but I can't tell her what I really think, not in her current condition. I expected you to act more responsibly. Your mother agrees."

"Yes, dear," said Connie's mother, who appeared to have been listening in.

Connie was silent. What could she say? Here was another set of people who thought she was reckless. Join the club, she thought sourly.

"Are you there, Connie?" barked her father as the line crackled and hissed at him.

"Yes."

"Well?"

"Well, what?"

"What've you got to say for yourself?"

"Nothing."

"Nothing?"

"What do you want me to say?"

This question seemed to floor her father.

"That . . . that you're sorry for getting Simon mixed up with your bunch."

"Okay. I'm sorry for getting Simon mixed up in the Society." That was partly true.

"And that you promise to try and keep him safe. Not let him do anything dangerous."

Connie was silent again. That was, of course, what she had already been trying to do.

"Connie?"

"I'll try."

"I don't want any more early morning phone calls telling me one of my children has ended up in the hospital with injuries from wild animals."

"I'll see what I can do," she said, trying hard to keep her bitterness to herself. It hadn't been her fault she'd ended up in Chartmouth's ER. Her father hadn't shouted at Simon for leading her into the jaws of the chimera—not that he'd been told about that.

When she put down the phone, she found Evelyn watching her closely from the kitchen table, where she was tucking into her fifth bacon sandwich of the day. Evelyn had developed a craving for bacon smothered in ketchup.

"Can he join?"

"Dad seems to think it's too late to stop him."

"Are you okay?"

"Kind of."

"That means no. Do you want to talk about it?"

Connie took a deep breath but at that moment, Mack stamped into the kitchen through the back door, holding up a pair of mud-splattered sneakers.

"I thought we agreed," he said tersely to Evelyn, "that

you're not to risk running on the moor with the banshees."

"We might've said something along those lines," Evelyn replied awkwardly.

"Then what are these?"

"Obviously, they are my running shoes."

"And why are they covered in mud?"

"Because I haven't cleaned them?"

"Evie!"

"Okay. Okay. Because I went running while you were in London. I changed my mind about the banshees."

Mack swelled with rage like a bullfrog preparing to croak. "But you know they're not good for the baby—not in the early months. All that spinning and wailing—think what you're doing to our child."

"She's fine," said Evelyn patting her stomach. "Isn't she, Connie?"

"Er . . ."

"Leave Connie out of this," intervened Mack. "This is between you and me, Evelyn Lionheart."

Connie realized this was really not a good moment to be in the kitchen. She got up to go.

"Connie, we haven't had our chat, yet," said Evelyn, stalling for time as a full-blown fight loomed on the horizon.

"It can wait," said Connie, slipping her hand free of her aunt and moving to the door.

The following day, when Connie got out of bed and opened the curtains, it took her a moment or two to realize what she was seeing. The sky, which had been barren and dry for months, was clouding over from the west. Fat drops of rain were pattering onto the dusty road. The drought had broken.

When she entered the kitchen, she found Evelyn and Mack having a cozy breakfast together, harmony restored. Tactfully, she decided to leave them in peace and take hers back upstairs. Besides, she had some reading she wanted to get through before Gard arrived for her next training session. She sat cross-legged on her bed, balancing a cup of tea in one hand and *The Early History of the Society* in the other. The book had been recommended to her by Mr. Dove, who'd been overjoyed at her interest in the subject. On any other occasion, she would have been fascinated to read about the establishment and spread of the Society in its early years, but ever since she'd taken it out, she'd been making her way slowly through the section on the later medieval period, trying to understand what it was the Trustees knew and she did not. So far, though she had learned a lot, Connie had not discovered anything she might not have guessed herself. The Trustees were right that here was a very different account from that given by Edward Alleyne. The book contained a long and detailed chapter on the first major calamity to face the Society: the rat-borne Black Death, or bubonic plague, as the modern writer explained. This writer, however, did not regard Guy de Chauliac as a hero; indeed, the universals appeared to be the villains of the piece, after Kullervo.

The Company of Universals, he wrote, *acting against the wishes of the rest of the European members of the Society, dispatched their champion to challenge Kullervo to single-handed combat. This rash decision was opposed primarily because the other members thought that the reduction of the Company of Universals to only ten (already half of them had succumbed to the Black Death) meant that de Chauliac's life was too valuable to be risked in this way. They sensibly urged that other options be tried first. The membership also feared that if de Chauliac's will broke, he could become a tool of Kullervo, making the existing disaster seem only a rehearsal for something far more serious.*

Connie had now reached the part where Guy set out alone to confront Kullervo.

There were no witnesses to what happened so we have only the vaguest idea of what took place. We know this much: de Chauliac sailed into the Arctic Circle, to the edge of the glacier where Kullervo had entered our world at the mark.

Connie pictured the man in her imagination, as he strode across the glittering white icefield, feeling for him in his loneliness and fear. Whatever the majority thought, she considered him a brave man to choose to face Kullervo.

The foolhardy challenger is thought to have survived the first hour of combat, matching the universal's weapons to each metamorphosis of Kullervo's, till finally—inevitably—his defenses were broken. But, clearly, Kullervo did not break his will for he did not join with him and no new disaster struck. As punishment, Kullervo took Guy and spent months exhausting him in the bonded encounter till the pain destroyed him.

Connie put the book down. Her memory had flitted back to the brief time she had spent in the air with Kullervo as he'd shifted from shape to shape, spinning her, dancing with her. That had been a bonded encounter, but its memory was almost sweet. She had for one brief moment glimpsed something in Kullervo, a joy at the myriad forms of creation, that she could relate to and respect. Was this the torture Guy had experienced? How could it be? But then, if her time with Kullervo had proved anything to her, it was that everything he did had its dark side. It was not so difficult to imagine him turning this game into a torment as he forced his companion to inhabit each form with him. Connie remembered the pain of encountering the fractured mind of the chimera. This beast contained only three natures in contention with one another. Imagine what it would be like to encounter form after form, creature after creature, each more complex, more terrible than the last? It would drive you into madness even if it didn't kill you.

Connie returned to the book.

It has to be allowed that after the universal's failed attempt to defeat the shape-shifter once and for all, the intensity of the Black Death declined. Kullervo was successfully distracted from pushing his plan to its conclusion. Humanity survived. But so did the plague. It would return on many occasions, though never so virulent as this outbreak, as if Kullervo was taking a playful swipe at humans, reminding us that he is waiting only for the right occasion to finish us off.

Laying the book down on the bedside table, Connie stared out at the rain streaming down the window. Kullervo would find the occasion one day. The Society should not be complacent and believe because it had always managed to forestall disaster in the past that it could do so in the future.

Kullervo was gaining in power. Almost all the weather giants had gone over to his side now. By its greed and carelessness, humanity was driving more and more creatures into his camp. The Society was losing touch with many of them, falling from its place of respect among the mythical creatures. Connie understood this even if the Trustees did not. She had heard the echoes of doubt and dissatisfaction in the minds of the creatures she had encountered. She'd heard them in her own mind for that matter. At night, they came back to haunt her when Kullervo tempted her with her uncertainties. If someone did not do something soon, it would be too late for the Society.

But do what? Connie was still no closer to understanding what it was she had to do to defeat Kullervo. She knew she could fight him for a time, like Guy had. Once or twice she had managed to undermine him, but that had been mainly luck that she had caught him unprepared. He would be ready for her if she issued a formal challenge. She doubted she'd last even an hour under those circumstances. Guy had been a mature, fully trained universal; she barely knew anything. As Col had bluntly told her, to face him like this would be suicidal.

So, was there a way to stop Kullervo or not?

9

Testing Times

Mrs. Clamworthy dropped Col and Simon at the Mastersons' on Saturday afternoon. The windshield wipers of her old Fiesta could hardly keep up with the downpour.

"Good luck!" she called after her grandson as he slammed the door shut. "I'll keep my fingers crossed for you."

Simon squelched after Col through the thick mud of the farmyard, which was already churned up by the passage of pupils, their mentors, and the examiners. He looked up at the sky, rain dripping off the end of his nose.

"They can't expect you to fly in this, surely?" he asked.

Col gave a hollow laugh. "You don't know the Society very well if you think a bit of rain will put them off. They'd probably arrange a weather giant if nature did not oblige—to make the test more 'realistic,' as my mentor puts it."

"Oh," said Simon. Most at home in front of his PlayStation, Simon was finding it hard to adjust to the outdoor life. "Okay, I s'pose I'd better wish you luck. See you later." He splashed away into the barn to be introduced to his mentor for the Nemean lions.

Col could hear the yawning roar of Simon's companion echoing in the rafters, which meant that the Society had finally succeeded in smuggling a lion into the country after some weeks of trying. He looked forward to hearing Simon's reaction later. He doubted if Simon would be worried about the wet weather once he'd met his companion for the first time.

"There you are, my boy!" Captain Graves strode across the yard and slapped Col on the back. "Pleased to see you are on time for once. I suggest you go and warm up with Skylark. The examiners are just finishing lunch. I'll bring them out when they're ready." The captain shook water droplets off his handlebar mustache, not much bothered by the rain that was streaming down his neck.

"Okay," said Col. "Er . . . who are they this year?"

"Clare Ridley—you remember, the winner of the dressage competition?—and Sergeant Middleton, the champion in the steeplechase."

Col remembered them very well. In the Society Games earlier that summer, where he and Skylark had again won the junior competition, these two riders had impressed him with their skill. Looking at them with their mounts, he knew that, though he and Skylark were good, they weren't *that* good.

"Why've they both come?" Col asked, thinking it a strange coincidence that the Society's two best riders had come to Hescombe just to examine a Grade Four flying test.

Captain Graves smiled proudly. "They've not said, of course, but my guess is they're talent-scouting for the Inter-Society World Championships next summer. You may be a bit on the young side, but you've shown talent— yes, indeed, you've shown talent—and I would bet that there's a third place in the British squad waiting for a young rider with promise."

Col swallowed. This was an honor he'd not even dreamed of: to be invited to be part of the British squad at fourteen! Wow.

"But before you get carried away, young man," said Captain Graves with an indulgent smile as he saw the look of wonder on his pupil's face, "there's the little matter of impressing them in today's test. Hadn't you better go and get ready?"

"Yes, sir!" said Col, sprinting off to the stables.

Skylark, you'll never guess! burst out Col as soon as he found his companion.

The white-winged stallion ignored this and arched his

neck proudly. *How do I look?* he asked Col, showing off his groomed mane.

You look great, said Col quickly, knowing how vain Skylark was on such occasions. At least, this time he hadn't asked Col to braid his tail with ribbons as he had at the competition. Col kept to himself the thought that all this gleaming mane would soon be wet and windswept in the rain outside.

So, what won't I guess? asked Skylark as Col vaulted onto his back.

Only that we've got Middleton and Ridley testing us. Captain Graves thinks they are talent-scouting for the British team!

Skylark gave a shiver of delight. *Well, we'll show them that they've come to the right place! We'll have to be in top form today, Col: focused and ruthless.*

Col felt his companion delve into his mind to explore their connection, deepening it so that their instincts were in harmony.

What's this? Skylark had stumbled across the anxiety and irritation Col was currently feeling for Connie, plus something else that he could not put a name to, yet.

Col hunched forward against the rain and urged Skylark into a warm-up trot. *It's Connie. She thinks she's found a way to take on Kullervo and win.*

And can she? The pegasus picked up his pace to leap a fence. They did not land but circled up into the air together.

Don't be ridiculous. No one has ever defeated him.

Have you no faith in the universal?

Of course, I do.

I think you are fooling yourself, Companion. You can't think straight when it comes to Connie; you never could.

Col groaned. *Skylark, this isn't a good time to discuss this.*

The pegasus snorted. *When would it be a good time?*

A whistle blew from below. Skylark and Col spiraled down to land perfectly at Captain Graves's side. Firewings, Skylark's mentor, gave an approving snort at his pupil's elegant descent. Also with Captain Graves were two people dressed in the British squad's navy flying jacket with a gold pegasus on the back. Clare Ridley, an athletic woman with shoulder-length brown hair, gave Col a friendly nod. Her formidable-looking teammate, Sergeant Middleton, was inspecting Skylark closely, water dripping from his close-cropped head, his jaw jutting forward. Col knew already that the sergeant would stand no nonsense.

"Glad to see you've got high presentation standards," Sergeant Middleton said to the pegasus, patting him on the shoulder before making a note in a leather-bound notebook.

Col looked down at his mud-splattered boots and then across at Sergeant Middleton's shining toecaps. He surreptitiously brushed at the dirt until he caught Mrs. Ridley's eye. She was laughing at him, so he stopped and grinned back. She was right: it was too late to do anything about that now.

"Right," barked Sergeant Middleton, "on my signal, take off and go through the first three basic maneuvers. At some point during this, I will make the signal for the emergency landing and I would like you both to descend as quickly and safely to the ground as possible, keeping yourselves under control at all times." He blew his whistle.

Col did not even have to urge Skylark forward: his mount was already galloping into the rain for takeoff. Gaining height, Skylark began to go through the pre-scribed moves—both of them sharing a secret yawn at the pedestrian nature of what they were doing. Left turn. Right turn. Forward dive and recover. Just as they reached the top of their recovery, the whistle blew again.

The mangy mule! Skylark snorted, plunging down in a beautifully judged emergency dive. *He waited till we were at the most difficult point!*

Of course, said Col, far from annoyed that they had a chance to display their abilities in something more exciting than boring turns. They landed with a neat thud next to Sergeant Middleton, who was looking smug as he enjoyed the trick he'd just played on them. Mrs. Ridley came over to him to talk. Col and Skylark waited while the two champions whispered together.

"I think we've seen enough of the Grade Four moves to know what mark to award," Sergeant Middleton said to Captain Graves. Col's mentor looked surprised: there were still many more moves that the examiners were supposed to test. "We thought we'd give the candidates a chance to show us their full repertoire. I don't think we'll waste any more time on Grade Four. What do you say, Clamworthy?"

Col hesitated. Was this a trap? Were they testing him to see if he was going to break the rules by doing moves he was not qualified for?

"What repertoire?" he asked innocently.

Mrs. Ridley smiled. "Oh, you can't fool us into thinking that you and Skylark learned to fly as you do by never going beyond Grade Four, Col."

Careful, said Skylark to Col in the privacy of their bond.

"Er . . . well . . ." said Col, wishing Captain Graves would help him out of this spot.

"We think you're both quite ready to do what you do best: fly. No limitations. You have our permission to do whatever you feel you've mastered, just don't attempt anything you can't do safely. We want to see what you're made of."

Captain Graves was struggling with his desire to allow Col and Skylark to show off before the British squad and his equally strong wish to stick to the rules. "Anything, Clare?" he asked.

"Yes, anything, Michael. Oh, don't worry. It's all official. We got permission from Kira and Windfoal before we came out here. They told us Col and Skylark had used some impressive unconventional moves in operational circumstances. We want to see them for ourselves."

"I suppose that's all right then," said Captain Graves as if he doubted what he was saying.

"Off you go," said Mrs. Ridley.

Col urged Skylark forward. Though the rain continued to stream down, it no longer mattered to him.

If they want the full repertoire, said Col with a chuckle, *they'll get the full repertoire. What do you say to Syracrusian Spiral, Athenian Dive, followed by Thessalonian Roll?* This was a little something he and Skylark had been working on in private. Theoretically, you couldn't do those three moves in sequence. He and Skylark were about to prove the theorists wrong.

You're on! said Skylark.

A good starting height was the secret to the success of the maneuver. They climbed up so that they were almost lost in the rain clouds.

Careful, hold on, Col, cautioned Skylark. *Remember my back is very slippery in all this rain.*

Get on with it, you old nag, teased Col. *I'll remember.*

With a kick of his rear legs, Skylark launched into the downward circle of the Syracrusian Spiral, twisting with perfect loops over an imagined spot on the ground (they had chosen the head of a startled Captain Graves). They then moved fluidly into the Athenian Dive, wings tucked in like an eagle plunging for the kill. Col clung close to Skylark's neck as his knees found little purchase on the pegasus's rain-slicked flanks. Both knew that they were at the point where the possible shaded into the impossible. So far, they had managed to stay on the right side of that line, but these weather conditions were threatening to push them over. Col braced himself for the final test. Just before they reached the level of the treetops, Skylark pulled away in a Thessalonian Roll, flipping both himself and his rider over in a three hundred and sixty degree turn. Col's fingers slipped but he dug them deep into Skylark's sodden mane. He kept his seat—just. Once righted, they glided down to land with barely a spray of mud in front of the judges. There was silence. Captain Graves was gaping: he had not known his pupil could do any of those moves, let alone do them together.

Finally, Clare Ridley spoke. "When I said no limits, I was thinking more along the lines of a few Grade Six moves—not moves right out of the rule book entirely."

Col's heart sank. Skylark's perky ears dropped back.

"Amazing," breathed Sergeant Middleton. "I'd have said you couldn't do that, but I just saw it with my own eyes. Amazing."

Col began to feel a bit more hopeful.

Mrs. Ridley was recovering from her surprise. "That's certainly given us plenty to think about. But don't try that again, will you, Col? Beginner's luck might run out."

"Oh, we've been doing it for over a year now," said Col quickly. Seeing their shocked faces, he added, "We had to do it when we were fighting Kullervo in Mallins Wood, which was how we discovered it was possible, you see?"

"I'm not sure what to make of that," said Mrs. Ridley. "What do you think, Will?"

Sergeant Middleton scratched his chin. "I think they should not do it again . . ." (Col held his breath) ". . . unless they're at the World Championships with us. That maneuver should wake up a few of our competitors, raise the bar on what we get up to."

"Yes," said Mrs. Ridley, her uncertainty vanishing as he gave the answer she wanted to hear. "Give us a few weeks and we'll be back in touch about your training for the squad. We might have a few problems with the age limit, but then . . . Anyway, that's our problem. Leave it to us."

"Great!" Col grinned at Skylark. Neither could believe their luck.

Captain Graves stirred. The rain was relenting and the sun peeping through a break in the clouds. "So what about their Grade Four practical?"

"It's a hard one," said Sergeant Middleton with a smile warming his stern face, "but I think they might just have scraped through. What do you think, Clare?"

"Scraped through with distinction, I'd say." She smiled back, nodding at Col.

❧

Connie and Gard had retreated to the front parlor for

her training that weekend. No longer allowed to go to the Mastersons'—too near the moor and the chimera, in the opinion of the Trustees—she and Gard had been forced to improvise a new routine. Today they were planning the next steps for her training. She had mastered the shield, sword, and helm—they were now second nature to her—and felt fairly confident with the hauberk, which she used to assume the protective powers of a mythical creature. The lance and the quiver and arrows were next on the list.

"So," grumbled Gard, leafing through the notes she'd made in the universal's reading room some months ago, "how is this quiver supposed to work?"

"I think," said Connie, leaning over to check her notes as she sat beside him on the old sofa, "it's a way of storing small bolts of energy from encounters to use later. It sounds quite vicious, actually—one of the warrior tools. The example given in the book was gorgon darts—like cold paralyzing stings. Not as powerful as the real thing, of course, but enough to take out an enemy for a few minutes. It said you could do the same with any other projectile power."

Gard raised his craggy eyebrows at her. His dark eyes gleamed under the overhang of his jutting forehead. "And the lance?"

Sitting next to him like this, Connie could smell his breath, which carried a scent like that of a sooty chimney.

"The lance is more powerful. It comes from the powers

of your companion. Unlike the sword, which the universal directs on his or her own, you guide it to the target together so it takes a bit of practice. It can't be stored up like the quiver and arrows. I think I did something like this with Storm-Bird the first time we met."

"I see." Gard got to his feet, creaking at the knees as his legs took his formidable weight. He walked to the fireplace and stood in front of it, deep in thought. "Can I ask you a question, Universal?"

Connie could tell he was concerned about something. "Of course."

He turned so he could study her face. "Why do you want to learn more warrior tools? Are there no defensive or healing tools that you could undertake first?"

She wasn't sure she wanted to admit the truth to Gard, knowing he wouldn't approve. "Oh, I'm just following the sequence of chapters in one of the books in the library. I thought that made sense." The book did indeed run in this order, but that was not why she was doing it.

"I had a long talk with Jade a few weeks ago," said Gard, turning back to finger the marble figurine of a white horse on the mantelpiece. "She told me you were talking about challenging Kullervo."

"Oh?" said Connie, trying to keep her tone light as if the subject was not of huge importance to her.

"You wouldn't be thinking of training yourself with the aim of taking him on?" he asked, stroking the smooth back of the horse with a chipped fingertip.

"I thought there was no harm in being prepared. I've met him three times already—I can't believe he's going to leave me alone now."

"No, he will not. But that is very different from seeking him out, as you well know."

Connie said nothing and looked down at her rounded writing:

The quiver: deadly against smaller foes, useful delaying attack against larger creatures. A warrior universal should keep a quiver full at all times.

"Do not try to lie to me, Universal," said Gard, tapping the horse as if to listen for flaws in the marble. "The uppermost layer of your mind is seething with the idea. It is pouring through you like a lava flow."

"I just thought . . ." began Connie, "I just wanted to understand. If there is a way of defeating Kullervo, I should do everything in my power to find it?"

"No!" said Gard sharply, the word ringing in the air. "Do not be tempted to think your skills are a match for those of the shape-shifter. Others have thought that and suffered the consequences."

"But—"

"There are no 'buts,' Connie. You should not be so quick to assume that as a universal you are always right. Instinct can lead you wrong. I remember Guy de Chauliac . . ."

Connie started with surprise, before she quickly reminded herself that the few hundred years separating her from her predecessor would seem but yesterday to the rock dwarf.

"I was serving as a Trustee with my companion at the time. Guy was headstrong. A loner. The universals under his leadership had stopped offering the shared bond to the Society, wanting to keep their powers to themselves. We were riven with petty feuds and rivalries as a result. I thought I understood him: I, who do not like to mix with others out of my element, believed I comprehended his desire to shut his mind away from everyone else. But I was wrong. He shut himself off because he was proud, too proud to share with others even the crumbs from the banquet of his gift."

"I think he was brave," said Connie boldly, not liking to hear another universal criticized so harshly.

"Oh yes, he was undoubtedly brave; I do not deny that. But was he right? We had other plans to combat the Black Death. Teams had been sent to places worst hit by plague to deal with the rats. We had begun to take action. It was not only thanks to Guy de Chauliac's foolish sacrifice that the plague was stemmed."

"But, Gard, both he and Reginald Cony felt that there was a way to defeat Kullervo. Reginald told George Brewer in those notes I showed the Trustees."

"Ah, George Brewer," said Gard thoughtfully, "now he

was another one. Until today, I had forgotten that I knew him." He moved to the other side of the fireplace and picked up the bronze statue of a bear rearing on its hind legs.

"Another what?"

"Another one who thought he knew what he was doing in the teeth of all advice. He also paid with his life."

"So who was he?" asked Connie, determined to get as many clues as she could from the rock dwarf.

"Do you not know?" said Gard, looking around the room. "We are surrounded by pictures of him, by his things," he held out the statue, "and you do not know?"

Connie gazed at the tarnished bear, unpolished over the decades since Sybil Lionheart passed away. A glimmer of the truth flickered into her mind. "He was my great-uncle? Sybil's husband?" she asked tentatively.

Gard nodded. "A companion to great bears. A good man in his way. Brave. Clever. Resourceful. He was the obvious choice to plan the evacuation from the Arctic Circle during the last big human war."

"What evacuation?"

"Kullervo was using the chaos to feed his rebellion. Creatures were angry; they choked in the city smog; they revolted at the cruel waste of lives as mankind slaughtered each other. We knew that the Earth cried out under the burden men had placed on her. Kullervo didn't find it hard to recruit for the army he was amassing in the north.

Those who wouldn't join him had to flee. Among them were many of George Brewer's great bears. He helped them escape to Scandinavia and northern Canada."

"So how did George die? How was Kullervo stopped?" Connie examined the picture of the young man holding her great-aunt's arm outside the church where they'd just been married. His expression was purposeful, determined. She could see how he might've come to be chosen to wrestle with the most difficult challenges.

"He was a great friend of Reginald Cony, as you know. Reggie told me that George led a team to confront Kullervo to negotiate the release of the creatures still trapped behind Kullervo's lines. It appears he also thought they could win some of the creatures back to their side and defeat Kullervo."

"And what happened?" Connie did not have a good feeling about the answer.

"They were all taken by Kullervo. Every single one. A useless sacrifice. It has gone down in the annals of the Society as our 'Charge of the Light Brigade' into the enemy's guns. The creatures they'd gone to save were released soon after: Kullervo has no desire to harm his fellow creatures, only humans."

Only humans, thought Connie. A creature that relished all natural forms but one.

"And it seems from the notes you found that George Brewer had other ideas we did not know about. He was thinking of mounting a challenge himself, and he not even a universal!" Gard put the statue back on the mantelpiece with a clunk. "This house has already offered up one victim to Kullervo; I do not want to hear of a second."

Connie shivered. She did not want to be a victim, but wasn't she one already? Kullervo had done enough damage to her over the last few years—invaded the most secret places in her mind; now he had sent the chimera to maim and kill her. If she just sat back as the Trustees advised and let others deal with the situation, she would be powerless to resist his next attack.

"But what if all of them—Guy, George, Reginald, Edward Alleyne—were on to something? Don't you think we should at least find out what it was?"

"They failed. They took grave risks and failed. Think no more about this, Universal."

Connie felt something build in her chest. No one seemed to understand! Her gut instinct was that this was a trail worth following, but every time she tried the Society erected barriers in her way. They were fighting a losing battle, support bleeding away as creatures lost confidence. Did the Society expect her to live out her life with Kullervo taunting her in her dreams, to be content like them to weaken bit by bit until she was no use to anyone? Kullervo wanted her to meet him at the mark. He expected her there.

"If he wants you there then that is all the more reason

for you not to go," said Gard firmly. Connie had neglected to raise her shield and had forgotten that Gard had access to her superficial layers of thought at that moment. "This is no joke, Universal. The Trustees have ruled on this. If you go against them, if you follow this path any further, there will be penalties."

"What kind of penalties?"

"You will be banned from access to the universal's reading room. Your training will stop. You might even be suspended from membership in the Society."

Connie gave a bleak laugh. "Oh, we've been there before, Gard, or is everyone's memory so short?"

"Yes," said Gard, his voice deadly serious, "we remember. But then you were acquitted—you had been wrongly blamed for something you could not control. But this you do control. You are not a little child, Connie: you are old enough to face the consequences of your actions if you disobey the rules in this way."

She made no reply but remembered this time to raise the shield so Gard couldn't hear the chorus of rebellious protests that'd struck up in her head. If there was a way of defeating Kullervo, she had to find it. She could not live with his mark inside her for the rest of her life, threatening at any moment to swallow her up. The others may not see it, but this was a slow torture that would exhaust her as surely as Guy de Chauliac had been worn out by Kullervo all those years ago. Whatever the Society rules, she wasn't going to stop asking questions. She would face the consequences when they came.

"So, shall we continue?" said Gard. He took her notebook and leafed through the pages. "Why not study the portcullis? That looks like a useful defense."

Connie nodded mutely.

"Let us begin," said Gard.

10

Candles

Autumn was passing swiftly. As the trees shed their leaves, becoming more ragged and skeletal each day, Connie found her mood becoming grimmer and more determined.

"What do you think, Connie?" Evelyn asked, levering open the can of paint in the middle of the empty guest room, which was about to be converted into a nursery.

Connie almost laughed when she saw the green paint Evelyn had picked out. It was exactly the same shade as the moor when the grass was lush and flourishing in spring. "Very nice," she said, returning to her task of scraping off the old wallpaper. "What are you going to do about those?" She gestured to the cans of blue paint Mack had bought. "Horrible color, don't you think?" said Evelyn, sniffing disapprovingly at the tins. "Not right for a baby."

"Oh, I don't know," said Connie lightly, "the color has a fresh, seaside feel to it."

"But I'm sure the baby'll be much happier with some earthy greens," said Evelyn, dipping in her paint brush and letting the syrupy mixture drip back into the can.

Connie saw that the nursery could quickly become a new battleground for Evelyn, and Mack if she did not think of something.

"I think he's afraid you'll make the baby into a banshee companion if you have it all your way," Connie said as tactfully as she could. "That's why he's given you the blue."

"What's wrong with being a banshee companion?" asked Evelyn sharply.

"Nothing," Connie said quickly. "But he wants to restore the balance. I wouldn't be surprised if he tries to get you to go swimming with the Kraken to even up the odds."

"Funny you should say that." Evelyn dropped the brush onto the paint tray. "I refused, of course. I told him it was way too cold to go swimming, let alone go anywhere near the Kraken." She seemed to be lost in thought for a moment, reflecting on Mack and his perspective on their child.

It seemed to Connie a good moment to suggest a compromise. "Well, who said the room has to be one color?" she asked. "Isn't that a bit boring? Why not paint part of it green and part of it blue? You could do a moorland wall and a sea wall."

If there was one thing Evelyn did not like, it was to be

accused of being boring. "You know, Connie, I think you're right. But you'll have to do the blue. The color makes me feel seasick. I'll do the green."

"It's a deal."

They finished preparing the surfaces and began to paint. Connie enjoyed the soothing rhythm of wiping the brush up and down on the wall with Evelyn doing the same beside her. It was rather like tapping stones with a rock dwarf.

"Do you know anything about Aunt Sybil's husband?" Connie asked, her mind quickly circling back to the subject that had consumed her for months.

If Evelyn was surprised by the sudden introduction of this subject, she did not show it. "Oh, not much: he died long before I was born."

"Didn't Sybil talk about him?" persisted Connie, thinking that if she could manage it without Evelyn and Mack noticing, she would stencil a seagull over her waves to sneak in an element of the High Flyers.

"Of course. She had been very much in love with him, but they were only married six months before he was killed."

"How did he die? Did she say?"

Evelyn put down her brush. The temperature in the room seemed to have suddenly dropped a few degrees. "I told you once. He was taken by Kullervo."

"Is that all you know?" asked Connie, pretending not to

notice her aunt's suspicious looks.

"Connie, why are you asking me all this?"

"I just want to know. I think it might be important."

"How important?" Evelyn had still not resumed painting. She had her full attention on her niece.

"You know, don't you?" Connie replied, laying her brush down on the edge of the can and wiping her hands on the old shirt she was wearing.

"Know what?"

"About my argument with the Trustees." The words that had remained unspoken between them for months finally emerged.

Evelyn nodded.

"And you agree with them?"

Evelyn sat back on her heels, shifting the unaccustomed weight of the baby from her knees. "I agree that you mustn't even think about challenging Kullervo, but—"

"But?" asked Connie eagerly.

"But I don't think you should be stopped from finding out all you can about defending yourself against him. You've had to fight him already and, though I hate to say it, will probably have to do so again."

Connie felt a rush of gratitude toward her aunt. She wished she had spoken to her sooner. She should've never forgotten that Evelyn had been the first to defy the Trustees when the Society had expelled her last year.

"And you won't stop me? Won't report me?"

Evelyn smiled and picked up the brush again. "Do you really think you live in a house where any of us will go running to the Society to tell tales? Even if I didn't agree with what you were doing, I'd never do that. I'd pack you off to your parents first. That'd keep you out of trouble."

Connie grimaced. "Thanks."

"What's more, I want to help you. I'll give you all that I know about George Brewer if that's any use."

"Brilliant! So what do you know?"

Evelyn left for a moment and came back with a bundle of old letters. "I thought we might get 'round to discussing this. If you hadn't raised it, I was going to. So I got these ready for you." She handed them over to Connie.

"Can I read them now?" asked Connie.

"They've waited over sixty years; they can wait a bit longer. We've got a room to prepare. But you can keep them as long as you need."

"Okay," said Connie reluctantly, tucking them into her pocket. She turned back to the wall. Now where should she put the siren? Flying with the seagull or on the rock with the dragon?

⁂

Connie and Evelyn got quite carried away with the mural in the baby's room. By the end of the day, it resembled nothing so much as a miniature version of the library in the Society's headquarters: a riot of creatures swimming, flying, and running. Evelyn was a bit scornful of the seascape at Connie's end, but Mack loved it. He thumped Connie enthusiastically on the back when he came in, making her spill paint all over his boots.

"And I left you the Kraken to do," said Connie handing him the brush and a can of black paint. "There's a space in the center."

"Right!" said Mack, rolling up his sleeves. "Time to watch the master at work."

"Master!" protested Evelyn, gesturing at her beautifully drawn circle of dancing banshees. "So what's this?"

"The work of an inspired amateur," replied Mack with a roguish grin.

Connie slipped upstairs. The letters had been burning a hole in her back pocket all day. She couldn't wait any longer to read them.

Sitting on her bed, picking the speckles of paint off her arms absentmindedly, Connie read her way through the small bundle of letters. Most of them were badly weathered as if they had passed through many a storm on their way from the Arctic to England. They smelled faintly of wood smoke. George's writing was how she pictured him: firm and resolute, commanding the reader's attention as it strode confidently across the paper. It was not until she reached the last letter sent from "somewhere in the Arctic Circle" that she found something to justify her intrusion on the past.

Dearest Sybil,

I write this in the knowledge that it is possibly my last letter to you. Either because I will succeed and be back with you very soon or . . . well we both know what might happen to either of us during these terrible times.

I received a letter from Reggie with the first installment of notes. I expect he told you about them before he was called up. I was right! It does seem that the key to combating the cursed creature is to survive the transformations until he adopts one that is weak. If you last long enough, he's bound to do this under the rules of the combat that he laid down. In his pride, he has declared that he has to keep changing form in answer to every counter-attack. Surely, eventually one of these will be something you can defeat?

I've been waiting for further information from Reggie but I don't know where he is.

Connie sat up: of course, the letter he was waiting for had never been sent! It had been left in the library.

If I know the army, they've probably packed him off to some training camp in the middle of nowhere where he's completely out of touch with the Society. Do you know where he is? We can't wait much longer as Kullervo is on the move and approaching our positions. We were thinking that between us we should be able to keep him at bay long enough. We have creatures and companions from every company here. Bruin is eager to take him on—you know what the bears are like!—and I must say I feel the same. If we don't hear from Reggie soon, we'll just have to do our best, even without the advice of our universal.

The griffin that carries this also brings my love. It is a good show that love weighs nothing or he would not be able to fly with the extra burden! Keep safe.

Your loving husband,

George

Connie could have wept as she put down the letter. Foolish, stupid, brave George: of course, he didn't stand a chance. You can't keep Kullervo "at bay" with only a few teeth and claws. The universal's mental tools were the only powers strong enough to keep him in check for any length of time. George had led others into a trap. Kullervo had probably crowed with delight as he saw them sledge their way to their deaths. Poor Sybil.

Moving to the window, Connie looked out into the darkness. She hoped she would never be so headstrong as to lead so many others to a pointless death. No, if she risked anything, it should be her own life and not that of her friends. Maybe it was just as well that she was in this alone. It should be between her and Kullervo—no one else. But when had he ever transformed into anything weak? Had George really been right? He was hardly likely to turn into a beetle for her to stamp on, was he? If there was a way, this wasn't it. George had found that out at the cost of his life.

In her plans to fight Kullervo, Connie had reached a dead end.

Connie was on her way back to London again, this time for Liam's birthday party. Unlike the hot sunny day when she'd last been to the Society headquarters, she was looking out of the train on a wet, chilly landscape. Not a proper winter's day, she thought to herself, no satisfying showers of snow, just a damp smudge of a day. Mack and Simon sat opposite her doing the end of year sports' quiz in the paper. But this time there was no Col to join in, no enthusiastic voice to shout out the answers and tease Simon about his team.

Connie traced his name on the window. She missed Col badly. She wanted to tell him about her preparations even if he did disapprove, hear about his training, just be with him, but Col had barely been in Hescombe since joining the British team. The selection had changed Col, she thought. He had renewed confidence in himself, able to be more generous about other people's gifts, including her own, now that he felt secure in his. The team was a very good thing for him—the only down side being that it had taken him away just at the time when she needed him. Not that she'd ever plucked up the courage to admit it to him.

Before going to Liam's birthday party, the Lionhearts and Mack called in at the headquarters to visit the library. Connie had a book to return and wanted to look up some new tools in the universals' reading room—"Before I'm banned," she added under her breath. Simon did not mind the diversion as he was pleased by the fuss made over him by the porter.

"I've heard about you, son," the porter said, holding out the book for Simon to sign. "Two companies, eh? How many badges have they given you?"

Simon proudly showed off his horse and lizard badges, which he had pinned to the center of his sweater.

"Treating you all right, are they, those Sea Snakes?" the porter continued. "If in doubt, you stick with us Two-Fours."

A companion to the cerberi, the three-headed guard dog, Connie realized, as the shadow of the porter's gift appeared in her mind's eye.

"Watch it, mate," said Mack good-humoredly as he buffed up his own lizard badge.

The porter was now used to Connie's presence and made no comment as she signed herself in.

"You know where to go," he said, waving them off. "Upstairs. First floor."

"I'll meet you in the café," Connie said to her two companions. "Give me an hour."

She ran up the stairs two at a time and then pushed the door open to the library. The light seeped into the chamber from the lantern dome, giving the room an underwater feel, like a sea grotto. This close to Christmas, there were few readers. A couple of pale faces rose at her entrance, blinking at her over their books like creatures disturbed from under the stones in a rock pool. Mr. Dove was sitting at his desk in the center of the room, nodding over a thick volume. Connie walked up to him and put *The Early History of the Society* softly on the desk in front of him. He started awake as if she had slammed it down and glared over the edge of the counter. For a brief moment Connie was reminded of the snake that guarded the universal's reading room. When he saw who it was, however, his expression changed and he smiled pleasantly at her.

"So sorry, Miss Lionheart. I should not have been asleep. You caught me unawares. Was this any good?" He held up the book she had just returned.

"Yes, very helpful, thank you."

"Funny bunch, your lot, weren't they?" he asked conversationally as he checked the book back into the library records.

"My lot?"

"The universals. Got into some hot water. A dangerous crowd, if you ask me. It's nice to have you with us, of course, but it's probably just as well there's only one of you."

Here it was again: the prejudice against the universals. She had met it in its extreme form in Mr. Coddrington, but she was surprised to hear it from the mild Mr. Dove. Still, she wasn't here to pick an argument.

"The key, please," she said, holding out her hand. It would be a relief to get away from all the other members. No wonder the universals had shut themselves away, if they had to deal with critical comments like this all the time.

Then a thought struck her. "Mr. Dove, can I look up a creature in your index, please?"

"No," he said, shaking his head, but added quickly when he saw her disappointment, "only because I have to do that for you. It's the rules."

"Rules?"

"Well, there are some restrictions on particular creatures, you know."

"No, I didn't."

"It's to stop unscrupulous companions taking advantage of prey, you see. For example, if you were a companion to the Scylla, we might want to ask why you were interested in finding out all there was to know about the selkies. Or a fire imp companion about a water sprite. Do you get the idea?"

Connie felt relieved. That was all right then. "That wouldn't apply to me, surely?"

Mr. Dove reached over for the volume she'd seen once

before when he had brought it before the Trustees. "I suppose not. But rules are rules, and even the universals are under some restrictions. What do you want to know?"

Connie cleared her throat. "Are there any books about Kullervo?"

"Ah." Mr. Dove put the book back on the shelf behind him. "We seem to have hit on one of those restrictions immediately." When she said nothing, he added, "I'm under instructions not to divulge that information to you at the present time."

"Says who?" she asked angrily, though she already knew.

"I've an order here from the Trustees. The restriction is to last until—"

"Until they think I can be trusted," Connie finished for him bitterly.

Mr. Dove gave her a sympathetic nod and leaned forward over his desk to whisper to her, "I personally do not approve of the decision—quite unfair to stop the spread of knowledge." He glanced around to check that they were not being overheard. "But might I point out that the order does not say you cannot look at the books? Who's to say that you did not stumble across the right work quite by chance when you were looking in the central shelves of the universal's reading room under 'C.'" He gave her a ghost of a wink, sat back quickly, and said in a louder tone, "So you understand that I have absolutely no choice but to refuse to look that creature up for you."

Connie gave him back a grateful smile. "I understand. Thank you."

Mr. Dove held out the universal's key on its blue ribbon. Connie was about to take it when the door to the library banged open, disturbing the centuries' thick layers of peace that had accumulated in this chamber.

"Stop!" shouted Mr. Coddrington, striding purposefully across the room. The sleepy readers sat up, staring at the little group clustered around the central desk.

"Mr. Coddrington!" protested the librarian. "What is the meaning of this? How dare you burst in here like an ill-mannered great boar?"

Connie went cold, recognizing her enemy on the warpath again.

"Stop right there, Universal! Don't give her the key, Dove!" cried Mr. Coddrington, thrusting himself between them.

"Why not? It's hers to take—it's her right," said Mr. Dove stubbornly. The key swayed in his grip like a pendulum. Connie was tempted to grab it and make a dash for her reading room. Mr. Coddrington would not dare pursue her past the snake; he wouldn't be able to put a foot over the threshold.

Mr. Coddrington swung around to glare at Connie as if he could guess her thoughts. His pale face was flushed with two bright spots high on his cheeks.

"Thank goodness I found out she had slunk into the

building. At least some of us are not lax about our duties!"

Mr. Dove sniffed at the implied criticism. "I had not heard that Miss Lionheart was to be denied entry, Assessor. I did not know that your zeal to persecute the universal had reached that height."

Mr. Coddrington turned back to the librarian. Connie noticed that most of the readers had left their places and come to stand in a ring around the desk. She met the gaze of one—an elderly woman with glasses dangling from a chain—and was dismayed to find that the woman was staring at her with a far from friendly expression.

Mr. Coddrington dug inside his jacket pocket and pulled out a piece of paper which he brandished under Mr. Dove's nose.

"Read this, Librarian. You'll find I have here an order, signed by all the Trustees, to ban the universal access to the reading room with immediate effect."

Connie's heart plummeted.

"It took a lot of lobbying to get this much, I can tell you," continued Mr. Coddrington, addressing the audience of readers, "but I managed finally to convince them, after vividly representing the consequences of a lack of vigilance against her unguarded activities."

Mr. Dove gave Connie an apologetic glance and gingerly took the paper. He spread it out on the desk in front of him and bent over to read it.

"Well? You see I have the authority," snapped Mr.

Coddrington, shooting Connie a triumphant look.

Mr. Dove cleared his throat. "It does appear to be as you say," he admitted. He turned the paper over, paused, then smiled. "But you seem to have forgotten something, Assessor. The paper has to be countersigned by the Senior Librarian. She is—unfortunately—away today, and I am afraid I really do not feel that I have the *authority* to sign for her on so weighty a matter in her absence. It therefore would appear that the order has not yet come into effect."

"But—!" spluttered Mr. Coddrington.

"I know, Assessor, that you would be the first to recognize the importance of following such protocols to the letter," continued Mr. Dove, enjoying himself immensely. "We have to observe the proper channels or where would we be, eh? I'm sure I've heard you talk on this subject numerous times in the past." He held out the key to Connie.

"Damn the proper channels," cursed the assessor, his face apoplectic with rage. He pointed an accusing finger at Connie. "She's a danger to us all. She's got to be stopped."

"But not by me—not until I have a direct order from my superior," said Mr. Dove calmly. "And as far as I remember, the New Members' Department has no authority over the library." He placed the key in Connie's hand.

Seizing her chance, Connie shouldered her way through the murmuring crowd and fled for the safety of the snake-guarded stairwell before someone else tried to stop her. She had forgiven Mr. Dove for his earlier slight against the universals. It was nice to know that she still had one or two allies in the Society.

⋈

Mrs. Khalid had organized Liam's first ever birthday celebration, complete with games, presents, and cake. At home, Liam was lucky if his parents remembered, and they had never gotten around to inviting any of his friends over. When Mrs. Khalid learned this, she had decided his eighth birthday would have to make up for all the ones he had missed in the past. Liam had made a surprising number of Society friends over the last four months and the room was packed.

Coming straight from the confrontation in the library, it took Connie a while to relax. She hadn't mentioned the scene to Mack or Simon, but after an hour she had begun to feel that here, at least, she was among people who liked her and did not fear her. Still, she felt too ashamed to admit to anyone that the Trustees had banned her from the reading room.

"Cake! Cake! Cake!" chanted Ahmed and Omar, Mrs. Khalid's sons.

There was a burst of applause as Mrs. Khalid emerged from the kitchen bearing a three-tiered cake aloft in triumph.

"Where are the candles?" called out Antonia Little from the corner next to Connie.

"Aha!" said Mrs. Khalid, producing eight big candles

from the inside of her robes like a magician pulling rabbits from a top hat.

"They're too big to go on the cake," Antonia said to Connie.

"I don't think they're for the cake," Connie replied with a smile.

Mrs. Khalid placed her creation in the center of the dining room table and then stuck the candles in eight holders around it.

"Omar, are you ready?" she asked her elder son, a tall, handsome boy with long black hair. He nodded.

"Lee-am, are you ready?" she said, turning to the pink-faced birthday boy.

"Yes!" he replied.

Mrs. Khalid took a taper and lit each candle, hissing under her breath. "Let game begin!" she said, stepping back.

Liam stood on a stool and cupped his hands around the first candle, a look of concentration on his face. When he took his hands away, Connie could see there was now a little fire imp dancing there. He swiftly moved around the table, summoning an imp to dance in each of the eight flames.

"Omar." Mrs. Khalid nodded to her son.

Omar stepped forward, flicking back his floppy fringe of dark hair. He hollowed his hands around his mouth and blew as if on an invisible horn. Connie sensed a rushing and tingling in the room. She looked up and saw the pale outline of a sylph burst into the room and circle overhead like a wheeling bird. Its body formed of nothing more than air, the wind sprite shimmered against the ceiling, its long hair rippling out behind it. Ragged wings streamed like a tattered pennant in its wake.

Connie nudged Antonia. "Up there," she said. Antonia looked up but could not spot it. "Look for the ripples as it passes in front of something."

"Ah, yes. I see it now!" said Antonia, catching a glimpse of long legs brushing past the curtains.

The sylph darted down to the candles and blew hard at the first one Liam had lit. Connie could see the imp struggling in the wind, shaking its fist furiously at the sylph, red sparks shooting ineffectually against its enemy. In a blink of an eye, the fire imp puffed out of sight: its flame extinguished.

"No, I put out the candles, not you!" Liam was calling. The sylph, however, was too much for one boy to cope with and had extinguished half the candles by the time Liam had rekindled two. "Connie! Help!" he appealed to the universal to come to his rescue.

"Go on, Connie!" said Antonia, pushing her up. "You're needed."

With a grin, Connie waited for the sylph to fly near her. As it passed, she caught a puff of wind and stored it in her quiver. As the sylph dipped to the cake, Connie released her arrow. The sprite was blown off course to become entangled with the curtains. The audience cheered. The delay gave Liam enough time to relight his last candle.

"I win!" he shouted exultantly.

"You win," conceded Omar, ruffling Liam's hair with brotherly affection.

The companion to the sylphs then strode up to Connie to congratulate her. He gave her a playful bow. "Victory is yours, Universal. How did you do it?"

"Thanks. It was an arrow from the universal's quiver," she explained. He raised one black eyebrow quizzically. "A mental tool. I've been practicing it recently. You catch some power and throw it back."

"Let's sing so the birthday boy can blow out his candles," roared Mack over the noise of the crowd.

When "Happy Birthday" had faded unmelodiously away, Liam stood on a stool, snapped his fingers, and instantly all the imps disappeared, taking the flames with them.

"No need for wind as a fire imp companion," he said proudly.

Mrs. Khalid applauded him enthusiastically from the kitchen door. "Well done, Lee-am," she called.

After slicing the cake into huge uneven slabs, Liam pushed his way through his guests to present Connie with the first slice.

"Here you are!" he said, thrusting it at her. "Thanks for your help just now."

"Any time," she said, licking the icing off her fingers. "I see your training is going well."

"It's fantastic. Mamma Khalid says we can meet some of the big ones in spring. She wondered if we could come down your way to do it. Not enough space in her back garden, she says."

"Of course. I'm sure Col and his grandmother can put you up," Connie replied.

Simon came over. "Well done, Liam. Those fire imps were cool."

Liam glowed under the praise. "How's the Athenian lion-goat-snake thing?" he asked.

"Nemean lion," Simon corrected him. "Very interesting. The Trustees think I might be ready to encounter the chimera soon. Can't keep Connie shut up in Hescombe much longer, can we?"

Liam looked up at Connie, who had turned very pale. "They've shut you up?"

"Not exactly. I'm not allowed out on the moor," she explained. That familiar feeling of sick dread had returned. She looked at Simon's happy face and wondered how he could be so blasé about the prospect of encountering the chimera. But then, he didn't know what he was letting himself in for?

"What've you done wrong?" Liam asked.

"Nothing," said Simon, "there's just this great, dirty brute out there that wants to eat her."

Liam looked shocked. "Do you want me to set a fire imp on it for you, Connie?" he asked.

"Thanks, Liam. But not this time," Connie said. She had to change the subject before she fought with Simon again about what he was doing. "Here, we've got you a present." She dug in her bag and handed him a box. "It's from all of us in Hescombe." Liam ripped off the top and took out a cell phone. "Pre-paid. Let us know when you need more minutes. Emergency calls are free, I believe, if you ever need the fire brigade," she added.

11

Portcullis

"I don't think I can get any further without practicing," said Connie to her mentor. "I now know what to do in theory, but I've got to try it out on someone."

"What about me, Universal?" suggested Gard, looking up from the notebook they had been studying together in the front parlor.

There was every chance that on the first few attempts she would fail to drop the portcullis in time, and Connie knew she would very much prefer not to allow Gard through her defenses. He might stumble upon the armory she had been amassing in secret. In addition to the sword, shield, helm, and hauberk he knew about, she had added the quiver, bow and arrows, the lance, and most recently the mace—a crude tool she did not like using, but she had to admit it was effective in smashing through most barriers.

If he saw those, he would know in an instant that she had not obeyed the Trustees in abandoning the idea of challenging Kullervo.

"How about Sentinel?" she countered. "He'd like that." She could trust the minotaur to guard the secrets of her mind labyrinth closer than she kept them herself.

Gard nodded. "You are right. He would be a good subject for the test. Where is he now?"

Connie dipped into her mind and sensed the minotaur concealed in a cave along the cliff not far from Number Five. This was his favored evening lookout post from where he could mount an effective watch over the universal. As the cave was so close to Hescombe, he had been disturbed on several occasions by unwary walkers on the beach but had so far managed to scare them away by bellowing and stamping. Locally, the cave had gained the reputation of being haunted. The tourist information center had even produced a leaflet on the subject that Sentinel had proudly tacked to the wall of his chamber in the abandoned tin mine.

"He's close by. Shall we go to him?"

"Yes. It would be good to get outdoors," Gard agreed.

Connie went first, checking that the coast was clear. The dark January evening had deterred most people from leaving their warm houses: Hescombe had a cozy, battened-down-for-the-night feel to it. Lights shone in the houses along the quayside. There was no one around to see the rock dwarf slip down onto the beach and crunch his way along to the cave with Connie at his side.

"Sentinel?" Connie called into the chilly blackness of the cavern, a deep groove in the liver-red rock face where the sandstone had been worn away by the churning of the waves. After a few more decades of attack, the sea might well succeed in punching its way through to form an arch, but so far it had only hollowed out a small chamber—at low tide, a place of rock pools and slippery seaweed; at high tide, an ever-moving floor of foam. Fortunately, tonight the tide was out, though Connie knew the minotaur had spent many nights of devoted service standing up to his waist in the surge.

"Universal," answered the minotaur, emerging at the mouth of the cave. His tawny hide matched the color of the sandstone that surrounded him, acting as a further camouflage. He bowed low. "I am at your command." He then turned to the rock dwarf. "Brother, you are welcome."

Gard returned the minotaur's bow. "We have come to ask you to assist the universal with her training. She needs to practice a new defense called the portcullis. Will you help?"

"Of course," said Sentinel, gesturing to them to take seats on the fallen rocks that littered the entrance to his temporary abode. "What is this portcullis?"

"It's a way of trapping an enemy when he has penetrated your first line of defense," explained Connie. "If I do it right, you should not be able to get beyond the entrance to my mind and be caught there until I release you."

Sentinel snorted, white plumes of hot breath puffing from his nostrils into the cold winter sky. "Trap me? You think you are strong enough to contain a minotaur?"

Connie laughed. "I've no idea. That's why I need to practice."

"We should begin," said Gard. "The universal is cold."

It was true. Her feet were frozen. A flake of snow fluttered out of the cloudy sky and settled on her knee.

"Okay. Are you ready, Sentinel?" asked Connie. The minotaur nodded. In unison, they closed their eyes to enter the shadow-world of the encounter.

Connie had hardly a moment to gather her thoughts before Sentinel came charging up to the portal to her mind and burst through.

"Not fair!" she exclaimed, breaking the encounter off quickly before he was able to enter too far into her thoughts. "You gave me no time!"

Sentinel gave a bellow of laughter. "An enemy does not wait for his adversary to be ready, Universal. Try again."

She looked at him suspiciously. From the smug smile on his face, she guessed he had plenty more surprises in store.

"Again," she agreed.

Closing her eyes, she rushed to be there first. On this occasion, the shadow-minotaur did not dash in; he stood waiting outside, pacing with his hands behind his back as if he had all the time in the world before making his move, his tail swishing lazily behind him. She knew what he was doing: he was waiting till she got bored or lost concentration. That would not do. She had a few tricks of her own up her sleeve that no one else knew about. It was time to play them.

"Okay. Drawbridge," she muttered. Mentally cranking on the winch that had appeared by the gate, she raised a heavy bridge out of the mists that surrounded the entrance, forcing the startled Sentinel farther in and cutting off his retreat. He made a dash for the gate. Connie had to abandon her drawbridge half-raised to cut the rope holding up the portcullis. It came crashing down, trapping Sentinel between the bridge and the strong lattice of the gate. The minotaur gave a bellow and charged back the way he had come, clambering nimbly up the sloping bridge and flinging himself over its lip to drop clear on the other side. Connie ended the encounter again.

"That was an improvement, Universal. The drawbridge was a clever move, but you must be faster if you want to catch a minotaur," Sentinel said, raising his curved horns proudly.

"Drawbridge?" asked Gard curiously.

"Er, just a little innovation of my own," said Connie quickly. "The two parts of the portcullis are hard to drop fast enough to catch the attacker. Even with the bridge, I didn't manage it." She could feel Gard's gaze on her, but she looked down at her feet, refusing to meet his eye.

"One more attempt?" asked Sentinel, clearly relishing the challenge.

Connie nodded.

They were both ready swiftly this time. Sentinel had decided to play this one straight. He charged at the portal and crossed the threshold.

Crash! Connie released the inner portcullis stopping any forward progress. Like lightning, Sentinel turned to retreat. *Crash!* The second gate clunked into place. She had trapped him. Undeterred, he threw himself at the gate to test its strength. It shivered, but held firm. He then charged the inner gate, horns lowered for maximum impact. The bull's head collided with the bars and a dull clang echoed around the gateway, but the portcullis stood firm.

Very good, Universal, the shadow-minotaur called out to his host. *I let you catch me, of course, to see if I could break out.*

The gateway rumbled with teasing laughter. Sentinel rested against the iron-lattice, gazing in on the mindscape to which he had been barred entry.

What are those? he asked, pointing to the weapons Connie now had ready by the entrance in case of need. She had forgotten they would be visible even from the gateway, arranged in rows so that she could seize them quickly if attacked. Dismayed, she ended the encounter.

When she opened her eyes, she found Sentinel staring at her, his dark brown eyes reflecting the lights of Hescombe behind her. "What did I see?" he asked her.

Connie felt uncomfortable under the scrutiny of her two companions. "That's my business, Sentinel. Can I have no secrets?"

He bowed. "I will keep your secrets, but will you not explain them even to me?"

"What secrets?" asked Gard sharply.

Sentinel said nothing, ignoring the dwarf. Connie shook her head. "Don't ask me, Gard."

"But it is my duty to ask you," Gard said, his fists clenched on his knees. She could tell he was angry with her and had guessed why she had chosen Sentinel to test her defenses rather than him.

But it was too late to worry about his feelings. What about hers? Connie was sick of even her innermost thoughts being patrolled by the Society. Was nothing of hers private? If she could not call her mind her own, then she was nothing.

"Is there a rule that says that the universals have no right to their own thoughts?" she asked.

"No. But you know why I ask. If you will not tell me, I will have to ask our friend. Sentinel, did you see anything that suggests the universal is preparing to challenge Kullervo?"

Sentinel reared backward in surprise. He had seen her

armory, of course, but had not realized she was amassing it for so serious a purpose. Connie turned pleading eyes to Sentinel, willing him not to fail her.

"I will not betray the secrets of the labyrinth," he said finally but with evident reluctance.

"So you did see something?" Gard persisted.

"I say nothing."

Gard stood up. "Universal, this is most serious. After all our discussions, you know what will happen if I discover proof that you have gone against the will of the Trustees."

"You have no proof," said Connie quietly, hating that she was setting herself against him in this way.

"Then show me what the minotaur saw. Prove your innocence."

"My mind and my thoughts are my own. You have no right to ask me that."

"I have no right but, out of friendship, I ask you to do this to put my mind at rest."

Connie got to her feet and turned to face the entrance. "Look, it's beginning to snow. I'd better get back. Thank you for your help, Sentinel. Thank you, Gard."

Quickly, she left the shelter of the cave and ran home along the high-tide mark, the snow whirling around her like a swarm of white bees, melting as the flakes hit the salty pebbles. She felt terrible turning away from Gard like that, but his mind would not have been "put at rest," as he called it, by an encounter with her. No one should see what Sentinel had glimpsed tonight. Her refusal to clear herself might well mean she would incur further penalties from the Trustees. If she let any creature encounter her, she might well end up in even hotter water. There was nothing else to do: she would have to keep to herself for a while and avoid all encounters.

When she reached home, she clattered through the kitchen, barely acknowledging Evelyn's and Mack's greetings, shouting something about needing to change into dry clothes. In the sanctuary of her room, Connie stripped off her outer layers and dived under her duvet, only then feeling safe from intrusion. With her feet off the ground, Gard would not be able to follow her.

Noticing that in her hurry she'd pushed her private notebook off the bed, Connie leaned over to pick it up. She had started keeping a second record of all the knowledge she was not supposed to have. It contained her practice records on the forbidden weapons, as well as the notes she had taken about Kullervo on her last visit to the universal's reading room. She flicked through the pages to remind herself exactly why she was risking so much to follow this path—and to bolster her resolve that she should, against her natural inclination, disappoint so many friends. The book Mr. Dove had directed her to had confirmed her fears. She should not have been surprised to find that Reginald Cony had been the author— of course, he would want to pass on the lessons his contemporaries had learned at such a heavy cost. The manuscript was not complete—it was a sketchy history of what was known about the shape-shifter, including a list of the known forms he adopted. From her own experience, she could add a few more. Reading it through, she realized that Reginald had been waiting in hope of hearing of one that could be defeated—some weakness in Kullervo's repertoire—but as far as Connie could see, all of them were equally formidable. Indeed, what Reginald had missed (he had never confronted Kullervo, Connie reminded herself) was that Kullervo's real strength lay in his ability to shift between his forms. It was not a single shape that was strong, it was the sum of them.

Reginald's introduction, which she had copied down, confirmed Connie's fears and to her, justified her course of action.

While his shape is ever-changing, Kullervo remains constant in one thing. He will seek you out, my fellow universal. You must be prepared. He has attacked humanity throughout our history and I believe his next assault will come soon. Mercifully, Kullervo has never found me. I have been too well protected and maybe my powers are too weak to tempt him, but even I in my old age must not be complacent. Perhaps it is safest for humanity if the universal gift does indeed die out as it seems to have done in my lifetime, but it goes against the grain to wish for the extinction of any creature. If anyone does read this account it means that the gift did not end with me. Be careful. Do not commit the same mistakes as I and my friends made. Be wise.

Wise? Connie put her notebook aside. The only thing she knew was that she knew very little.

❧

Connie hadn't seen Col at all during the Christmas holidays, and it was not until the day before they returned to school that she ran into him at Jerrard's, the bakery on the High Street. She'd been sent out to buy some bread; he was there stocking up on croissants before leaving for his training.

The bell rang as she entered the shop, but Col didn't look around as he was busy paying for his purchases.

"What'll you have today, love?" asked Mrs. Jerrard, bustling forward to serve Connie.

"A sliced wholemeal, please," Connie said. Col turned on hearing her voice, a full paper bag clutched under his arm. "Hi, Col."

"Connie! How are you?" He waited for her to finish at the counter and followed her out. "I haven't seen you for ages."

"No, you haven't. I know you've been busy."

He looked guiltily pleased with himself. "You could say that. It's been frantic."

"I like the jacket."

Col turned a little self-consciously to show off what

only a Society member would recognize as his team stripe. "Thanks."

"Tell me all about it."

He glanced at his watch. "I really should be going. . . ." But they hadn't had a chance to speak for so long, he couldn't just walk away. He quickly filled her in on the details of the rigorous schedule he and Skylark had been given, the weekends on Exmoor, the plans for a trip to the Alpine training at Easter.

"Sounds brilliant." Connie felt a little sad that his new role was taking him away from Hescombe, but she wouldn't allow herself to feel envious. She only wanted what was best for him, and this was clearly it.

"How about you, Connie?"

"Same old thing, you know."

"Meaning?" Col pulled her over to a bench in the bus shelter.

"Meaning everyone's convinced I'm reckless; I'm grounded, not allowed out of Hescombe; and I've been banned from my reading room."

"What!"

"Mr. Coddrington's doing, but the Trustees agreed."

"Why?"

She shrugged.

Col ran through what Connie had said. There was only one explanation for the drastic action by the Trustees. "You haven't given up your idea of taking on Kullervo, have you?"

Connie rubbed her hand across her brow wearily. "I'm not exactly seeking a battle, if that's what you mean. I just want to be prepared."

Col hated the idea of her facing Kullervo alone again. "But you should let us look after you—keep you safe."

"Yeah, like you did from the chimera?"

He swallowed. "Yeah, well . . ."

"You see: it's going to come. I've got to be able to defend myself." She kicked a stone into the gutter. "And you're hardly ever here, so what do you care?"

As soon as she said the words, she wished she could take them back. Her feeling of being abandoned by almost everyone had slipped out.

Col exploded. "Don't you dare say I don't care!"

She held up her hands. "Sorry, I didn't mean it like that."

But Col wasn't letting it go. "You're getting so wrapped up in being a universal, Connie, you're not listening to others anymore. Everyone's saying it. They're scared stiff you're going to do something stupid."

"I won't."

"I wouldn't bet on it."

She turned to him. "So you think they're right to stop me from learning anything?"

Col sat stiffly, wondering how this conversation could have gone so wrong. "Yeah, I think I do."

Connie sprang to her feet and stalked off without even saying good-bye.

He couldn't let her go like that. He just wanted to make her see that she had to be safe. "Connie!"

Her response was to break into a run, disappearing around the corner to the harbor. Col ran to catch up, thinking he would find her and put his arguments properly, but when he reached the quayside, she was gone.

⊰⊱

"Connie?" It was Dr. Brock, not Col, who later found Connie hidden in the weather shelter, clutching a mangled loaf of bread. She had been crying but was attempting to hide this fact from him when he sat next to her.

"Having a hard time?" he asked gently.

"Just a bit," she admitted, sniffing.

He passed her a large white handkerchief from his pocket. "Want to talk about it?"

"Not really," she said in a deadened tone of voice.

Dr. Brock thought he could guess the cause of today's upset. He had heard rumblings among the senior members of the Society, complaints that the universal was going off the rails again, this time of her own volition. He knew that the Trustees were soon coming to Hescombe to confront Connie about her behavior. Steps had already been taken against her which he knew must be painful.

"Well, if you ever do need to talk about it, remember I'm here for you," he said kindly, patting her wrist.

"Thanks, but I don't think anyone can do anything."

Dr. Brock sat, gazing out at the boats at anchor and the

seagulls strutting along the quayside. "I wanted to talk to you about something, Connie."

"What?" she asked, suspicious that he would lecture her on her deviations from her training agenda. It'd be just like Gard to arrange for her to be taken to task by those she was closest to, in hopes that they'd get through to her.

"Have you felt anything odd recently? Anything out of the ordinary?"

This was not the question she'd been expecting. "Like what?"

"The dragons have sensed something strange going on up on the moor. The rock dwarves say they can't tell who's out there. Parts of it now seem almost always to be swathed in fog. It might, of course, just be thanks to this strange winter we've been having, but I'm not sure." Dr. Brock settled back on the seat beside her.

"I haven't been near the moor for ages. You know that. Not allowed."

He turned his blue eyes on her. "Indeed I do. But will you try for me now? Tell me what you sense from here?"

Connie closed her eyes and turned her thoughts to the moor. It was no good: at this distance, it was a confused babble of voices like a badly tuned radio. She opened her eyes again to find his gaze on her still. "Sorry, I can't make anything out. It's beyond my range. And I think I've a headache coming on."

Dr. Brock nodded in understanding. "Oh well, it was worth a try. Don't break any rules now, but you'll let me know if you sense anything?"

"I will."

He got up to go. "Don't stay out long, will you? It's too cold to sit here all day."

She watched him walk away, straight and purposeful. A shadow passed over the pale sun, momentarily dimming his snowy hair. Connie looked up. For an instant, she could have sworn she saw the back of a weather giant pass over, hurrying westward, but now the mass of cloud had resolved itself into drifts of gray vapor. Still, the clouds were moving west even though the breeze was against them.

12
Kelpies

March arrived in a series of howling storms, bringing trees down and flooding low-lying meadows. It seemed to Col that every day for the past few weeks he hadn't been able to go outside without a raincoat and boots and always returned soaked to the skin despite these precautions. His intensive training schedule had passed in a blur of wind, rain, and aching bones, and he was relieved to have a weekend off for a change. Sometimes it was impossible to balance being a member of the Society and having normal friends. He felt torn but knew there was little he could do about it.

Worst of all, weeks had gone by and he had still not made up with Connie. At school she'd been distant, almost as if she was purposely freezing him out, as if she was afraid he'd hurt her by probing too deeply into what she was thinking and feeling. She avoided Society meetings and stayed indoors as much as possible, a complete change from her usual behavior. Gard was tight-lipped as to what he thought of his pupil's behavior, but even Col, so rarely in Hescombe these days, could sense that things were coming to a head between the universal and the Society authorities.

With all that to worry about, Col decided he needed a ride on the moors with Mags. It would help him summon up the courage to corner Connie and sort things out.

"Glad to see the sun's out for once," Col said to his grandmother on his way out the door.

Mrs. Clamworthy looked out the window despondently. Her water sprites loved the floods as it gave them more scope for their wanderings. "Still, there's more rain forecast," she said, brightening up at the thought. "You've checked that the chimera's not about, I hope?"

"Of course. Simon says it's gone off further onto the moor."

"Just stay near the cottages. I don't trust that creature to keep away."

"Okay. I shouldn't be back late," Col called as he splashed down the garden path to fetch Mags.

"Don't forget we're having an early dinner with Liam!" she called.

"As if I would!" he replied, leaping the ditch.

Col guided Mags up the farm track leading out to the open countryside. New shoots were pushing through the soil in all directions. A clump of snowdrops, past their prime, had shriveled and turned brown in the shade of a bank of daffodils. Birds sang in every hedge, declaring their territory.

Feeling both he and Mags would enjoy a good gallop over firm ground, Col headed up the track toward the Devil's Tooth, now a small incisor on the horizon over the back of Masterson land. Hooves splashed through the deep puddles, spraying Col's jodhpurs with black speckles. Here and there, where the grass was still in the shade of a boulder or clump of bracken stalks, the frost lingered, dusting the ground like icing sugar, but the rest had melted away in the morning sunshine. Down in the hollows, mist lingered in thick swirls, making the high places of the moor look as though they were floating on clouds.

"Careful!" Col checked Mags as he veered to the left toward some bright green grasses. That was boggy ground, home to the kelpies, the water horse tricksters. He knew better than to go down there.

But Mags would not stop fretting. Something was definitely spooking him. The mist swirled and gathered around them with unnatural speed, yet Col could see no other cause for alarm.

"What's the matter?" he crooned to the horse, patting his neck in reassurance. Mags side-stepped and tossed his head.

The air chilled a few degrees. Col could hear a strange clicking from close by. There was definitely something in the mist—lots of somethings. He pulled on the reins, thinking to make a quick retreat, but then an icy touch pinched the back of his neck. Mags reared and Col, already unconscious, tumbled from the saddle. In a panic, the horse bolted, leaving his rider out cold.

Mrs. Clamworthy knocked on the door of Number Five and came in without waiting for an answer. She'd interrupted the inhabitants as they relaxed in the aftermath of their supper. Mack was sitting with his feet up on the table, yawning, while watching Evelyn fuss around at the sink. His wife seemed to be unable to rest, refusing his pleas to take her considerable weight off her feet, instead insisting that the sink needed cleaning. Connie had her head down over a pile of school books, pretending to do her homework, while really reading her practice notes and running through her new tools in her head. She looked up when Mrs. Clamworthy came in and immediately knew that something was wrong.

"Mum!" said Mack, leaping to his feet. "Have a seat."

"No, no, dear," said Mrs. Clamworthy in a fluster. "I thought you had Gard with you. I was expecting Col back for dinner—we've got Liam and the Khalids staying—but he's not come in yet. I thought Gard might be able to tell me where he is."

Mack steered his mother farther into the room, but she shrugged off his attempts to remove her coat. "Sorry, Gard's up at the Mastersons' as the Trustees have just arrived," said Mack, not looking too concerned to hear his son was out wandering.

Evelyn put down her dishcloth and crossed the kitchen to put an arm around her mother-in-law.

"Don't worry, Lavinia. Connie can summon Gard through that thing they do." She looked expectantly at her niece. Connie put her pen on her pad.

"Of course," Connie said hesitantly. She and Gard hadn't been speaking since the incident of the portcullis, and she was reluctant to let him into her mind when she knew it was littered with evidence of her disobedience. But if Col was lost, she had to help him.

"Would you, dear?" said Mrs. Clamworthy gratefully. "It would take a great weight off my mind just to know where he is."

"I'll do it right away," Connie said, her hesitation vanishing. She went to the back door and planted her feet firmly on the stone path. *Gard!* she called into the bedrock. *Can you hear me?* There was no reply. Was he sulking or was he somewhere he really couldn't hear her? *Gard, this is important.* Still no answer. It was not like Gard to fail to respond to a summons—whatever his feelings toward her at that moment. She went back into the kitchen.

"Sorry, he must be inside somewhere."

Mack strode over to the phone and rang the Mastersons'. "It's busy," he said, putting it back down.

"I know," suggested Evelyn, "why doesn't Mack drive you up to the Mastersons' and you can talk to Gard yourself? That would be better than sitting here worrying about things."

Mack grabbed his jacket from the peg. "Can I take your car, Evie? I don't think Mum's quite up for the back of the bike."

Evelyn tossed him the keys to her little car. "As long as you remember to treat my car like a lady and take the corners slowly. And be careful of the gears. They're tricky if you're not used to them."

"Hah!" said Mack. "There's not much I don't know about engines."

Evelyn was about to protest, but Mrs. Clamworthy had no time for an argument. "I won't keep him long, Evelyn," she interjected. "Why don't you sit down. You look tired out."

Evelyn gave a wan smile and patted her tummy. "I will. When junior here stops kicking me to bits."

"Ah, yes, Mack was just like that," Mrs. Clamworthy replied on her way to the door. "Squirmed like a squid until the day he was born."

"And why aren't I surprised?" Evelyn muttered.

"What was that?" asked Mack sharply.

"Go on," scolded Evelyn, shooing him away with a wave of her hand.

The back door closed, and the kitchen fell silent again. Evelyn winced as the sound of grating gears and an over-revved engine resounded in the lane. Connie tried to return to her work but it was no good. She kept turning over in her mind what might have happened to Col. Was he just out late and had forgotten that he was supposed to have dinner with Liam, or did he have an accident? It then occurred to her that there was a way for her to find out without waiting around for Gard.

"Would it be okay if I went over to Uncle Hugh's?" she asked abruptly.

Evelyn gave her a shrewd look. "Why? It's dark already."

"Well, I thought if I got near enough to the moor, I might be able to sense Col through his gift. If I find out where he is, I can let you all know."

Her aunt sighed and slumped into a chair, taking a breath against the discomfort of nine months' worth of baby thumping her in the ribs. "I suppose it'll be okay. I'll send Mack to fetch you when he gets back from the Mastersons'. But they'll probably find Col first, or he'll have turned up of his own accord."

"Probably. But in that case, I still get to see Uncle Hugh and Simon," said Connie, pulling on her outdoor clothes. "Anyway, I've been meaning to check out what's happening on the moor for Dr. Brock. I could do that while I'm up there."

"You're not to set one foot on the moor, Connie."

"Of course not." Connie dug her bike lights out of a drawer in the dresser. "But I don't have to go any further than the field near the cottage to sense what's happening. I won't go on my own, I promise."

⫘

When Connie reached Hugh's cottage she found it dark. This was highly unusual—not quite as strange as Col's disappearance, but she could usually count on her great-uncle to be home at this time of night. She wondered where he was, until she found a message for Simon tucked in a bottle on the back step. The note told Simon, who was expected back late from seeing Liam, to put himself to bed as "the old man" had gone to a trivia night in Hescombe with Horace Little and Dr. Brock. Connie smiled as she read the name of the team they had formed: the Old Dragons.

But there was someone else at the cottages always on the watch for her: Wolf, Rat's Alsatian, threw himself against the fence separating the two properties, making it shake alarmingly as he attempted to break through, barking fit to burst. The noise brought Rat outside.

"Hi, Connie," he said. "Thought it had to be you."

Connie leaned over the wooden panel and scratched Wolf on the head. He whined ecstatically. "Hi, Rat. Have you seen Col?"

Rat shook his head. "Nope. He's having dinner with Liam, isn't he?"

"He was supposed to, but he never showed up."

Rat shrugged. "Well, he's not here."

Connie looked out over the dark fields leading up to the moor. The eight wind turbines revolved their ghostly white arms in the night. The plantation could only be seen as a darker shadow against the sky. A thin paring of moon peeped over the treetops, shedding little light. "It's very late for him to still be on the moor. I thought I might be able to sense if he was out there. Will you come with me to the edge of the field? I've promised everyone I won't go any further, but I'll have a better chance of finding him if I'm as close as I can get."

"Okay," said Rat. "I'll just grab a flashlight."

He came back a few moments later with the powerful lamp his dad used to fix cars. It acted like a small headlight as they made their way past the wind farm. Connie led them up the far side of the field away from the plantation, not wanting to revisit that spot.

"Come on, let's get away from here," she said, picking up the pace.

Rat nodded sympathetically.

They climbed until they reached a gate at the top of the field. Here the tidy farmland gave up its grip on the earth, leaving the moor to its own devices. Sheep bleated in the darkness. The grass hissed in the light breeze. Everything seemed normal. Rat switched off the light, understanding without being told that Connie's gift could see far better without this distraction.

Connie dipped into her mind, feeling out for the mythical creatures and their companions abroad at that moment. She had not opened up for some time, having chosen to remain closed away from others. But what was this? The moor was seething with their presence—too many to distinguish. It was like turning over a stone and discovering an ants' nest bustling with activity. She opened her eyes and looked over at Rat, who was leaning on the top bar of the gate, chewing peacefully on a stalk of grass.

"Rat, something's really not right. Where have all these creatures come from?"

"What creatures?" Rat asked, letting the stalk flutter to the ground.

"I've never felt so many up here before. Has the Society called a meeting I don't know about?"

"Not unless I don't know about it, either. What's going on?"

Connie reached out into the darkness again but ended the attempt with a shake of her head. "There's too many of them." The hair on the back of her neck was on end. "Something tells me they're not friendly. We'd better warn Dr. Brock." She made a move to go.

"What about Col?" Rat snagged her jacket.

In the shock of finding all those creatures congregating on the moor, she had almost forgotten the reason for her visit. "I don't know if I'll be able to spot him in all this noise."

"But what if one of those unfriendly creatures has got him?" Rat was craning his neck to see if he could make out anything in the twilight.

Rat was right. She couldn't give up now. Connie took a deep breath and tuned back into the humming on the moor. Dragon. Banshee. Stone sprite. Kelpie. Hundreds of images flickered through her mind like a kaleidoscope. Concentrate. A companion to pegasi. A gold link amid the many. There: she had found him. He was not far or she never would've sensed him. In fact, he was only a short distance away, possibly just over the brow of the hill on the track up to the Devil's Tooth.

"He's almost within call," she told Rat. "A little to the north of us."

Rat turned the light back on and swung his leg over the gate. "Come on. I'll need you to help me find him."

Connie hung back, the promise to her aunt still fresh in her mind. The grass whipped at her legs in the stiff, rainy breeze. "But I'm not allowed on the moors!"

Rat jumped down on the other side. "Don't be pathetic. We're not going far. Or would you prefer Col to be attacked by one of these unknown mythical visitors?"

"Of course, I wouldn't." What did it matter if she got into more trouble with the Trustees if she could help Col? From the way he was so still, it was possible he had fallen and hurt himself. Connie clambered over the gate and set out in pursuit.

"This way!" she called as Rat veered off too far to the left, heading down toward the wet, low-lying ground. "It's dangerous down there—full of kelpies and will-o'-the-wisps. They'll lead you into the bog." She ran to catch up with him.

Rat grinned. "See, that's what I like about you, Connie," he said, "deep down, you don't care about the rules, either."

Connie wasn't sure if she should take this as a compliment, though it had clearly been intended as one. Guilt filled her as she thought of what her aunt would be saying at this moment, sure that it wouldn't be flattering. "Let's get this done as quickly as possible," she said. "Follow me."

She led them onto the track and turned right heading uphill. She was soon out of breath and had to pause to ease a cramp. Rat, who spent most of his time roaming on the moor, was unaffected by the climb; he took the opportunity to holler into the darkness, flashing his light like a beacon.

It picked out a body lying by the side of the track.

"Col!" Rat dashed forward and pulled Col's head and shoulders onto his lap.

"W-what?" Col said groggily.

Connie touched his hand; it was icy cold. "How long have you been here?"

"I dunno." He groaned and then flinched with the pain of aching muscles.

"What's the matter with him?" Rat asked Connie anxiously.

Col was still wearing his riding helmet. He didn't look as if he'd hurt himself. Connie ran her hands quickly over his forehead and neck, finding a tender patch of skin just below the hairline. Col flinched.

"Rat, shine the light here. I think a stone sprite must've touched him. I've seen marks like that before." She had, on her own skin after touching one; only the universal's shield had held off their numbing attack.

"But I thought they lived in the ground. How could it reach his neck?"

"Good question." Connie checked the surrounding area and again felt the hum of hundreds of creatures gathered not far away. "But we don't have time. We've got to get off the moor. Can you walk, Col?"

"I think so." He flexed his frozen feet.

"You missed dinner," Connie said gently, unbuckling his helmet.

Col gave an agonized groan. "I bet Gran's worried sick."

"Hadn't you better call to tell her you're all right?"

Col's fingers were so cold by now that he fumbled his phone as he dragged it from his pocket, and it fell on the stones with a crack. Rat picked it up for him and examined it in the light. It was dead.

"Great," said Col. "It's really my day, isn't it?"

"Don't worry. You can use my phone." Connie pulled hers out of her jacket pocket.

"On second thought, let me do that for you," said Rat,

intercepting the phone to dial Col's home number.

"She might still be at the Mastersons'," Connie called out, helping Col to his feet. "The number's in the address book."

Rat nodded that he had understood.

"Mags," Col murmured as his wits came back to him. "Is he all right?"

"I'll find him. Don't worry." Connie whistled into the darkness, but there was no response.

Col stumbled a few paces, trying to bring the circulation back to his dead limbs.

"Mags!" he shouted hoarsely into the darkness. "Mags!"

Rat joined them. "Need the light?" Col nodded. "By the way, your gran says you're to go to bed when you get home and ordered us off the moor immediately."

"Not without Mags," said Col. "Shine your light down there."

Rat slowly moved the beam over the rough terrain, stopping each time it caught on a rock or horse-shaped tussock of grass. The moor was eerie in this half-light, a place of strange shapes and dark menace.

Connie grabbed his arm. "Look, there!" she said, pointing to three small silhouettes in the middle distance. "He's wandered off with the Dartmoor ponies."

With a preliminary pitter-patter, rain began to fall, building into a steady downpour. Rat turned his collar against the wet, having neglected to bring a coat.

"We'd better go and get him," Connie said anxiously. "I really don't like the moor tonight: there's too much going on." She dipped into her mind again to check for any activity near them and caught the tail of a slippery presence before it disappeared. "In fact, we'd better make this quick. I think my friend is on the move."

"Your friend?" asked Rat dimly.

A look of alarm flashed across Col's face. He shook himself out of his daze. "The chimera." He grabbed Connie's arm and pulled her along after him. "Look, Connie, we'll get you on Mags, and you can ride back to the cottages. You'll be safe there."

Connie broke into a run. "It's not just me I'm worried about," she gasped. "What about you and Rat?"

"Let's deal with one thing at a time," said Col, though his mind was whirling. It would be the perfect end to the day to find himself face-to-face with the beast that had almost killed his friend. "Where's Icefen?" he asked Rat.

"Miles away," said Rat, running to keep up with him. "No go."

The boys exchanged a look, agreeing that their priority was to get the universal away from danger. They'd worry about themselves after.

When they reached Mags, he was cropping the grass with his new friends. He didn't protest when Col gave Connie a lift up onto his back, twittering to greet her. But no sooner had she settled in the saddle than Mags snorted and reared in alarm as a new scent reached him on the breeze. Connie tumbled off backward, her fall broken by Col who was still standing at the stirrup. Mags whinnied and would have bolted if Rat hadn't made a grab for the reins in time.

"Mags!" cried Col. "What's got into you?" His horse's eyes were rolling in their sockets, full of terror.

"He can't help it," said Connie. Poor Mags: first stone sprites, now the chimera. She realized how lucky they were he'd stayed near Col and not run for home.

With Col's aid, she scrambled back on. She did not need to dip into her mind to know that the chimera was loping toward them: the breeze also carried a triumphant roar of pleasure.

"You've got to get on!" she shouted. "There's no time to run."

"He'll be too slow with all of us," said Col. His eyes fell on the ponies, which were still grazing, the scent and sound of the chimera not having disturbed them yet. The scraggy black-haired one perked his ears forward, as if listening for Col's voice, his eyes welcoming. The bay munched the grass as if nothing unusual was happening. "We'll ride those! Come on, Rat."

The two boys sprinted over to the horses and leapt on their backs before the animals knew what had hit them.

"Yah!" yelled Col, grabbing a lock of tough black mane and spurring his mount forward. The horse gave a whinny of surprise and bounded away, closely followed by his brother and Mags. The three fled down the hill in an erratic zigzag.

"Not that way!" cried Col as his beast turned to the right despite his signals, relentlessly heading down to the marshy ground. Rat sped past, his mount tossing its head.

Connie pulled Mags up before he lost his footing in the boggy ground. "Stop!" she cried. She'd realized why those beasts had shown no signs of being alarmed by the chimera. "Those aren't horses!"

But it was too late. The creatures propelled their riders into the treacherous marsh and then vanished from beneath them, giving a whinny of laughter as they melted back into the mists.

Col and Rat fell into the bog. The kelpies had ditched them.

13

Trap

"Run!" Col shouted at Connie while he floundered in thick, evil-smelling mud.

"No way! I'm not leaving without you!" Connie dismounted and stumbled to the edge of the mire, frantically trying to think of a way of saving them. She could see Rat, thanks to the light he was still holding—but he was waist-deep and sinking.

Mags heard his master and had no hesitation in obeying his command. When Connie's back was turned, he gave a shrill whinny and bolted down the track, heading for the safety of the cottages.

"Mags!" Col shouted in warning, but Connie was too slow to catch the reins; her fingers made a snatch at thin air. She had to let him go; she couldn't spare any time: Col and Rat were inches from drowning.

"Stop moving!" she screamed at Rat, who in his panic was struggling against the irresistible suck of the bog.

"That's easy for you to say!" he yelled back.

"Spread your weight—lie flat!"

"I'm not putting my face any nearer this stuff," Rat protested.

"Just do it!" growled Col, realizing Connie was right. Their sinking would be slowed if they tried to float on the surface. He spread-eagled himself, gagging on the foul gas that belched from the mud each time he stirred.

Looking up at Connie in the desperate hope she'd come up with a plan, Col saw a flicker of flame appear in the darkness and then go out.

"Chimera!" he cried.

Connie spun around, just in time to see the chimera leaping down the hill toward them. Seeing it was her only escape, Connie took a leap onto a tussock of grass sticking out of the bog like an island. It sagged under her weight but didn't sink. Out of the shadows loped the chimera, its lion's jaws open in an exultant grin, the black cobra head swishing excitedly. Then, catching a whiff of the stagnant air of the marsh, it stopped short at the edge and lowered its snout to sniff. The serpent darted to the lion's forepaws and fluttered its tongue on the mud-crusted surface, testing the ground. With a howl of disappointment, it began to pace to and fro, its amber eyes glaring at Connie. It was calculating whether it could leap upon her and not tumble into the mud. When the lion's eyes met hers, they both knew it could not. But the chimera had other methods of attack.

And so do I, Connie thought. Her armory was prepared, her shield at hand.

"Col! Connie!" gasped Rat behind her. He was now up to his chest and could see nowhere to go but down.

The beast stopped on the edge of the firm ground closest to the universal and took a deep breath. Swiftly, Connie delved into her mind and pulled out her shield to hold in front of her. A torrent of flame spouted from the lion's jaws. She knew from experience that the shield would hold for a short while. Steam hissed in the air as the silver vapor of the shield evaporated under the onslaught. With a quick sleight of hand, she made a grab at one of the tongues of fire licking at the edge of the dissipating shield. From where Col was lying, it looked as though Connie was surrounded by a silver halo of cloud, battered by an intense flame.

The fiery torrent ended as the chimera paused for breath. It ran its pink tongue over its flame-scorched lips, relishing the approaching moment of the kill. It knew the feeble protection was no match for a second bout of fire: the universal would be his.

Connie threw her shield aside.

"Connie!" yelled Col in dismay, seeing his friend standing unprotected only feet from the creature. He had no idea what she thought she was doing. It seemed pure madness to cast away the only barrier between her and the flames.

As the shield disappeared, almost instantaneously in Connie's hands appeared a long bow, strung with gold. Reaching behind her, she pulled a single arrow from the glimmering quiver on her back, strung, and fired. Her aim was true. The arrow, blazing with the chimera's own fire, flew through the air and pierced the flank of the goat. The terrified creature panicked at the sting of unaccustomed pain. It fled, forcing its bolder brethren of snake and lion to flee with it as it hurtled off into the darkness, screaming with agony.

Col gave a feeble cheer, not wanting to move more than absolutely necessary as the mud lapped at his ears.

Connie turned on her island to face him. "Right." She took off her shoulder bag and threw one end to Col. The bag fell short. She tried again. This time as she threw it, Col took the gamble of lunging and grabbed it in his fingers. Connie knelt down to steady herself to pull him clear.

"No!" said Col. "If you do that, we won't be able to reach Rat: he's too far in." At that moment, the flashlight winked out, sunk beneath the bog.

"Rat!" Connie screamed. "Are you still there?"

"Hurry!" came Rat's strangled voice as he spluttered out a mouthful of rancid water.

Col grappled at his waist, trying one-handed to remove

his belt. He got it free, though every move he made pushed him in deeper. He threw the end to Rat. Only Rat's head, forearm, and hand were still above the surface, and he could not grip the belt unless it fell exactly in place. On the third throw, Rat caught it and took a firm grasp of the buckle.

"Pull, Connie," said Col. "Slowly!"

With hands slipping on the slimy, mud-covered strap, Connie began to heave her friends toward her. The effort was immense: two boys weighed down by the sucking mud were almost too much for her, but she dug deep and found the strength. After six heaves, Col was free, having reached the firm ground of the island. He passed the belt holding Rat to Connie and pulled himself out. Together, they hauled Rat hand over hand out of the bog. He coughed and spluttered as he crawled onto dry land. The only problem now was that this left the three of them tottering on the frail refuge.

"Should we stay here and wait for help?" Col asked, turning to Connie.

"No way," said Rat. The brown water was creeping over his shoes as the island sank under their weight. "I'm not going in there again." He spat out a mouthful of mud. In the moonlight, the only part of him that shone white was the area around his nose and eyes: the rest of him was slimed in mud.

"The chimera?" Col asked Connie.

"It'll be back once the other two regain control from the goat. We've got to get to safety," she said. There was no more she could do against the chimera. Surprise would work only once.

Over to the south, the roar of an angry creature reverberated in the air.

"Let's go then," said Rat. Gathering himself for the leap, he jumped to the firm ground where the chimera had so recently stood, the grass blackened by its flame. Col followed him.

"Come on, Connie!" Col called, holding out a hand to help her. It was a good thing he did for, without the benefit of a running jump, Connie fell a pace short and was thigh-deep in the bog before he and Rat hauled her out.

"It's blocking our way to the cottages," she panted, sliding in her shoes as she ran up the hill. She felt exhausted but knew she couldn't give in to tiredness now. "Make for the Mastersons'."

The three of them ran back the way they had come, hitting the track and making faster progress on the clear path. But they could not hope to outrun a chimera.

"Where are the dragons when you need them!" cursed Col, stumbling over a boulder in the dark but managing to stay on his feet.

"I can't summon help on the move," Connie said. "Let's get to the Devil's Tooth. It'll buy us some time, and I can call Gard from there." The thought darted into her mind that after this, she would be in serious trouble: ignoring warnings, going on the moor, using forbidden weapons. But that seemed the last of her worries just now.

With limbs like lead, Connie clambered up the hill to the base of the tor. Col gave her a leg-up onto the summit of the granite rock and pulled himself after her. Rat scrambled up the other side. The top of the Tooth formed a flat platform in the burnt-out patch of moor. It provided just enough room for the three of them to crouch.

All were silent while Connie concentrated on sending out her distress call.

Gard! Help!

Nothing.

Please talk to me! Help!

But there was no answer. There was going to be no second lucky escape from the Devil's Tooth.

"The stone sprites are blocking me," she explained to the others. "There's hundreds of them in the ground between us and the road. Even if we ran for it, they'd get us first."

"Can they reach us here?" Col asked.

Connie nodded. "But I think I can use my shield to stop them if you stick close to me." Connie immediately found herself squeezed in the middle of a tight embrace from both boys. Rat was even stepping on her toes. "But not that close!"

Rat gave a forced laugh and stepped back a little. "Sorry," he said, "but just now you seem the only thing between me and my death."

There was little anyone could say to that. Connie bowed her head, concentrating her energies on holding up the shield. Rat crouched down beside her. Despite everything, Col felt a surge of warmth just looking at his friends being so brave in the face of such dire danger. It didn't matter what others thought of them; he knew there was no one else he'd rather be with in a crisis.

"So, we're trapped," Col said, his voice calm as he faced the truth. He also found comfort in standing so close to his friends. Especially to Connie. If the end was coming, at least it was good to be with them. "Is there no way of getting a message through?"

Connie shook her head. "Not to Gard. Not unless someone comes close enough to hear me, but all I can sense are our enemies."

"You forget we've got the technology," said Rat, not yet downhearted. He pulled out Connie's phone from his hip pocket. It was wet and black with mud. He wiped it clean and punched the buttons. Nothing happened. "But it broke."

Col swore softly.

"But you've still got the universal with you," Connie said determinedly. "I'm not beaten, yet."

Col felt very proud of her at that moment. Connie was right. They were not giving up yet. "What's the plan?" he asked, confident she would come up with something.

"I'm working on it." Connie hunched forward, gazing over the edge of the platform.

Without warning, the chimera leapt out of the darkness. Connie screamed as it attempted to mount the tor, swiping at her with its razor-sharp claws. Moving with quick reactions, Col and Rat heaved her out of its path just in time. The chimera gave a deafening roar of disappointment and fell heavily back to the ground, its claws skittering on the bare granite. Col could feel Connie shaking in his arms.

"I think the lion's back in charge," said Rat grimly.

"But I don't think it can reach us up here," Col added, looking hurriedly around to see where the beast had gone.

"But *they* can." Rat pointed to the ground below.

Looking down, they saw movement in the rocky earth at the base of the Devil's Tooth. It seemed to be bubbling and seething like a hot spring. Bursting out of the surface of the rock were many pairs of long-fingered, emaciated hands. Creeping, crawling hands that made flesh shrink just to look at them.

"Stone sprites," breathed Connie, her face creased in concentration. "I'm keeping them off with my shield."

The hands grew into long, spindly arms, flailing around in the air like plants in a gale. They seemed to be snatching, feeling for something. For warm flesh. Next, the crust of the rock split and rounded humps emerged, like the backs of whales rising above the sea. The rest of the sprites surfaced: heads slung low on scrawny chests, skeletal jaws and teeth, angular legs and arms. When they scuttled free of the rock, they resembled giant pale spiders, luminous body hanging down like some obscene cradle held up by four long limbs. Their joints clicked like pebbles grating on stone each time they moved.

"I guess now we know how they reached me on Mag's back," Col said with a shudder.

Hundreds of these foul creatures scratched at the base of the tor, looking with hungry eyes up at the three warm bodies that Connie was keeping out of their range.

Universal. Universal. We want the universal! they chanted in thin, bloodless voices, battering on the shield already damaged by the encounter with the chimera's fire.

Connie could also hear the hysterical voices of the chimera hissing, roaring, and bleating against her defenses.

Come down! the lion roared. *Face us!*

He wants you! bleated the goat.

It's you he's after, hissed the snake.

We'll take you to him, growled the lion.

The three friends had reached a desperate dead end. Connie was tired, at a loss for how to save them from this trap. Without much hope, she wondered what words could do. She raised her hand for parley. Col and Rat saw her lift her right hand and stand up straight. They looked at each other, wondering what was going on. In Connie's mind, the voices of the creatures relented, giving her space to speak.

Who wants me? she asked, though she could guess the answer.

Your companion. He has come to claim you, tittered the snake.

Connie said nothing, ending the parley to think.

"Any ideas?" asked Col hopefully when he realized that Connie was back with them from the inner world of her gift.

"Yes, but you're not going to like it."

"If it's better than being frozen or eaten, I'm listening," said Rat.

"It's better than that." Connie took a deep breath, knowing before she spoke that Col would refuse. But she wasn't going to lead them into a hopeless fight with creatures far more powerful than them. That was what George Brewer had done. "We can make a deal."

"That sounds good," said Rat quickly.

"What kind of deal?" asked Col, his suspicions aroused. "You don't mean—?"

"It's me they want. If I go down to them, they might let you go."

"But they'll eat you alive, Connie! You can't do this." Col grabbed hold of the back of her jacket as if she'd been about to throw herself off the rock.

"They won't. They're working for Kullervo. They'll take me to him."

Col let go of her and sat back. "And that's better, is it?"

"I promise I won't let him take me over like last time. I'm prepared for him," Connie pleaded, begging Col to understand, to give her his support. She was finding it hard enough to stick to her purpose and had no energy to fight him, too.

"But he'll kill you," Col said in a monotone.

"He might. Or I might defeat him."

A spark of understanding ignited in the depths of Col's eyes. "You're not thinking of challenging him, Connie? You're not still thinking of that?"

She said nothing. Rat stirred uneasily. Time was running out. They could not sit up here all night. Sooner or later, one of those creatures would break through the shield and get them.

"Col," said Rat, "listen to her. She's right: either she goes down and we have a chance to get away and find help, or we all get killed for sure."

Col cursed and kicked the rock. He knew they were telling the truth; he just didn't want to hear it. He grabbed Connie and pulled her toward him.

"Don't give in. Don't challenge him," he whispered furiously in her ear. "Just hold him off until we can get help."

This was the signal she had been waiting for. Connie knew she had to go now while she still had the courage. She gave Col a wan smile, touched Rat on the arm in a gesture of farewell, and then slid her way down the rock. Seeing their quarry approach, the stone sprites scuttled to her side, following her like the rats after the Pied Piper. But none of them could touch her: her shield surrounded her now like a silver mist, placing her beyond their cold reach.

Col watched her walk forward to where the chimera was pacing, its tail flicking with an angry twitch. He realized that he was watching the bravest person he knew risk her life for him. The knowledge was almost unbearable.

Down among the stone sprites, Connie looked through the silver haze of her shield into the implacable eyes of the chimera.

I'll come with you, if you let the others go free, Connie said, her voice firm despite her fear.

You will drop your shield? yawned the lion, displaying its row of yellowed teeth and ridged red maw.

Yes, I'll drop my shield. You'll be able to take me without a struggle. But you must promise to let my friends go free.

The snake's head slithered forward to the edge of her shield and stared in at her, its eyes gleaming with malice in the silvery light. Slowly, the cobra nodded.

You agree? Connie asked.

The snake's head nodded again; the lion face smiled enigmatically.

Connie wasn't sure if she could trust this promise, but what choice did she have? With great reluctance, she dropped her shield, leaving herself unprotected, within reach of the jaws of the chimera. As soon as her guard was down, the snake's head lashed around and struck her to the ground. Her head hit the earth, her mouth full of dirt. The chimera paced lazily forward and bent its lion's face to her. A rough tongue licked her bloodied cheek, its breath hot and reeking.

You taste good, the creature said.

Connie closed her eyes, anticipating the bite of teeth into her flesh. She nearly screamed, but she knew that the chimera fed on her fear and would be goaded into tormenting her further if she showed weakness. But it had no intention of eating her: it opened its jaws and once more Connie found herself in the grip of its mouth as it carried her away.

In the pale glow coming from the stone sprites, Col and Rat watched in horrified, impotent silence. Rat had to haul Col back as the chimera struck Connie. "Don't be stupid!" he hissed. "Don't waste the chance she's bought us!"

Once the chimera had disappeared into the darkness with their friend dangling from its mouth, and the stone sprites in pursuit like an army of gray crabs, Col grabbed Rat. "Let's run for it. Get help."

A downdraft of wings hit Col as he was about to slide down the smooth-sided tor. Rat yelled. Looking up, Col saw Rat caught in the claws of a black dragon that had swooped in from the west. Col cried out in protest, but then felt his own jacket pierced by talons, and he was torn off the rock face. Above, he saw a white dragon. Its pink eyes glared down at him as if it considered him a very pitiful prey.

Hanging limp in the clutch of the dragons, Col and Rat were carried away into the night sky.

14

Challenge

Connie thought the nightmare of the journey in the chimera's mouth would never end. The creature was running eastward across open moor, jumping streams, clattering across roads, intent on reaching its goal. Each leap, each bound seemed to punch a little more air out of her struggling lungs and dig deeper bruises in her ribs. All Connie could tell was that they were heading toward Chartmouth. A flash of a car headlight and the chimera cowered for a moment in the shelter of a hedge. Once the noise of the engine had faded, it leapt onto the tarmac and loped swiftly down the hill. To her right, Connie could hear the whisper of the trees in Mallins Wood.

Help! she cried out to any friendly wood sprite that might be listening but no answering voice met hers. Why was no one around to hear her?

The chimera's sharp sense of hearing sent it bounding into the shelter of the trees as another vehicle approached, this time a truck grumbling its way slowly up the steep hill out of Chartmouth. Had the creature lost its senses? Connie wondered. It seemed intent on dragging her into the heart of a human settlement. Even the chimera, as insane and divided against itself as it was, must realize that it stood no chance in these surroundings. Connie felt a faint glimmer of hope that they would be spotted and she might be saved.

Once the truck had gone, the chimera set off again, undaunted by any fears of being discovered. The time was late. Traffic was light on the roads, and the chimera slipped into the outskirts of Chartmouth unseen. It turned away from the houses onto the half-built industrial site, deserted at this hour. Connie's hopes of being rescued faded as she realized it knew exactly where it was going. She was bumped along tarmac, her dangling hands grazed by the grit. Then the terrain changed: she was being dragged over weeds, half bricks, dirt, and litter. Bounding along a perimeter fence, the chimera paused at a break in the wire and went down on its belly to squeeze through, trailing Connie on the ground as it did so.

Gard! begged Connie. But still no reply. A cold tide of stone sprites was flowing through the bedrock, freezing all communication.

The chimera loped across the empty parking lot to a

huge white building which was surrounded by storage tanks, ranging from turret-like cigar-shaped cisterns to two vast drum containers. The building itself was floodlit, gleaming against the night sky like the white castle of a modern giant. A gas flare burned perpetually in the sky above: a fiery flag marking the home of Axoil. The chimera had brought her to the oil refinery.

The chimera slipped in through an open door. Connie glimpsed a guard slumped in the shadows outside; his dog whimpered pleadingly at her, but there was nothing she could do to help. She could feel her jacket beginning to split at the seams as the creature clattered up several flights of iron stairs, through some hanging plastic strips, and into the central hall of the processing plant. It padded along a walkway, the steel structure ringing under the hooves of the goat, to drop Connie at the feet of Kullervo.

The shape-shifter had assumed his favorite form, a midnight blue eagle, and was perched on the railing, his dark shape a black void against the clinical white light bouncing off the walls. His shoulders were hunched as he brooded, hooked beak glinting like a scythe waiting to cut down anyone who came in reach.

Connie lay face down with a horrid sense of déjà vu, remembering how they had first met.

"You have hurt my companion." Kullervo's voice echoed harshly in the cavernous room. "How is this possible?"

Pleased by its successful labors for its master, the

chimera sat on its haunches and licked its paws. Kullervo shifted shape, melting briefly into a dense dark mist before resolving into the form of a gigantic chimera; he stood so that Connie was between his forepaws and could see in minute detail the ebony sharpness of his claws close to her own skin. Watching the second chimera appear, Connie's abductor shivered with pleasure. The cobra-headed tail slithered to curl around its fellow, an intertwined knot of snakes. The lion-head sniffed the scent of its brother, recognizing the dominant male in its pride.

She gave her word to drop her shield, it purred subserviently.

Ah. Being selfless no doubt. A human weakness, Kullervo sneered.

Connie scrambled to her feet, away from the claws, and raised her shield. It shone brightly even in this light, the four points of the universal's sign glittering like diamonds. With lightning swiftness, the chimera leapt away from Kullervo to block her escape, landing on the steel walkway with a clang.

"Well," rumbled Kullervo in amusement, "that promise did not last long."

"I never promised how long." Connie staggered backward so that she was pressed against the railings. She stood between the chimeras, a mouse caught by two cruel cats intent on playing with her before the end. The Kullervo-chimera yawned and settled down on the walkway, rear hooves tucked to one side, snake tail undulating lazily over its back caressing its conjoined elements. Kullervo raised a paw to his mismatched eyes and studied it.

"A most intriguing shape," he mused. "I like adopting this form. It has an enticing sense of danger as the three natures try to tear each other apart. Do you like it?" He turned his gaze to Connie. She said nothing. "You've experienced an encounter with our friend here, I believe," continued Kullervo. "I was most jealous to hear about it. I would have enjoyed seeing you share this form. But there is still time for that."

"Time?" said Connie, amazed to find that she could speak despite her terror. "The Society will find out where I am. They'll come for me. Hadn't you better run before they get here?" But she knew her threats were hollow— and so did Kullervo. The refinery was the last place anyone would look for her even if Col and Rat did succeed in raising the alarm.

"Oh no, Universal. We have plenty of time. Your friends are busy fighting my army out on Dartmoor. Even as we speak, the first clash of the dragons is taking place. They will have no chance to spare a thought for you—I have seen to that. They are hopelessly outnumbered and unprepared because, foolishly, they have not let their little universal near the moor to give them early warning of my massing forces." Kullervo smiled, showing a row of white teeth.

"But the refinery—it can't be long before someone notices we're here!"

"Ah. You are right. Thank you for reminding me. I have a little diversion planned to keep the other humans busy, too." Kullervo nodded at the chimera. "You know what to do. Bring our guests when you have finished."

With a nimble leap, the chimera disappeared through the plastic screen and out of sight.

"What's it doing?" Connie asked fearfully, her thoughts going back to the guard she had glimpsed on her way in. Was the chimera going to attack anyone who came to the gate?

"Giving intruders a warm reception. This place has been doing its best to heat up the atmosphere; I thought it would be fitting if we hastened the process."

"What do you mean?" Her shield wavered as Connie realized what was happening.

"Fire." Kullervo shimmered fleetingly into the dark, flickering form of a fire imp before taking shape as the eagle once more.

"But you'll kill us all!"

"Only the humans." The eagle croaked as if pleased by her swiftness to grasp the situation. "And not before you and I have concluded our business together. You, Companion, will survive if you do my bidding."

Somewhere in the depths of the building, a fire alarm began to ring.

"What business? You don't think you can persuade me to let you use my powers, do you? I'll never do that."

The eagle took a pace nearer and lifted a talon toward the shield. "This flimsy defense will not hold. You will be mine."

"Never!" Connie gritted her teeth and clung on to the barrier. "You'll have to kill me first."

"Oh no, I'm not thinking of killing you. If you refuse me again, it will be your friends' lives at stake."

Connie heard footsteps behind her. She turned around quickly to see Col and Rat being pushed through the screen, the lion's jaws at Col's back, the snake hovering by Rat's neck.

"But our bargain!" Connie exclaimed to the chimera, her shield fading in shock.

Never promised, hissed the cobra in Connie's stunned mind. She raised her shield again and thrust the creature's presence from her.

Kullervo crowed with laughter. "Never trust a two-faced creature, Companion. Bring him." He pointed a claw at Col.

With a swipe of the lion's paw, Col was sent flying across the walkway, colliding with the railing before falling at Kullervo's feet.

"Careful," the eagle chided the chimera, "I do not want my guests to fall needlessly to their deaths. I have a far better use for them."

The chimera growled, less compliant now that Kullervo was no longer in his chimera form.

Connie saw that Col was bleeding from many scratches. He raised his head, and his eyes met hers. He seemed to be trying to apologize for having let her down, for having allowed himself to be captured.

"Oh yes, I will have great pleasure in killing this troublesome one," said Kullervo, turning his vicious eyes to Connie to see that she was hearing every word. "If you don't agree to help me end once and for all the destruction brought by humanity, then I will have to find something to make you obey me. Perhaps I'll start with your friend. I have been feeling peckish." He tapped his beak on Col's shoulder, rolling him over so that he was facing straight up at his captor. "If you do not give in, I'll eat him. Where shall I begin?"

"No!" screamed Connie. She heard a scuffle behind her and a crack. Rat was knocked back by the snake as he'd attempted to leap to his friend's aid. "Don't you dare touch him!"

"So, you will be mine then?" asked the eagle gleefully, pawing at the meal before him with the talons of his right foot.

Col tried to push off Kullervo's hated touch, but he was pinned to the floor. "No, Connie. Don't give in!"

Overwhelmed with terror, Connie couldn't think straight. This wasn't how it was meant to be at all. When she had given herself up to the chimera, she had thought it was only her own life she was risking, but now she had to bear the responsibility of her two friends. Kullervo knew her too well: she could be brave for herself, but not on behalf of others.

"I see you need more time to decide," he said, beating his wings and shifting shape. The mist coiled and twisted, forming into a nine-headed hydra, black scales glowing like jet in the harsh light. "Tie them up . . ."—one head darted down to flicker its tongue over Col as if tasting his scent; another slid to Connie and grinned—". . . till dinner time."

Suddenly, there was a deafening boom from outside; the ceiling lamps went out and a wailing alarm echoed around the processing hall. The only light inside the building now came from the silver shimmer of the shield and the gleam of Kullervo's eighteen eyes. Beyond the windows the flicker of flame danced joined by the muffled noise of another explosion. Connie's eyes began to water as the air carried with it the trace of acrid fumes. Kullervo seemed very pleased with these signs of his plan's progress. Two heads rose to look out of the window.

"Good, good. Very dangerous, oil fires," he hissed. "The fumes more harmful than the blaze itself. It will keep away unwanted visitors, but I advise you to decide quickly—or you all burn."

He gave a spitting hiss into the shadows behind him,

summoning more assistance, and Connie heard feet clanging on the stairs. Stone sprites scuttled into view with rope dangling in their teeth. Two went to Rat, two to Col, and the remaining six surrounded Connie, protected by her shield. She heard Rat cry out with shock as their cold pinching hands grasped his wrists.

"Don't hurt them!" she begged.

"Then I suggest you drop your shield and let my sprites tie you up like a good girl." Kullervo laughed, the bubbles of foul gas bursting from the snake's head bobbing before her.

Reluctantly, Connie let the shield fade. The six creatures pounced on her, grabbing at her ankles and wrists. One had its freezing hands at her throat, constricting her breathing with its icy touch.

"Oh no, you are not to damage her," said Kullervo, half-heartedly restraining his followers, unaware that beneath his very nose Connie was secreting away some cold darts in her quiver.

The stone sprites bound the three friends to the railings. They saved particular malice for the universal, lashing her so tightly she could barely move. Col and Rat were on either side of her, out of reach. The stone sprites scuttled off, their task done, the sound of their clicking joints disappearing into the shadows. Connie almost preferred it when she could see them: it was worse to imagine them waiting to pounce somewhere in the darkness.

The hydra slid over to Connie and curled in a half-moon around her.

I will leave you to reflect on my offer, Kullervo said with one of his many mouths. *Offer! Offer!* echoed the others. *Be sure to have your answer ready when I return. I will not be long. There is someone I want you to meet.*

The hydra reared up over the walkway and slithered down like a python hanging from a branch. Twisting around the walkway below, Kullervo slipped off into the darkness.

Left alone, the three friends felt the huge weight of the silence that had fallen between them. Col, shifting painfully on his scratched legs and back, knew that one of them must speak. He must help stiffen Connie's resolve to resist Kullervo, even if it meant condemning himself and Rat.

"Are you okay, Connie?" he whispered. A series of loud cracks and bangs exploded, indicating that another blaze had erupted outside. "Sorry we couldn't get away."

"It would've been no good," she replied despondently. "They're all busy fighting Kullervo's army. There's no one at the Mastersons'."

"You know what?" said Rat, trying to sound cheerful, "I'd have liked to have been in a decent battle with Icefen but . . ." He couldn't finish the sentence.

"But now we're tied up here like turkeys for Christmas," said Col with a hollow laugh. Silence fell again.

"I'm scared, Col," said Connie in a small voice.

Col could see her sitting straight-backed against the railing, her face deathly white.

"Me, too," Col said, desperately trying to think of something to encourage her, some bright thought. "But you must stay strong. This isn't about us: it's about all of them out there. Think of all those beautiful, wonderful people you'll be saving—and the creatures who try to defend us. If you let him use you again, he'll destroy us all."

Connie choked on her tears. "I can't send you to your death. I just can't."

"You must!" he growled.

Connie felt something crack inside her. "I'm going to do it: I'm going to challenge him. It's the only way."

"No!"

"I've said all along that it would come to this." She was close to panic.

"But you've been forbidden by the Trustees," Col countered, wishing he could give her a hug as he could see she was falling to pieces before his eyes. "They had a good reason."

"Stuff the Trustees," interrupted Rat.

"Shut up!" said Col. "You don't know what you're asking her to do."

"I'm only asking her not to feed me to that monster!" Rat shouted back. "I don't want to die, even if you do."

"Of course, I don't want to die!" Col yelled at him, wishing he had his hands free so he could throttle Rat, "but we'll only die later if Connie can't hold out against him—and so will millions of others. That or he'll torture her to death."

"Ah, that's what I like to hear," hissed Kullervo, sliding back onto the walkway and writhing past Col to stop before Connie. He seemed to swell in size in the presence of their argument. "Friend at war with friend—my favorite human trait."

Col and Rat both shut up, neither of them wanting to give Kullervo the satisfaction of hearing them disagree.

So, have you decided, Companion? asked Kullervo.

Connie nodded, keeping her eyes on the floor. She wasn't brave. She was a coward.

And what is your decision? the hydra asked, its tongues like black ticker tape fluttering in the air in celebration.

Connie raised her head and looked briefly across at Col, her interior struggle evident on her face. Col shook his head, but she turned her gaze on the nearest head of the hydra.

"Meet me at the mark. I challenge you to single-combat."

15

Voice from the Past

"No, Connie!" cried Col, straining at his bonds to reach her, to stop her from doing this, but she ignored him.

"But I want a proper bargain this time. No tricks. They must be set free first." She gestured with her head to Rat and Col. "And all the other humans you've got trapped here. I want to see them walking out to safety. Then,"— her voice almost disappeared—"I'm all yours."

Kullervo dissolved and reformed into the shape of a great bear, thick blue-black fur shining in the light coming through the high windows. He moved toward Connie, the walkway groaning under the weight of his vast bulk. He raised a sharp-clawed paw in the air. Connie closed her eyes, not wanting to see her death approaching. She felt the rush in the air as the claws passed close to her neck, the soft pelt brushing her cheek. The ropes that bound her fell to the ground.

Very well, growled Kullervo. *They go free. The stone sprites will drag the other humans clear of the fire to a place where they can be found. I would make them walk away like you ask, but unfortunately, they are all out cold.* The bear growled with laughter.

They're not dead? she asked.

Not yet—and thanks to you, it looks as though they will live another day. His snout nuzzled the top of her head. *Just one more day before you surrender to me. We both know that you have bought them only a temporary reprieve.*

Temporary or not—I'm taking it, said Connie with determination, getting to her feet and away from him. Even upright, she did not reach the thigh of the great bear.

How can she possibly hope to defeat that? Col marveled.

But she doesn't expect to win, another voice in his head whispered. She's going to sacrifice herself to let you survive.

"Connie, it's not too late. Please change your mind," Col urged her.

Kullervo turned to him. "I am getting tired of the bleating of this little one. I will be pleased to get rid of him." He raised his paw. Connie shrieked, unable to stop herself, fearing he was about to strike.

The bear swung his head toward her. *Do not be concerned,*

Companion. Our bargain will hold for a little longer. He cut through Col's bonds.

"Run, boy. You are free. Take your chance. But you'd better hurry: the chimera is on the prowl outside and, though I command it in most things, I cannot be answerable for how it chooses to satisfy its appetite."

Col scrambled to his feet, dodged past the massive forepaws of the bear and ran to Rat. He swiftly untied the knots holding Rat to the railing and hauled him to his feet. The moment Rat felt his bonds loosen, he made a dash for the exit. Col hesitated and glanced at Connie, who was standing still as she watched her two friends escape. No way could he just run. He sprinted back to her and swept her into a tight hug.

"If we get out of this," he whispered in her ear, "there's something I want to ask you."

"I'll look forward to it," she said bravely, though without much hope. "Give my love to . . . to the others."

Col felt a paw push on his back.

"Get away from my companion. She is mine now," growled Kullervo.

With a final desperate hug, Col turned and ran after Rat, each step costing him worse pain than anything he had experienced so far that night. Bursting out of the side door, he was pulled up short by Rat, who had pressed himself against the wall.

"Stone sprite!" Rat warned.

To their left, Col could see the pale outline of a sprite dragging a man away. The guard dog barked and snapped at the creature, but its teeth made no impression on rock.

"At least Kullervo's keeping his part of the bargain," muttered Col as they watched the stone sprite pull the man into a warehouse, separate from the refinery building. "They should be okay in there."

In contrast, the refinery itself was clearly in grave danger. Between the boys and the main entrance a fire now raged. The battlements of the oil castle were under siege. Great billows of black smoke belched into the air, lashed by red tongues of flame from burning cisterns. A wall of fire separated them from the emergency vehicles that had rushed to the scene. The boys could hear the wail of sirens in the night, but they had no chance of reaching help that way.

"We need to get out," said Col.

Rat jerked on his sleeve and nodded over to their right. The dark form of the chimera was slinking between the two big drum containers, scorching their metal sides with bursts of its flame. Fortunately for Col and Rat, it was too preoccupied by its game to notice them. With stone sprites on their left, a chimera and a wall of fire on their right, they had no choice but to make a dash straight ahead to see if they could find a way through the high fence.

"On three," breathed Col, waiting for a moment when the chimera had its back turned. "One, two, *three!*"

The boys burst from their hiding place and sprinted across the parking lot, hitting the fence with a clatter.

"Look, there's a gap!" cried Rat, dragging Col through the entrance used by the chimera.

The boys paused on the other side of the fence, at a loss for what they should do.

"Should we go to the police?" Col asked, knowing the idea sounded ridiculous. What could they do against Kullervo?

But Rat nodded. "We've got to give it a try."

It seemed miles as they ran around the perimeter of the refinery, stumbling in the dark over weeds, bits of masonry, and an abandoned supermarket cart that'd been left in this no-man's land. They finally made their way onto the access road. In contrast to the desert they had just left, this was teeming with people. Seven fire engines were parked as close to the fires as they could, hoses trained on the blaze. Firefighters with blackened, sweaty faces jogged by carrying more equipment, jostling the boys out of the way.

"What on Earth are you doing here?" A policeman strode over from his car and clamped a firm hand on the shoulders of both boys. "The order to evacuate the area was given half an hour ago—and that includes you two."

"But—!" protested Col, trying to wriggle free as the burly policeman pulled them away.

"No buts," said the policeman.

"But we were in there," Rat shouted at him, trying to get

it through the man's thick skull that there was another emergency for him to deal with. "Our friend's in there."

Rat's words had started a completely new train of thought in the policeman's head. "You were in *there*?" He dropped his hold on Col and began to pat Rat's pockets, checking for matches. "Not indulging in a little bit of arson, were you?"

This wasn't going well. If the policeman had his way they would be spending the rest of the night answering questions at the local station.

Col caught Rat's eye. Rat understood.

"Now!" yelled Col.

With a twist to equal Skylark's Syracrusian Spiral, Rat slipped free from the policeman's hand and ran off to the left. Col darted to the right.

Rat had plenty of practice dodging the police so he knew back-up would be after them. As Col sprinted through a depot belonging to the local dairy, Rat made a dash across the road and pulled Col into the darkness of an unlit alleyway. "Keep still," he hissed.

A police car zipped past, heading away from the refinery, blue lights flashing.

"We need to reach help," panted Col, "but it's going to take too long on foot."

Rat pulled out Connie's phone but it was still dead.

"Remember, she said everyone would be up on the moor," said Col.

"Not everyone—what about your dad? You can't get the Kraken up onto the moor."

"You're right. And Evelyn will be home, even if he's not."

"And what about the Khalids? Aren't they staying at your house? I doubt the Society will have sent them up there—at least, not the boys."

Col nodded. "Let's split up: you go to my house; I'll fetch Dad. He'll know what to do." Col felt a sudden powerful desire to see his father, to hand over responsibility for tonight's mess to someone he could trust to have Connie's best interests at heart. Mack had fought to save Connie last year—he would do the same now.

"But we're still miles from Hescombe," said Rat. "We need transport—the police'll pick us up in an instant if they find us running down the road."

Col gazed around him for inspiration. The answer was obvious. "I wouldn't normally suggest this but . . ."

Rat was quick to catch on. "We'll need to get the keys." Without pausing for further thought, he picked up the metal lid of an old milk churn lying in the passage and chucked it through the window behind them. An alarm bell began to sound inside the dairy, but all the workers had been evacuated and there was no one, not even a night guard, to stop the two boys from climbing in and ransacking the garage until they found the keys. "Here, put these on, too," said Rat, throwing an overall and cap to Col. "You're a mess."

Col gave a grunt of laughter for they both knew that, if anything, Rat looked worse.

The boys dashed over to one of the electric milk trucks standing idle in the yard. The evacuation had come as the dairy workers were halfway through loading up for the morning's deliveries. The truck was stacked with crates of milk and orange juice. Rat grabbed a couple of cartons from the back before slipping onto the seat beside Col. "Let's go," he commanded, ripping open a juice and downing it thirstily.

Col checked the controls, relieved to see the truck was simple to drive and with a top speed not much faster than a bumper car. The engine whined into life and purred out onto the roadway. Slowly but steadily, they made their way along the road. Col had to pull over a couple of times as more fire engines and six ambulances passed.

"They must've found the workers in the warehouse," Col noted grimly. They looked at each other, both wondering what had happened to Connie by now. Was she still alive?

A police car slowed beside them, the driver peering curiously at the milk truck making its way as fast as it could away from the refinery. Col pulled his cap low over his eyes. Rat put his feet up on the dashboard and began to whistle cheerfully. The policewoman lowered her window.

"You do know you were supposed to have evacuated an hour ago?" she called to them.

"Yes, officer," called Rat politely. "We're just on our way now. My brother here said we couldn't let our customers down, you see."

"Well," said the policewoman tersely, "if you're making deliveries anywhere downwind of the refinery, you'll find all your customers have gone."

"No, no, we're on our way to Hescombe."

The policewoman gave a curt nod. "Then hurry on out of here. But I'll be complaining to your bosses at . . ."—she glanced at the side of the van—"at the Sunnyside Dairy that you didn't get out quicker."

"Er . . . yeah, sorry."

"On your way, then," she said finally, deciding that, what with the fire and the evacuation, there were too many other things to worry about to waste her time on them.

Col breathed a sigh of relief and put his foot down on the accelerator. The police car sped past, leaving them following slowly in its wake.

❧

Once Col and Rat had left, Connie felt a huge weight of responsibility lift from her shoulders. She thought she could bear to face anything that might happen to her, but she couldn't have watched Kullervo torture her friends before her eyes. There was silence between Connie and the shape-shifter as they listened to the boys' footsteps clattering away on the stairs.

Satisfied, Companion? grunted the bear, ambling over to

her on four paws and nuzzling her again with his velvety black snout. Connie shuddered in revulsion and dodged away. The creature did not seem deterred by her rejection of his touch. *I am certain you will not be like the others, Universal. None of them understood me like you do. They all fought to the end—their end—but not you. You will be different.*

Connie said nothing, still standing against the railing.

Those men from the Society were proud creatures, all of them. They only thought of me as a monster to be destroyed. They did not realize, as I know you do, that humanity is the monster that must be wiped out.

Bitterly Connie said, *So you killed them all—Guy de Chauliac, George Brewer, and I don't know how many others.*

The bear settled down at her feet, throwing out an arm to hook her away from the edge; so she came to rest between his forepaws like a tiny cub. His warm breath, scented of honey, stirred her hair as he growled softly above her. *Yes, there were many. But that is nature's way. The weak perish; the strong survive. You should not blame me for being what I am.* Connie sat tensely in his embrace, trying to control her terror. *And you will find that even I can be merciful. I did not kill them all.*

Surprised, Connie turned her head and gazed up at him to see if he was telling the truth. His blazing eyes were shadowed by no lie that she could detect. *Are you telling me that you did not kill Guy de Chauliac?*

The bear grunted. *Oh no, I killed the universal. He was a*

feast that could not be resisted. No, I kept alive one who offered only a mouthful, who had no powers for me to consume. He raised his snout and growled a low rumbling summons into the shadows. "Come forward, Companion to Great Bears."

Connie heard the tap of a walking stick and the wheeze of halting breath. Out of the darkness stepped an old man, bent under the weight of long years of suffering. He limped forward, trailing a dirty fur cloak on the ground. Several of the fingers that grasped his staff had lost their tips, as if he had once been severely frostbitten. He came to a halt by the bear and bowed.

"Master," he said hoarsely. He then raised his gray-skinned face, deeply scored with lines, to peer at Connie. "I am honored to meet you, great-niece."

16

Human Companion

Col dropped Rat at the top of the High Street, leaving him to dash to the Clamworthys' house while he puttered on to Shaker Row. The milk truck seemed to be going infuriatingly slowly—only twenty miles an hour downhill—and he was on several occasions tempted to abandon it to continue on foot. But Col knew that in his exhausted state it was quicker to remain where he was.

The milk bottles rattled and clanked as he turned into the Row. He saw that Evelyn's car was not parked outside. His heart sank. It looked as if his father was not there. But he had come all this way: he had to check. Leaving the truck outside the gate, he clattered around to the back door.

"Dad! Dad!" he yelled, bursting into the kitchen.

"Col! Thank God!" It was not his father who answered but Evelyn.

Col couldn't see her anywhere. "Evelyn? Where are you?"

Evelyn gave a long agonized groan. Col now spotted her doubled up on the floor by the empty fireplace. "It's the baby. It's coming. I've tried the hospital . . ." She stopped, another wave of pain hitting her. Col ran over to kneel at her side. "But all the ambulances are at some fire. They've called the midwife, but she's been evacuated from her home. They said they'd try to send a doctor . . . aargh!" She swore again, waiting for the agony to fade.

Col did not know what to do first. "Where's Dad?" he asked quickly.

"I don't know," she said, panting hard. "He hasn't come back. But there's no time for that. I think it's almost here. You've got to help."

"I'll be with you in a minute," Col said frantically. He called his home. There was no answer. He called the Mastersons' and Shirley picked up the phone.

"Yes?"

"Is my dad there?" he asked without even giving his name. But Shirley knew who it was.

"Get off the line, Col," she said angrily. "Don't you realize there's an emergency on the moor? I'm running headquarters as everyone else is out there."

"Even my dad?"

"No, not your dad. He left with your gran before the alarm. Now hang up the phone."

"Forget the moor, Shirley," Col hissed so Evelyn

wouldn't hear. "Kullervo's got Connie at the refinery—that's the real emergency. Get a message to the others."

Col slammed down the phone as Evelyn gave a groan. Glancing between the door and his stepmother, Col struggled with what to do next. Really, there was only one thing he could do. He couldn't abandon Evelyn, not now.

Just as Col turned to Evelyn with shaking hands, the back door flew open and the doctor rushed into the kitchen carrying a heavy black bag.

"Sorry I wasn't here sooner, Evelyn," she said, rushing to her patient's side. "The hospital switchboard was in chaos—they only just got through to me."

Col sighed in relief.

⁂

Many anxious minutes later, Col was the first one to pick up the baby from the cocoon of towels, feeling its warm wetness and the beating of the tiny heart in its chest.

Assuming that Col would know where everything was, the doctor dispatched him to fetch fresh clothes for Evelyn and those that had been set aside for the infant. After a few false starts, Col dug out one of his father's nightshirts for Evelyn and then went through to the nursery. Turning on the light, he stood for a moment in silent admiration. Winged horses revolved with dragons in a mobile over the baby's cradle. The Kraken writhed darkly in the center of the wall. Banshees and wood sprites circled in endless dances across a green field. The room reminded him of Connie's wall of encounters.

Connie.

Grabbing a pile of clothes, he leapt down the stairs two at a time and back into the kitchen.

"You'll be okay now, won't you?" said Col, dumping the clothes beside the startled doctor and dashing to the door. "I'm off to find Dad."

Evelyn smiled up contentedly over the black hair of her baby. "Yes, your brother and I will be fine. Thanks, Col."

When Col ran out of Number Five, he thought he would have no choice but to drive the milk truck back to Chartmouth, though the chances of getting there in time to be of any help were remote.

But fortunately, there was a much swifter means of transport waiting for him. He felt a prickle at the back of his neck before he heard the clatter of hooves landing on the tarmac behind him.

Skylark! he cried, never having felt so relieved to see the pegasus in his life. *You're just in time!*

Skylark trotted forward a few paces so his companion could mount. *Where've you been, Col?* the pegasus asked. *I've been looking for you all over the moor! It's a nightmare out there—casualties being ferried back to the Mastersons', reinforcements arriving from all over the country—I couldn't get a word of sense out of anyone. Finally, I found Mags, and all he would tell me was that you'd been attacked.*

We were, but there's no time to explain. Let's get going.

Where to? asked Skylark as he began to gallop down

Shaker Row to reach take-off speed.

To the refinery. The bumpy ride was replaced with smooth strokes of wings as Skylark's hooves left the ground. *Kullervo's got Connie there—or he did a couple of hours ago.* Col could not bring himself to imagine what might have happened since. *I think Rat, Dad, and the others set off earlier. I hope Shirley passed the message on to the rest of the Society members. The attack on the moor's a diversion.*

Skylark neighed, shaking damp droplets from his white mane. He had been flying all night scouring each valley and hilltop for his friend and was exhausted, but he found new determination hearing of the threat to the universal. *Perhaps Shirley did. I saw Dr. Brock and Argot heading toward Chartmouth some time ago. I wondered what they were up to. But the Trustees and our volunteers were still trying to hold back Kullervo's army. I feared that he might have you with his forces.*

How are we doing?

We're paying a high price—the dragon twins were both injured by that renegade weather giant, Hoo; at least one of the dragons is dead. Six of the rock dwarfs were attacked by stone sprites and have been reduced to rubble—it's terrible. I couldn't see any more, but I know that scores are being treated by Kira and Windfoal at the farm. They could do with the universal's help right now.

Connie can't help—she might not even be alive. Oh, Skylark! Col stopped speaking, his thoughts choked off by the grip of fear.

They were now flying over Mallins Wood. Before them, Col could see great plumes of black smoke rising into the gray dawn sky. The blue and red lights of the emergency vehicles flashed below: there were at least twenty vehicles parked haphazardly in front of the fire. A fringe of gold flame blazed on the tops of the two drum containers like twin volcanoes on the verge of erupting.

Where can we land? wondered Skylark, looking down at all the humans scurrying like ants around a burning nest.

In no-man's land, said Col, steering him around the curtain of cloud. *There's another way in. I bet that's where Rat would've taken everyone.*

Col was right. When they landed not far from the hole in the fence, they found a small knot of people and creatures gathered outside the perimeter. All looked grim. Mack was talking earnestly to Rat, Col's grandmother, Mrs. Khalid, and Liam; Dr. Brock was huddled in the middle of a group of four that included Simon, a Nemean lion, an Amalthean goat, and a great snake. Omar Khalid was standing just inside the fence, arms raised like a conductor, directing the activities of six sylphs who were busy keeping the smoke wall intact to hide their presence, as well as blowing the poisonous fumes away. Argot stood guard in front of Omar, his emerald eyes fixed on the prowling presence of the chimera, which was striding in the middle of the empty parking lot, jaws open in a mad grin, ready to pounce on anyone who tried to reach the door. Not that any human could have survived in there now: smoke, accompanied by the occasional belch of flame, issued from the building. Col felt sick. He could see at a glance that there was no sign of Connie among the little band of Society members.

Mack strode over and gave his son a clumsy embrace as Col dismounted. "Are you all right? What kept you?"

Mrs. Clamworthy swooped on her grandson and gave him a trembling hug.

"I'll tell you later," said Col quickly to Mack. This did not seem the moment to break the news of the new arrival. "What's the plan?"

Mack sighed. He looked wrung out with anxiety. "There's been no sign of Connie or Kullervo. The stone sprites scuttled away about ten minutes ago—they were blocking our path, too, and we hadn't worked out a way past them. Now we've got just the chimera to deal with and the fire. And Kullervo," he added as an afterthought.

Col was on the verge of asking if Mack thought there was any hope, but he bit his tongue, knowing it was pointless. They had to continue as if there was still a chance Connie could be saved. Instead he asked, "So, what first?"

"The chimera," replied Mack. He turned to Dr. Brock. "Ready?"

The doctor nodded and, steering Simon by the arm, ducked through the wire mesh. The three companions followed: the lion, a magnificent tawny giant with a mane of black fur; the goat, who was of a size to match the lion, with a white, silky fleece and great curling horns; the snake, as thick as a tree trunk and at least sixty feet long by the time it had unfurled to wriggle through the fence. Dr. Brock said some final words to Simon, who nodded and took five paces forward. The three companions closed ranks around him, the snake coiling protectively around his feet, the lion at his right shoulder, the goat at his left.

The chimera stopped prowling and gathered itself for a roar of challenge. Who were these who dared to invade its territory? No one in the little group of four companions flinched, though Col put his hands over his ears at the deafening, hated sound of that creature's voice. Simon closed his eyes—the last thing Col would've done standing within an easy bound of the chimera—and raised his arms to touch the silky fleece of the goat and the rough pelt of the lion. The snake's tongue flickered across his shoes.

Then, slowly, Simon raised his right hand and pointed it directly at the chimera.

The chimera leapt backward as though it had been struck and gave an angry bellow. The attempt to bond with it, to command its obedience, seemed to send it further into madness. Horrified, fearful for Simon's safety, Col watched the chimera shake its lion-head in agony, the snake tail lashing, hooves sparking on the tarmac like flashes from flint. Desperate to end the voices now speaking in its head, the creature leapt toward Simon, attempting to silence the source of this suffering. With reflexes of lightning, the Nemean lion pounced to intercept, knocked the chimera sideways, and came to rest with his two great paws on the chimera's chest. At the same instant, the great snake slid forward and swiftly curled itself around the chimera's tail before it could sink its fangs into the lion. Joining the melee, the Amalthean goat galloped forward and stamped on the kicking, struggling hooves. The creature now pinioned, Simon walked calmly to the head of the beast.

"Don't forget its fire!" Col breathed, while he watched amazed at Simon's courage.

But Simon wasn't concerned that he would receive a blast of flames for his trouble: he sensed, as no one else could, the change within his companion creature. It had recognized the superior strength of the king of lions; the tail was curled in fraternal embrace with a far greater snake; even the goat stopped struggling hysterically as it realized that neither flight nor fight would save it.

"Be at peace," commanded Simon, laying a hand on the chimera's mane and stroking it. The chimera shivered. Even from where Col was standing, he could hear the deep rumbling that now came from its throat: it was purring. Simon stood up and nodded to Mack.

"Good," said Mack, ducking his head as he came through the fence. On this signal, the others followed him. "Now for the fire."

Kullervo left George Brewer alone with his great-niece, pacing off to see the progress of the fire he had started. The firefighters were making little impression. Every time they had begun to gain control over a blaze, a new one erupted in a quite different part of the refinery. The fire had now reached the staff canteen, and the building itself was aflame.

"Magnificent, isn't he?" said George Brewer, watching the great bear stalk off into the night. He turned and sat down beside Connie, groaning as he lowered his worn limbs to the floor. "I didn't understand, you see? I didn't understand what he was really like when I attacked him."

Connie didn't want to hear praise of Kullervo. She hadn't yet recovered from the shock of seeing a dead man come back to life. "So why did you let everyone believe you were dead? Why didn't you come home?"

"I wanted to, at first," said George. He gazed up at the flames flickering outside the windows, his face drawn with the memory of the early years in Kullervo's service. "Until I saw that his way was better. He thought you might come along."

"What? How could he know?" Connie hugged her knees, resting her head on them, wishing she was anywhere else but here.

"The eyes, my dear: the mark of the families to which universals are born. You've all had them, you know, all you universals. Sometimes the universal gift can lie fallow for many generations, but the eyes remind us that the bloodline persists to be discovered again one day. Your great-aunt Sybil had them, too, you know, showing that the Lionhearts still carried the gift."

"He knew about her eyes?" Connie asked in a hollow tone of voice. "How?"

"I admit he did extract that from me." George shuddered as if the memory was painful. "When he found that out, he said he would spare me because I might be useful to him one day. And so I am, it would seem." He gave Connie a feeble grin. He'd lost most of his front teeth—Connie wondered if they had been knocked out; his hands and face bore many scars. Pity stirred in her.

"Useful? How so?" she asked gently.

"To explain to you, my great-niece, that it is no good fighting him. I should know: I watched many good men die at his hands."

"And you still serve him!" exclaimed Connie, now in disgust.

George shook his head. "You don't understand. It was *we* who attacked *him*—it was *I* who led them to their deaths. I have paid for my error ever since. Don't fight him, my girl."

"I am not your girl. You're not even my uncle." Connie got up to distance herself from him. "You left my greataunt thinking she was a widow. You never cared about what happened to her, did you?"

"Oh, I cared," George said sadly, and Connie knew he was speaking the truth. "But he wouldn't let me go. He calls me his pet human." He gave a humorless laugh.

"Better to have died than live like that!"

"Do you really think so?" he asked as if giving serious thought for the first time to this suggestion. "I would've preferred to die at the beginning. That was until I realized his way was right. I have been living in the north all these years with nothing to do but watch as humans heated up the world. It seemed to me that our reckless, greedy burning of fuel was like a sailor on a wooden raft setting light to his own vessel just to keep warm, paying no heed to the consequences. My disgust and hatred of my own kind grew as I watched the ice melt, the polar bears lose their habitat, the creatures being driven closer to the edge of extinction, and I found I no longer thought my own life was of any value. It no longer mattered if I lived or died: only if they survived. And they will survive only if you help him." He raised his scrawny hand to clasp her sleeve. "Join with him. Help Kullervo save the world from humanity."

Connie could see the mad gleam in George Brewer's eyes as he looked up at her. His years of isolation in the snowy wastes of the Arctic had unhinged him. If he could say those words and mean them, then he must have forgotten what it was to love another human. Having felt nothing but fear for the past few hours, Connie was flooded with the comforting warmth of the most powerful emotion she knew. She realized she had not forgotten for one moment what it was to love—not only other creatures but her own imperfect fellow humans; what she felt for brave, proud Col; for crazy, vibrant Rat; for argumentative, grumbling Simon; for complex, caring Evelyn; for her loving yet disapproving parents; for Jane and Anneena, innocently unaware of any of this; even for brash, courageous Mack; and for all her other friends. Yes, they were worth dying for. That was her greatest strength.

"I will not join with him. But I won't fight him. He'll have to kill me," Connie said.

An angry growl rumbled in the darkness. The walkway creaked as the great bear bounded back in. Kullervo took a swipe—Connie instinctively ducked, but the blow was not aimed at her. George Brewer was flung the full length of the walkway, smashing into the far wall. "You failed me!" snarled Kullervo. "All these years of waiting, and you failed me! You are a pathetic, useless human!"

"Sorry, master," George whispered as he slid to the floor. He did not move again.

Kullervo turned back to Connie, his rage now deadly cold. *So, you are going to refuse me after all? Just like the other universals I had to kill?*

I have no choice, she whispered. *I'm not a murderer.*

You had a choice and you chose to die. You chose not to save your fellow creatures just to protect your own kind. I despise you for that. You are not worthy to be my companion. He sniffed her hair, the saliva from his jaws dripping on her shoulder. *I will have great pleasure in exhausting your powers. Though young, you have proven stronger than many of the others and will make a good meal for me. Shall I start now?*

Connie took a pace backward and faced him, raising her shield so that the compass etched on its surface blazed into his eyes. She saw herself mirrored there—sharp and clear in the light of the shield. It gave her an idea.

She took a breath. "Not so fast, Companion. I challenged you to meet me at the mark."

Kullervo gave a growl of delight. "So you are going to fight after all? If I must kill, then I prefer my prey to resist. The hunt is no fun without a chase."

"Meet me at the mark," Connie repeated.

The minotaur had taught her that an enemy will not wait; Connie closed her eyes and dashed to arrive first at the wall of encounters, the place deep in her mind where all the creatures with whom she'd bonded had left their mark and where Kullervo's dark void was found. She could hear the hiss and suck of his presence through the wall, so close that it was hard to say where her mind ended and his began. But she was not going to let him in this time to take her over; nor was she going to exhaust her weak armory in a futile defense of the barrier. She was going to do what no other universal had done: she was going through.

Abandoning the shield, Connie launched herself through the mark, diving like a seabird from a cliff. The wall of encounters crumbled and collapsed behind her. Her shadow-body lost its form once it was in the black void on the other side. She became a waterfall of silver tumbling down to meet him. She was in a place she had never been before—inside the shape-shifter's very being. The mind of Kullervo stretched away on all sides with no beginning or end, appearing to her like a starless sky over a dark blue sea. But the waters were alive with potential, poised to shift into a new shape in the blink of an eye. Though starless, the sky was not without light. Flickering shapes—like the patterns cast over the North Pole by the Aurora Borealis—etched themselves briefly across the heavens before winking out. As she fell toward the waters below, Connie saw that these patterns were reflected beneath her, the forms that Kullervo had mastered rippling in the sea, an endless stream of possibilities, bodies to inhabit, powers to assume.

But there was one possibility Kullervo had never anticipated: his waters were about to receive a new form in the shape of an uninvited guest.

Kullervo had no time to prepare himself for the unexpected attack from the girl he thought he'd subdued. The meeting of the two tides—the powers of the universal and of the shape-shifter—was like the meeting of two oceans at the continental cape. They crashed together, mingling, creating great shock waves.

I challenge you—you must take my form, Connie urged the

darkness. *You must.* She brought the imprint of herself into the very collision that sent his water soaring in the air. She wanted to give him knowledge of the human form—its wonders, its limitations, its strengths. But she received only rejection in return.

The dark waters fled from the silver tide that swept through them. Even so, they could not escape mingling with the weak creature that they hated more than any other: a human.

No! stormed Kullervo. He fought back, but he could no longer assault the frail mind of the universal as he had done in the past. Connie had totally abandoned herself to him and had left nothing behind for him to attack. She could not go back now even if she tried. She had become him, and he had to become her. Kullervo rose up into the form of a weather giant to blow the silver waves away, but the tide of the universal twisted around him, pulling the nascent form back into the sea. He writhed into the many-armed shape of the Kraken to cast her aside, but he could get no hold on the elusive being and it slid through his grasp like quicksilver.

I'll crush you! cursed Kullervo. *I'll stamp out every trace of your being, you foul creature, you monster!* Images of rampaging creatures flickered across the sky like flashes of lightning.

Take my form, the universal challenged him again. *Defeat me that way if you must.*

Then the silver waters rose to the surface and began to

close in around Kullervo's darkness like a glove enveloping a hand, squeezing him into the tight confines of the form of a young girl.

Find out what it is to be human, she urged him. *We may be weak. We may be destructive. But we are part of this world, too. Acknowledge this and I'll let you go. I'll become whatever you want.*

Never! howled Kullervo, battering against the prison of the shape he most despised and had always resisted. He was not going to succumb to this trial she had thrust upon him.

Connie sensed his resistance and sought for a way to soften it. If only they could be brought to understand each other, she thought, maybe they could find peace? She was prepared to risk it, but would he?

You see, I can love even you, Kullervo—what we could have been—what we could still be. Remember—you once showed me. A shared memory crackled between them like an electric current as they relived the dance in the air—she had tumbled and twisted in the cloud of his being as he turned into dragon, phoenix, griffin. The silver water diverted from the human form it had been trying to take and assumed the form of each creature as they remembered together their dangerous game. But Connie had made a perilous concession. Kullervo took advantage of this lull in her onslaught and continued to play through the changes—fire imp, great bear, eagle. The shifts were coming faster and faster—Connie could not wrench him back on the path to take the human form. Instead she found herself being spun into more and more shapes—stretched into a great snake, sprouting the wings of a siren, heads of a cerberus, tail of a salamander. Hydra. Chimera. It was agony.

I take you, Universal! roared Kullervo, exulting in her pain as he forced her to assume shape after shape. *But this is even better than before, better than any of the others I have encountered. I have you here, inside me, you'll never be exhausted, never escape. This game can go on for all eternity!*

No! gasped Connie, suddenly aware of the terrible danger she was in, scrambling to escape the kaleidoscope of shapes he was shifting her through. *I challenged you to take my form. By the rules of the combat, you cannot refuse!*

Rock dwarf, wood sprite, kelpie, gorgon. Kullervo cackled with glee as he dragged her through more shapes, delighting in displaying the endless variety of his repertoire. Connie was drowned in pain beyond anything she had ever felt or imagined. She could feel her sense of self beginning to disintegrate under the onslaught; the silver tide was in danger of dispersing and being mingled forever with his darkness.

What was it like to be human? She could no longer remember. She could not even recall what she looked like. Just let the pain stop, she cried. But she knew it would not.

Nemean lion, cyclops, pegasus.

Suddenly she remembered—not her own face, but that of Col, the companion to pegasi.

Then came Rat, her aunt, Mack, Anneena, Jane—

images of all the people she loved were seared into her mind with a power that only death could extinguish. The pegasus dissolved and out of the waters rose a silver Col, laughing as he flew on Skylark. Beside him, Rat emerged from the waves, chewing calmly on a piece of straw— Anneena waving her arms enthusiastically—Jane reading quietly—Simon grumbling about something—Evelyn dancing with Mack. Everywhere Connie looked, she saw the silver shape of the people she loved rising out of Kullervo's waters, even her parents, who appeared watching the scene with characteristically shocked expressions.

What are these abominations? screamed Kullervo, striking at the human shapes with clawing waves.

Finally, out of the water rose a silver girl—among her friends once more, Connie could remember herself. The silver shapes joined hands with her in their midst, forming an unbreakable circle.

Will you not learn to love this form, too? she asked Kullervo. *We could be joined together as equals—live in peace.*

Never, he cursed her. *I reject your way utterly.*

Then, my friends, let us complete the challenge, Connie said to her circle.

On her signal, they dived down into the dark waters that so hated them, taking into the very heart of Kullervo their knowledge of what it was to be human. His darkness and hate fought back, but used to invading the minds of others and bending them to his will, he discovered he was bound to hers; for he and his companion were equals: there was no force in him that could break her grip when she carried the challenge to him. Her love for humanity transfused like fire into his soul. It was a power beyond anything he knew. The universal whispered to him that if he embraced it, too, he might find there something to satisfy the emptiness inside him, the void that drove him to assume the shape of others. But he rejected her offer, attempting to push the knowledge away as if it was a poisoned chalice she held to his lips.

As the silver radiance shone ever brighter, penetrating the darkest corners of his being, burning it away, Kullervo had nowhere to run from the searching light of the universal, no dark shadows he could twist to his purposes. His whole being was now ablaze as the elements disintegrated— water burned.

Never equals! Not on your terms! he howled, his voice frail now like ash blown away on the wind.

Then I take you. You are mine, the universal said sorrowfully. *Forever.*

The silver girl stood alone on the barren rock. The dark tide had been consumed in the fire. Nothing remained but her.

17

Return to the Elements

Connie opened her eyes. She was sitting propped up against the railing. The heat in the room had built unbearably since she had last been conscious. She coughed—the air reeked of oil fumes. Raising her head, she saw that Kullervo had gone; the great bear that had towered before her had disappeared. She corrected herself. No he hadn't, he was still here, with her—

He now *was* her.

She clambered slowly to her feet and held out her hands. They glowed in the darkness with a strange silvery sheen as though they had been dipped in starlight. Taking a breath, she thought of a new form, a different shape: a sylph. Her body dissolved into a silver mist and then reshaped into the long-limbed, flowing form of a sylph before swiftly slipping back to become a girl again.

A faint round of applause—*clap, clap, clap*—came from the place where George Brewer had fallen. Reminded of the danger they were both still in, Connie dropped her hands and ran to his side.

"Uncle George, let me help you," she said, easing an arm under his head.

The old man coughed. "No, my dear, you've done enough. I've seen what you've become—and it's beautiful. Sybil would be proud." He patted her on the arm. "Do you know . . ." His voice sank to a whisper. "I think your way was best . . . after all." His last breath came in a soft hiss, and Connie knew that his broken body had released its spirit.

A cloud of smoke belched from the stairwell. She had to get out. But what could she do with the body of a man everyone thought had died years ago?

A fire imp whizzed into the hall overhead and ignited a pile of printouts stacked by a computer. The plastic casing of the machinery began to sag and melt like candle wax.

"Leave him to us!" sang the fire imp. "His spirit is gone. We'll return his body to the four elements."

Yes, that was the way it should be, thought Connie, laying the old man's head gently on the floor; nature should get back what we had borrowed.

No longer afraid of the blazing room around her, Connie walked toward the exit. This stairwell was also on fire; the plastic screen dripped molten droplets onto the floor. No one—or nearly no one—could escape that way.

With a silver-shimmer like a heat haze, Connie dissolved into the flickering form of a fire imp and passed through the flames.

⁂

The chimera tamed, Mack beckoned Mrs. Khalid and Liam forward. With a protective hand around the boy's shoulders, Mrs. Khalid stepped across the parking lot and past the creature. It made no attempt to stop them, its eyes now closed as if it had fallen into sleep. Mrs. Khalid led Liam toward the heart of the fire: the two drum containers, burning more than a hundred feet away, the heat so intense even at this distance that Liam's brow was shining with sweat. Deciding they were close enough, Mrs. Khalid leaned down and pointed Liam to the one on the right, then turned to the other. With a quick confirmatory glance at his mentor, Liam raised his hands to the sky as if cupping the hot draft of wind in his palms. In unison, two great tongues of fire ignited with an echoing whoosh. The flames leapt into the sky from the top of each drum. But they did not go out: they remained, flickering and dancing, taking the shape of two fire imps. They were as tall as skyscrapers, a vivid angry red, waving their long spiky fingers in gestures of rude defiance at the thin jets aimed at them from the engines on the other side of the wall of smoke.

Mrs. Khalid turned back to her charge. "Remember, Lee-am, though bigger, they are the same."

Liam nodded, his tongue sticking out between his teeth in concentration. On Mrs. Khalid's signal, the fire imp companions called to their creatures. Distracted from their game with the firefighters, the imps looked down on the two tiny humans below and held out tapering limbs of flame toward them, inviting them to the party. Mrs. Khalid shook her head, though for a moment Liam looked tempted.

"Now!" she called.

The fire imp companions clicked their fingers together, and the fire imps were snuffed out, leaving curling plumes of smoke rising to the sky.

At the same moment, a tongue of strangely silvery flame issued from the stairwell directly in front of their group, darted into the air, and disappeared. Even before the smoke cleared, Col was running across the open space between him and the rear door to the refinery. He dashed past Liam and plunged into the building without a clue what he was going to do. He just knew he had to reach Connie. He would have continued recklessly into the smoldering stairwell if a hand hadn't grabbed his belt and pulled him up short.

"You aren't thinking of going in there again?" asked a familiar voice. "Because I wouldn't recommend it."

Col was speechless. He grabbed hold of the arm that was restraining him to check that it was real.

"Let's get away from this smoke." Connie coughed.

In a daze, Col stumbled after her. Once outside, he grabbed her to stop her from running farther and stared into her face.

"You're alive," he said at last.

"So it seems," said Connie faintly. Her hair glistened in the dawn-light as if it had been dusted with silver.

"But, Connie, what about Kullervo?" Col glanced behind them as if he expected to see the shape-shifter bound from the building.

He didn't get an answer as a tidal wave of people hit them. Mack enfolded Connie in a bear hug; Rat squirmed through to give her a slap on the back; Simon hung onto his sister around the waist; Liam was hopping up and down to touch any available inch of skin; Dr. Brock kissed her on the cheek once Mack had allowed her to surface for air; Mrs. Clamworthy squeezed her hand as if she would never let go. Even Omar Khalid waited his turn to give her a relieved embrace.

Finally, Connie pushed her friends away gently. "Sorry to have kept you all waiting," she said as if she was only late for dinner. "Shouldn't we go?" She nodded to the thinning smokescreen.

Mack grinned. "Yeah, we'd better get out of here. Explanations can wait."

"But Kullervo?" asked Dr. Brock urgently.

"He's . . . gone," Connie said, meeting his eyes. "Forever."

"I can't believe it, but if you're here it must be true."

Dr. Brock gazed at her in wonder. "Connie, I want to know exactly what happened, but first we must get the news to the Trustees and stop the battle." Argot rose to his feet and snorted to his companion. Dr. Brock sprinted across the tarmac and vaulted onto his back. "And we must spread the message to Kullervo's forces. See you at the Mastersons'!" the doctor shouted as the red dragon propelled into the air.

Mack turned to his son, still standing in a daze a few feet away. "Col, you'd better get Skylark out of here before he's spotted. Simon, you and your companions lead that monster to the farm across the moor—but hurry! Connie, Rat, Liam—let's go before we're arrested."

Simon was about to rush away when Connie caught his arm. She gave her brother a hug, just for him. "Great job, Companion to Chimera," she said in a low voice, nodding over at the sleeping beast. "I'm proud of you."

Simon smiled back but was too choked up to say anything.

"Well, what're you waiting for?" Connie smiled. "Don't spoil it all now by getting caught!" She pushed him away. He stumbled off, but not without turning once or twice to look back at his sister to make sure she was really there.

Col knew how he felt. He hadn't gotten over his surprise at seeing her walk out of the burning building. No one should've been able to survive in there—let alone walk away from Kullervo.

"Col, are you going to stand there all day?" bellowed his father, seeing that his son was still rooted to the spot.

Realizing the answers were not going to be given just then, Col shook himself out of his stupor. There was another miraculous event he had witnessed this night and it was about time he shared it. He jogged over to his father. Blocking the gap in the fence was Simon astride the Nemean lion. Once on the other side, the three creatures— lion, goat, and snake—led the chimera into the gray shadows of the dawn, cutting across no-man's land to reach the open moor.

"Congratulations, Dad," Col said when he came alongside Mack.

Mack threw an arm around his shoulders. "It was nothing. The others did most of it, as you saw."

"I know," said Col with a grin. "But it's not every day you become a father for the second time."

Connie gasped. Mack froze. Col could've sworn he heard the cogs grind as Mack's brain adjusted to this new piece of information.

"What?"

"Yep. An hour or so ago. At home. Mother and baby are fine." Col could see Connie smiling broadly on the far side of his father.

Without another word, Mack broke into a sprint, pushing Omar and Rat out of the way as he dived through the fence and raced off into the twilight. A moment later, the sound of grating gears and a screaming engine indicated that Mack was making a fast getaway in Evelyn's VW.

Mrs. Clamworthy put her hands on her hips. "Typical!" she said in exasperation. "We've got seven people to get home, and he takes one of the cars without so much as a single passenger!"

"It's all right, Gran. I can take someone on Skylark," said Col, looking hopefully toward Connie.

The universal shook her head slightly, refusing his unspoken offer. "Mrs. Clamworthy, you take Liam and the Khalids with you. Rat can go with Col," she said, guiding Mrs. Clamworthy over the rough ground to where the old lady's Fiesta stood waiting.

"I can't do that. What about you?" protested Mrs. Clamworthy.

"Oh, I'll be fine. I just need a little time to myself to get used to . . . to recover. I'll find my own way home." Mrs. Clamworthy gave her a questioning look, but Connie smiled and shook her head again. "It's no good asking. I'm not going to explain. You'd better go."

"If you insist," said Mrs. Clamworthy, giving in to the new-found authority in Connie's voice. No one listening to her could doubt that she would get home safely.

"See you later." Connie turned from them and began to walk off across no-man's land, following the route taken by her brother and his companions. Her slight form was soon swallowed up by the shadows, except perhaps for a faint glimmer of silver in the half-light.

Skylark neighed, reminding Col there were only a few minutes left of semi-darkness for them to make their escape unseen. Col leapt onto his back as the Fiesta stuttered into life. Rat scrambled up behind him and hung onto Col.

"What do you think happened?" Rat asked once they were airborne.

"I don't know," mused Col. "And I'm not sure we're ever going to find out. Connie's different. She seemed older somehow—more mysterious."

"She was *cool*," pronounced Rat, squirming in his seat to get a parting look at the smoldering refinery.

"Yeah, she was cool," agreed Col.

⚜

Connie was lying on her bed, supposedly resting, when she heard footsteps on the path. At first, she didn't move. She was still reliving the events of the past few hours, concluding with her flight home in the form of a silver pegasus. Col would like that one, she thought with a smile. But so much had happened, she was so different, she didn't know where to begin. She felt like a tiny stream suddenly swollen with a flash flood: all she could do was wait for the torrent to pass so she could absorb what had taken place. She was a universal still—yes, she could sense her powers within her—but now she also had Kullervo's gift, the imprint of his nature, mingled with her deepest self. If anyone visited her mental landscape today, they would find a vast ocean of silver lapping peacefully at their feet, waiting to curl itself into new forms.

"Connie!" Mack called up the stairs. "Jane and Anneena are here."

Raising herself from her pillow, Connie straightened her clothes, checked in the mirror that she had resumed her shape properly, and hurried downstairs. She found her friends in Mack and Evelyn's room bending over the cradle where the new baby was sleeping, an awed expression on their faces.

"He's so tiny," whispered Anneena, putting the tip of her little finger in the clasp of one of his curled hands. He gripped it instinctively and shifted in his sleep, mouth feeding on air.

"Look, he's dreaming of milk!" said Jane softly. "Let's leave him in peace."

They tiptoed down to the kitchen. Evelyn was sitting with her feet up by the fireside. Mack was washing up at the sink; he looked distinctly shell-shocked. Connie hoped the excitement of last night had not been too much for him.

"Is Mack okay?" she asked her aunt quietly as Jane and Anneena fetched their presents. "He looks a bit . . . a bit odd. He's not still worried about what happened at the refinery, is he? And the battle on the moor—that's over now, isn't it?"

Evelyn smiled sadly. "Oh yes. I think we're both feeling a bit mixed up. It's strange to be grieving for those who died during the battle while feeling so happy to have a new life in the family. It feels all wrong somehow." Evelyn sighed and closed her eyes. "At least, Kullervo's sudden disappearance meant that the Society avoided a slaughter at the hands of his supporters. It could have been much, much worse. We all realize that."

Connie braced herself. "Tell me who we lost."

"Three dragons, six rock dwarves, two pegasi, a great boar—I'm afraid the list goes on. Ten human companions were injured, two seriously so."

"And Kullervo's supporters?"

"I don't know. They must have suffered losses, too. They retreated in confusion, led by that weather giant Hoo. You remember him, I think."

Oh yes, Connie remembered him. He had abused his position as a Trustee and allowed Kullervo to invade her last year.

"Kullervo may be gone, but the weather giants will not give up," added Evelyn.

Connie sighed. "You're right. We've given them too much cause to hate us humans. The world's gone mad. I sometimes think it's like the chimera. We shouldn't be fighting these creatures—we should be doing what we can to keep the Earth fit for all of us to live in."

They sat together in silence. Inside Connie's head, a

wail of grief reverberated. She felt the urge to shift into a banshee to spin out her misery in their mind-numbing dance. It seemed the only way open to her to dull the pain of being part of this world.

Upstairs, George Clamworthy let out a cry in his sleep. Instinctively, Connie rose to comfort him, but the baby had settled again before she could reach the door.

Evelyn patted the chair beside her. "Sit down for a moment. I want to tell you something. You have to realize that you are not to blame for these losses. You cannot be everywhere and save everyone. You conquered Kullervo: that is enough—more than enough."

Connie knew her aunt was right. She'd had no choice last night. But still, so many had died.

"Life is full of the bitter as well as the sweet. Your victory—our little George—these are what you should be thinking about now." Evelyn held Connie's gaze, trying to fathom what was going on behind her niece's eyes. "Something's happened to you—I can tell. I wasn't the only one to become someone different last night."

"How do you mean?"

"I became a mother. I think the change has been as great for you, maybe greater. Am I right?"

Connie shivered: that was exactly how it felt—she had shed the skin of her old life and transformed into something new.

"Yes, I've changed. But I can't explain it."

"I understand. I can't tell you yet what it's like to be a parent. It's as if my center of gravity has shifted into that baby—it'll take me a while to regain my balance."

Further discussion was prevented as Anneena came back carrying a magnificent bunch of flowers for Evelyn. Jane followed with several bags piled high with food.

"Here's your lunch—thanks to Anneena's mum," said Jane. "So, tell us, Connie, what were you doing last night when all this excitement was going on—the baby, the fire, the evacuation—don't tell me you missed out on it all?"

Connie felt caught between her friends' interest and the fascinated gaze of her aunt and Mack, neither of whom had heard any details yet of what had gone on inside the refinery and both of whom had been itching to ask.

"I . . . er . . . I was somewhere else," Connie said.

"Oh? Where?" persisted Jane.

"Somewhere new. A place I'd never been before. Nature-watching."

"Didn't you notice the fire from there?" asked Anneena, sensing there was something strange in their friend's answer.

"Yes, but I didn't think much about it, I was too caught up in . . . in other things."

Anneena signed in frustration. "Typical! It's just like you, Connie, to go around with eyes only for badgers or something when half of the county is on fire! You always seem to miss out on the real excitement. Remember how you slept through that tornado last year?"

"I remember." How could she forget?

"It's a good thing Jane and I keep our eyes peeled for you. You stick with us, and we'll see you don't miss out on the next adventure."

"Er . . . thanks. I'll do that."

18
The Company of the Universals

Of course, the defeat of Kullervo and his supporters couldn't be allowed to pass without marking it with the biggest event the Society had ever organized. First, in a simple ceremony out on the moors, the Trustees honored the dead and wounded from the battle. Connie saw for herself how intense the fight had been as many members gathered bore the marks of fresh scars. Kullervo's supporters had been merciless toward the creatures they believed had betrayed them by allying with humans.

To them, we are the monsters, Connie thought sadly. Anger washed inside her like a tide as she stood with the others in the chill breeze to say farewell to their friends and comrades. She felt she couldn't bear the pain of it.

If this was what it was like for you, Kullervo, she told

the shape-shifter inside her, I can understand how part of you was driven to violence to silence this agony.

Connie barely felt like taking part in the celebration of her victory, but everyone expected her there. It took her some time to shake off the melancholy mood that had settled over her out on the moors. She wandered about the Mastersons' farm aimlessly, watching the preparations and avoiding conversation when she could. The farm had been commandeered by the Trustees for the event, and mythical creatures and their companions continued to pour in from all over Britain. A huge bonfire had been lit in the paddock, and dragons were already warming up for the most magnificent fireworks display in their history, breathing out practice sparks of silver over the upturned heads of the crowd. Dr. Brock and Argot flew over, blasting the barn roof with emerald flame that lingered on the ridge like a crown for a few moments before disappearing, leaving no trace of its passage. The crowd cheered, neighed, whistled, stamped, and made every other noise known to animal-kind, entreating the Sea Snakes to start the entertainment for real.

"Later!" shouted Dr. Brock from Argot's shoulder. "It's time to eat!"

Volunteers with flushed faces were manning the barbecues and tables, all of which groaned with food to suit every palate: sides of meat, bowls of creamy desserts, stacks of cakes, and pyramids of fruit and vegetables. The platters of gleaming fish were surrounded by a crowd of enthusiastic selkies—Arran in their midst with his arm draped around Jessica's shoulders. He was balancing a herring on his nose and making everyone laugh and clap with appreciation of his skill. With a flick of his neck, the herring sailed into the air; Arran stood beneath with mouth wide open—only to find his supper intercepted by Argand, who flew over and took it in one gulp.

Rat was ecstatic because he and Icefen had been given express permission to use the frost wolf's breath to wipe clean the memory of any humans that came across the gathering.

Connie, standing with Sentinel at her side to keep off the crowds of Society members, was a still spot in the swirling masses that surrounded her. She watched Rat and Icefen bound off into the night on the trail of a small group of paratroopers who had been so unwise as to exercise on the moor that night. They did not stand a chance, thought Connie—the soldiers, that is.

Rat's mentor, Erik Ulvsen, turned up five minutes later on an even bigger wolf than Icefen.

"Off hunting?" Erik asked delightedly when Connie informed him where his pupil had gone. "Excellent." Frost wolf and rider took off after Rat.

Liam slipped under Sentinel's guard and shyly took Connie's hand. Simon, who was keeping an eye on him for Mrs. Khalid, gave his sister a hug.

"That looks fun," said Liam, watching the frost wolves bounding over the fields. "Do you think Rat'll let me have a go?"

"I'm sure he'd love to," said Connie, her spirits lifting a little when she saw Liam's look of delight.

"Maybe I could come along for the ride on Rex?" suggested Simon. When Connie and Liam looked blank, he added, "The Nemean lion. I'm sure he could carry two—would you like to come, Connie?"

"I might later. But I'll make my own arrangements for a ride." It was Simon's turn to look puzzled. "There's something I've got to tell you. . . ." She stopped, sensing someone approaching from behind them. She knew without turning that it was the soft-footed companion to Storm-Bird.

"Universal, the Trustees would like to speak to you," said Eagle-Child.

"Tell me later," said Simon as he and Liam stood back to allow the Trustee to guide Connie into the stillness of the barn. Sentinel followed at a discreet distance.

Connie had known this moment would come—the moment when she would have to account for the conquest of Kullervo. But what could she say when even she didn't understand everything that had happened? It was going to take her a long time to get used to her new gift, and she had a shrewd suspicion it would take others even longer. Over the last few years, she had been brought face-to-face with the prejudice against the universals in the Society:

what would they do when they discovered that she had become even more unusual, placed herself even further beyond the stretch of their understanding?

Indeed, what had she become?

Walking into the center of the circle of Trustees, Connie sensed that emotions in the room were running high. The dragon Morjik crouched in the shadows like a rough-hewn rock of green granite. Only the glitter of his ruby eyes showed that he was glowing hot with life. Kinga was sitting between his forepaws, his ancient head resting on her lap. Storm-Bird croaked once from the rafters, seen in the darkness as a blacker shadow in the night. Windfoal gleamed with snowy purity at the western side of the barn, her long mane sparkling like the froth of a waterfall tumbling over her powerful shoulders. Kira, dressed in an orange and yellow kikoi, brought a vibrant dash of color into the room, making an exotic contrast to her unicorn companion. The Trustees for the Elementals, both past and present, sat still like pieces from a chess game in which two boards had been mixed up: Gard's northern solidity of a Scottish king pitched against Mr. Chan and Jade, both from an antique Chinese board, lines fluid and graceful as willows.

Despite the silence that reigned in the room, Connie perceived that the Trustees were at once delighted and wary: overjoyed that Kullervo appeared to have been defeated at long last, but afraid of the one who had achieved it.

Without pausing to be asked, Connie threw out the links of the shared bond and waited for them to come to her.

Greetings, Universal, said Gard, stomping through the portal to her mind, stopping on the threshold to take a curious look at the silver ocean that now lapped there.

Hello, she said simply. Rising from the waves, she conjured an image of herself to stand with him, head bowed.

The other Trustees joined them, paddling ankle-deep in the water, bemused by the change that had come over her mind. Morjik stirred the water with a claw, sending concentric waves rippling off into infinity. He growled in recognition, seeing for the first time the ocean that he had sensed in her long ago.

When it was clear she was going to say no more, Gard spoke again. *You took a terrible risk in challenging Kullervo.*

Yes, it was terrible.

Will you tell us what happened?

I'm not sure I can explain. I took him at his weakest and . . . and now he's no longer a threat to us. That's all I can say.

So is he gone?

Yes—and no.

You speak in riddles, Universal.

Only because I've become a riddle, even to myself.

The Trustees pondered her words.

You broke the rules, Universal, said Kinga finally. *We should expel you for that.* But she was smiling.

Are you going to? asked Connie, not much worried by this

threat. *In that case, I should mention that I had the unanimous support of the Company of the Universals. I was acting on their behalf.*

Eagle-Child laughed, his voice echoing from the waters. *We have agreed that you can stay in the Society this time.*

The universals always were a law unto themselves, grunted Gard. He rubbed his brow, still pondering the new landscape she had revealed.

Thank you, said Connie, *I'd like to stay in the Society—that is, if you think you can cope with me.*

Oh, said Kira, splashing her toes in the warm water as if it was the Indian Ocean, *I think we're used to you now.*

Oh no, you're not, thought Connie to herself.

With a slight nod of her shadow-head, Connie raised a soft bed of silver sand under Kira's toes, glistening with shells, to honor the Trustee's holiday mood. Kira gave an astonished gasp, bent down, and pulled out a curved conch shell. Putting it to her ear, she smiled at the universal: *I can hear the waves of my home!*

Eagle-Child was crouched on the portal, looking gravely at the water. Connie shivered and around him sprung up tall prairie grass, hissing softly in the wind. He stroked his hand across the tops of the grasses and began to hum a song of his people. Storm-Bird swirled overhead, flying in the clouds that raced across the silver sky. Flashes of lightning scored the canopy with sharp gashes of light.

What is happening, Universal? marveled Gard.

Connie shook her head slightly, denying him words of explanation; instead she sent him a stream of molten rock, curling it around him like a climbing rose and letting it set in a fantastical sculpture. He stepped away, leaving the stone flowers suspended delicately like an arch. Jade and Mr. Chan moved closer to examine it, wondering at its fragile beauty.

This goes beyond explanations, said Kinga as Connie now turned her attention to the Trustees for the Sea Snakes, surrounding them with a sudden growth of thick primeval forest. Kinga ran her hand over the rough bark of an oak, its roots nestled on a bed of moss. Turning to her fellow Trustees, Kinga added, *The universal has become something we've never seen before in a human companion.*

I think, Universal, you are now one of us, growled Morjik. *A mythical creature. Or should I say: you are all of us.*

Connie laughed softly. *Yes, that's it. You're all here, and always will be, part of me.*

Kinga shook her head. *Something wonderful has happened to the universal—we can all see that and we must understand it. But I do not think this is a matter that will be grasped in one visit. Let us enjoy her victory for we still have many battles to fight if we are to save the world for all creatures. The universal's task is far from over.*

Connie ended the encounter. They returned to the present in the barn, feeling relaxed and peaceful.

"I know," said Connie. "The threat from Kullervo may

be gone, but his army is still out there. There are many more Axoils and many angry creatures who would want to punish humanity for our greed." She looked around the circle, feeling a great tie of love binding her to each of these marvelous creatures. "I feel as if my work has only just begun."

⧉

Col waited anxiously outside the barn. He knew that Connie was closeted with the Trustees, but he wasn't worried about that: what could they do to the Society's hero, the girl who had beaten Kullervo? No, he was worried for himself and for what he was going to say next. In the last twenty-four hours, he had gone from not understanding what love was, to seeing it in action as Connie sacrificed herself for him and Rat. She had opened his eyes to his own feelings, and he didn't want to let this moment slip away. And Skylark, relieved that his companion had finally come to his senses, had sworn he wouldn't speak to Col again unless Col did something about it.

Connie came out with Sentinel, looking happy. She spotted Col through the throngs of people and began to push her way toward him, greatly assisted by Sentinel who took his bodyguard duties very seriously. She had almost reached him when Omar Khalid intercepted her. She turned aside to speak to him.

Col watched as Omar bent low over his friend, talking intently. With a pang of jealousy, Col saw Omar raise his

301

hand to stroke Connie's arm. She was blushing. If Col didn't do something quickly, it would be too late—for him. He pushed through the crowd and broke in upon the private conversation. "Sorry to interrupt," he lied cheerfully. "Omar, do you mind if I borrow Connie for a moment?"

Omar clearly did mind but was too polite to say so. "Of course," he said graciously. "I hope I'll see you later, Connie."

Not if I have anything to do with it, Col vowed silently. "Can we go somewhere I can speak to you on your own?" he asked Connie.

She nodded and let him lead her away. Connie expected that he wanted an explanation, and she knew he deserved one. If there were anyone in the world that she would tell the whole story to, it would be Col.

His determined attempt to get her on her own almost failed as Mr. Coddrington arrived in their path. Sentinel snorted with anger. Connie placed a restraining hand on the minotaur's sinewy forearm to prevent him from charging.

"Miss Lionheart—Connie, if I may be so bold—may I say how delighted I am to see you safe and sound?" said Mr. Coddrington smarmily, reaching out to shake her hand. Connie snatched her hand away, leaving him grasping air. The assessor frowned.

Connie looked with distaste at the companion to weather giants, remembering all the pain he had caused her. And now he had the nerve to pretend he was her friend! A wave of silver-blue anger welled up inside her, tempting her to shift shape, to crush the insignificant creature before her. It was time he got what he deserved.

"Mr. Coddrington," she said with a dangerous edge to her voice as she struggled to contain her anger. It was frighteningly difficult to stop herself from lashing out. "No, you may not. You've never been my friend and never will be."

"Miss Lionheart," protested Mr. Coddrington, bristling defensively at her tone, "don't think that just because you are a universal you can get away with such impertinence to a senior member of the Society!"

"And don't think you can get away with bullying me anymore, Mr. Coddrington, or you'll find you've picked a fight you've no hope of winning. Keep out of my way in the future or else." Connie began to walk away.

Col gaped at this new side to her character but hurried to follow.

"Or what?" shouted Mr. Coddrington at her back. "You can't do anything against me!"

"Can't I?" said Connie calmly. With an action so quick that Col could barely make out what she was doing, Connie conjured the universal's bow into her hands, strung, and fired it. An arrow, bearing a sharp cold sting of stone sprite, whistled through the air and slapped Mr. Coddrington on the cheek. He was instantly frozen to the spot, a look of horrified indignation on his face. "Come on, Col."

Col tripped after her, dumbfounded at what she had done. "Will he be all right? I'm not worried about him but, I mean, won't you get into trouble?"

Connie shrugged, though she was still shaking. For a moment, she had felt something inside, a presence that goaded her into attacking. The balance of power between her and the part of her that was Kullervo was a delicate one: she had almost lost it.

"He'll be fine. It'll wear off in a few minutes. Anyway, I'm in trouble enough already." She left this comment hanging as an invitation to Col to find out more. While walking the knife edge of her new nature, she would've liked to confide in him. Would he—would the others— think she was a monster? That was her greatest fear. But Col was too preoccupied by something else and didn't take up her invitation to ask more.

They escaped the crowds and left Sentinel guarding the pathway to the stables. Col turned to her.

"Connie, do you remember what I said last night—that I had something to ask you?"

Connie nodded. "Yes."

In the darkness away from the party, Col could have sworn she still glistened with that strange silver sheen he had noticed earlier. "I've been a complete idiot waiting so long, but last night helped me see you for the first time."

She gave him a strange look. "There's more to me than you think."

Col grinned. "I know that. You're the girl that beat Kullervo." He was bright red now and not meeting her eyes. "I realized that I want to spend more time with you—and no one else, except for Skylark, of course, but that's different." He laughed nervously. "So I just wondered, would it spoil things if . . . if I asked you to go out with me?"

This was the last question Connie had been expecting, but she already knew what her answer would be—the answer she would have given him months ago if it had crossed his mind to ask her.

"No, I . . . er . . . don't think it would spoil things."

"So, will you?"

"Yes . . . but you might be getting more than you bargained for." It was only fair to warn him, she thought. "I've changed since last night."

Col just felt relieved that she agreed. He'd been a fool not to ask her before. It had taken a close shave with death to understand his true feelings. "Last night changed me, too, so I'm not worried about that," he said, finally getting the hug he had missed out on that morning. He ruffled his fingers through her hair. "Look, no sparks." He laughed and hugged her close.

Connie smiled, feeling more completely happy than she ever had in her life. She would tell him about

Kullervo—but not yet. This moment was too perfect to spoil.

⚜

When Connie and Col returned to the party, arm in arm, they found that their presence had hardly been missed. Mack and Evelyn had arrived, Mack bearing the baby in his arms triumphantly, holding him up like the World Cup. Argand flew around them, breathing joyous golden flames into the sky, forming a glowing circle of fire to mark the little one's arrival. Spotting Col, Mack skillfully avoided the elderly lady members who had come to coo over the child and dumped the baby on his older son.

"You know what my greatest achievement is?" Mack asked as he put his hand on Col's shoulder.

"No," said Col, not really wanting to hear about his father's exploits just then.

"It's having two smashing sons. Thanks for what you did last night. I know I don't say this enough, but I love you." He would have enfolded Col in an embrace if the baby hadn't started crying at that point, feeling the squeeze of his over-enthusiastic father. Evelyn rushed over, but not out of concern as Col was doing fine, nursing the baby on his shoulder like a pro.

"See," she said proudly to Connie, "he cries like a banshee already!"

"George swam like a fish when I bathed him," said Mack, giving Connie a wink.

Connie looked up at the circle of fire and then down at the little bundle sniffing on Col's shoulder. George Clamworthy blinked back at her with his mismatched eyes: one green, one brown. Her instinct had been right. She was no longer alone: the Company of the Universals had a new member.

DATE DUE		
NOV 0 5 '10		
NOV 1 1 '10		
12-20-10		
OCT 1 7 '11		
MAR 16 '12		
APR 11 '12		